BAD LIES
A Novel

Bad Lies

A Novel

Thomas B. Jones

NORTH STAR PRESS OF ST. CLOUD, INC.
Saint Cloud, Minnesota

First Edition: September 2014

Printed in the United States of America

Published by
North Star Press of St. Cloud, Inc.
P.O. Box 451
St. Cloud, Minnesota 56302

northstarpress.com

AUTHOR'S NOTE

Anyone writing about the past needs to admit and disclaim certain things. So here goes.

Bad Lies is first and foremost a work of fiction. The main characters in this novel are decidedly fictional and a product of the author's imagination. What happens in *Bad Lies* with regard to the 1948 St. Paul Open and surrounding events falls into the same category—fiction. So, as you have no doubt read before, ". . . any resemblance to actual persons, etc. etc."

On the other hand, I have featured individuals, events, and places that most familiar with local and national history during the 1940s will recognize. This historical base for telling the novel's story is, I trust, carefully constructed. If I do allow my imagination and plot necessities to alter what we know about some individuals, events, attitudes, and places connected with the post-World War II era of history, such reshaping is minor.

With all that admitted, let me extend heartfelt thanks to some good folks for their encouragement, talent, and expert opinion. Of course, none of these individuals stand guilty of what readers might find mistaken, lacking, objectionable, or dead wrong in this novel. That said, here's to Joe Chambers, Donna Blacker, and Susan Nathan.

●●●●●

Iwo Jima 1945

A *sloping wall of dark volcanic sand lay beyond the landing zone. Private John O'Donnell struggled to near the crest and spread-eagled on the ground. Tiny, abrasive particles of ash, the air-born product of Mount Suribachi's frequent eruptions, scoured his face as enemy machine gun rounds churned the blackened sand. Marines scrambled in all directions, frantic to escape their exposed position and the withering enemy fire.*

O'Donnell moved sideways, rolling, crabbing away to a tumble of rocks high enough to afford him cover. He fought his way toward the few men remaining in his squad, hunkered down behind another high terrace of sand. Weeks of island assault training kicked in, and the men maneuvered away from danger, making good a brief escape from the killing. But ahead waited thousands of starving, ragged, desperate enemy troops ready to die for their emperor, holed up in a daunting network of caves, blockhouses, pillboxes, and tunnels. In his bones, O'Donnell knew his chances for surviving yet another Pacific island battle weren't worth a plugged nickel.

A half-mile east of the beach, a Japanese machine gun emplacement wedged into a bluff brought O'Donnell and his squad to a halt. They huddled in a large, rain-soaked gully, returning fire without much effect. O'Donnell found good cover under a ledge topped by a lone, stunted banyan tree. He dug into the lava rocks beneath, gouged out a shallow foxhole and burrowed into it, pulling his helmet down to cover his face. Volcanic sand spilled back over him like a pail full of coffee grounds.

•••••

A LATE AFTERNOON SUN fell slowly in the distance, providing smudged backlighting for those still trapped across from O'Donnell in the gully. A young lieutenant had called a tank up, and it fired with precision at the machine gun nest before rattling off in search of another target. The lieutenant screamed at the others to advance, his voice stuck at a high, nervous pitch. He bolted out of the gully, legs churning and feet slipping in the ash. O'Donnell readied to follow, but heard a powerful thud behind his foxhole. In the wake of the blast that rumbled through the gully, he was propelled into a hard ledge that overhung his position. His skull struck rock. He blacked out, pretzeled under a blanket of ash and rocks. Blood trickled through his hair and across his face, mixing with lava cinders to form a sticky crust.

After a time, O'Donnell sensed someone kneeling beside where he lay. The man's dark skin identified him as one of the black Marines ordered to carry ammo between the beachhead and the front lines.

"Is anyone left?" O'Donnell tried to focus on the man's face.

The black Marine scanned the gully. "Just you, me, and Charlie Gibbs over there."

O'Donnell could make out someone twenty yards away, duck-walking from body to body, checking for signs of life. Gibbs turned to say something, but instead threw up his hands to protect himself. A volley of shots rang out. Rifle fire shredded Gibb's face and chest.

O'Donnell and the black Marine trained their weapons on the gully's back edge. Three Japanese soldiers rushed into view, uniforms scrubby and torn, rifles aimed at the spot occupied seconds before by Gibbs. The black Marine and O'Donnell opened fire from their position with lethal effect. One of the enemy clutched at his chest and toppled into the sand. Another of the ratty crew staggered a few yards forward, fell to his knees, and crumpled sideways. The remaining Japanese soldier scurried away.

The black Marine raced up the gully bank and disappeared in pursuit of fleeing enemy soldier. He returned within minutes, a bloody knife held loose in his hand.

"We need to hole up and see what happens," he told O'Donnell, pointing to an abandoned pillbox on a small hill ahead.

The pair made slow progress toward the pillbox, O'Donnell struggling up the incline, still dizzy and off-balance. In the distance, he could hear the sounds of battle rippling across the island, but it seemed as if his little piece of Iwo Jima had been disconnected. The black Marine angled his way above the entrance to the pillbox for a look inside.

"Ain't exactly the Ritz," he informed O'Donnell.

Within the dark walls, O'Donnell could hardly see a thing. The black Marine crawled to a slit in the concrete and peered through it. In an instant, a strange, murky green color illuminated his face, spreading a fantastic glow into the pillbox, lighting the interior like some carnival ghost house.

"That's one damn crazy moon." The black Marine slid away from the opening. "They're still sending up flares and firing artillery like there's no tomorrow. We need to sit tight for a couple of hours."

O'Donnell didn't need an invitation and plunged into a deep, dreamless sleep despite sitting upright in the cramped quarters. He awoke to find himself bouncing head down, thrown like a sack of laundry over his rescuer's shoulder. Small arms fire crackled in the distance, and O'Donnell lapsed in and out of consciousness as the black Marine strained to make it over hostile terrain to the beach, enduring a lash of heavy, cold rain, pressing on until O'Donnell lay on a stretcher near a line of wounded men.

O'Donnell pushed up to one elbow, reaching to shake hands. "I'm John O'Donnell."

"Isaac Dawkins." The black Marine ignored O'Donnell's outstretched hand. "Most folks call me Flash."

"Sweet Jesus. I owe you," O'Donnell said.

Without a word, Dawkins walked away, soon obscured by the smoky darkness and heavy rain spreading over the evacuation zone.

St. Paul 1948

T HE JAZZY, LATE-MODEL Buick Roadmaster crunched down the gravel driveway, tailed by a large dog bounding happily and barking like a hound from hell. O'Donnell didn't share his dog's excitement. The past had come calling. O'Donnell didn't much like the remembering.

Flash Dawkins emerged from the Buick. He stood by the driver's side with an amused expression. "Long time no see."

"Damn sure," O'Donnell said. "Glad to know you made it."

"You didn't think I'd let those Jap jungle rats get me, did you?"

O'Donnell caught Cosmo's collar as the dog made another circle around the car. "I tried finding what happened to you. No luck though."

"More fun to surprise you."

After that day on Iwo Jima, O'Donnell ended up on a hospital ship with a concussion and shell fragments in his back. Along with all the other wounded in the island fighting, he'd earned a trip across the Pacific to Hawaii. After two weeks recuperating, O'Donnell's reassignment orders sent him to Honolulu where he served until early 1946. He'd made a few inquiries to see what might have happened to the black Marine, but O'Donnell didn't get far with the bureaucrats, and eventually gave up trying. Back stateside, O'Donnell did his best to fit into a normal life. He pushed thoughts about the war years into a remote corner of his mind—at least until the day before. That's when, out of the blue, Flash Dawkins phoned.

"Johnny-boy. It's Flash Dawkins. Remember me? Friend of mine and I are coming out your way tomorrow. We got some business to discuss." With that said, his caller hung up, leaving O'Donnell holding the phone without a clue how Flash Dawkins had found him and what the hell the man wanted.

"Let me introduce you to my special friend." Flash pointed at a man emerging from the Buick. "Just another little surprise."

O'Donnell couldn't believe it. Joe Louis, the heavyweight champion, pushed the car door closed, trying his best to fend off a frantic welcome from Cosmo, who'd twisted out of O'Donnell's grasp. O'Donnell hustled to corral his loopy mutt, but not before Louis issued a sharp command. Cosmo dropped down to all fours, ears laid back, a worried look in his eyes, tail barely moving.

"It's okay," Louis winked at O'Donnell. "He's down for the count."

O'Donnell offered a handshake to Louis and congratulations for his recent title defense against Jersey Joe Walcott. "Is it true you're planning to retire?" O'Donnell asked.

"That's right. Had enough of the fight game. I'm devoting my time to relaxing and playing some serious golf."

The St. Paul newspaper had reported a few days back about the boxing legend arriving in the Twin Cities for some sort of celebrity golf tournament. Louis had a longstanding passion for the game, and apparently he loved to mix in some serious gambling when he played.

"You ready for this crazy fool." Louis rolled his eyes, pointing a finger at Flash. "Cocky sucker been driving me nuts for damn near a year now."

"Come on now, Champ," Flash said. "I'm your secret weapon on the golf course. Don't forget that."

O'Donnell guessed Flash lived up to his nickname without much effort, yet he knew precious little else about the man standing in front of him. He brushed past O'Donnell and up the cabin steps, standing on the porch like he owned the place. "What's for breakfast?"

O'Donnell didn't figure bacon and eggs would settle his debt.

3

THE THREE MEN RECLINED on the porch, balancing breakfast plates on their knees, sipping mugs of coffee. O'Donnell did his best to find out what happened after last seeing Flash on the landing beach. Flash ignored the questions, going on about his travels about the country as Joe Louis's personal golf pro and partner in high-stakes matches.

"Since I put this hustler on the payroll, I've knocked five strokes off on my handicap." Louis said. "He knows how to win a bet, too."

"Like the man said, there's a sucker born every minute. We're just scratching the surface." Flash grabbed a slice of toast off Louis's plate.

The two men jibed back and forth, revealing what O'Donnell felt was an uneasy friendship. Louis set his plate down next to the old rattan chair where he sat. He waved off Flash's conversation. "You finished with baseball, Johnny? Heard you threw your arm out."

"That's right," Flash said, jumping back into the mix. "You were supposed to be some hotshot pitching prospect."

"I already told you he was good," Louis said. "You listen to anything?"

"I was okay," O'Donnell said. He'd quickly worked his way up through the Brooklyn Dodgers' minor league system to the St. Paul Saints—the Dodgers's Triple-A farm club. "I threw too hard, too soon. Now I can't throw a curve without my damn arm feeling like it will drop off."

O'Donnell didn't have much heart to say more about his ball playing days. It should be like water under the bridge. But in his heart, he hoped it wasn't. "So, forget my sob story. What brings you two here?"

"First off, the Champ played in the Elks' Midwest Golf Tournament yesterday," Flash said. "Plenty of loose cash from the locals needing to find a home I'm telling you."

"But we're up here for something a little more serious." Louis pulled his chair closer to O'Donnell. "Been reading the local news, Johnny?"

"Sorry. Not day by day." O'Donnell's lake cabin stood a few miles past the St. Paul city limits, and the *Pioneer Press* didn't deliver door to door that far away. Besides, reading the sports section during baseball season didn't exactly put a smile on O'Donnell's face. World news and the local happenings usually weren't much more promising.

"Then you missed the article about one of our friends," Louis said. "You heard of Teddy Rhodes?"

"Can't say I have," O'Donnell said.

"Next to Flash here, Teddy Rhodes is probably as good as we have in the game of golf."

"Glad you qualified that," Flash said. "Best black golfer this season is me. Ain't no doubt I'm better than most anybody ever tees it up."

Louis hesitated and glared at Flash. He seemed ready to say something to the younger man, but shook his head instead.

"Rags Rhodes had plans to enter the St. Paul Open," Flash said. "Sort of a challenge to the old *status quo*. I'm taking his spot."

"Johnny, you understand what we're up against in the sports world, right?" Louis asked. "Aren't many pro sports most of us can play and earn a decent living, but Jackie Robinson's given us a new angle. Maybe I have too. Anyway, thing is, we can always use a little help, especially when it comes to breaking into the game. It's a long road, but we all got to jump in and do our part."

Flash stared hard at O'Donnell. "You believe that's right?"

"I believe that's right." O'Donnell felt good saying so. As a nineteen-year-old Marine, he'd seen first hand what black-skinned Americans were up against. Despite the fact black Americans had been allowed to enlist after 1943, they still had to live with segregation in the Marine Corps. They trained at a separate facility attached to Camp Lejuene, and only white officers could lead the black troops. Growing up in lily-white Minnesota hadn't much prepared O'Donnell for what was going on. He didn't like what he saw.

"You know about the Professional Golf Association?" Louis asked.

Except for occasional rounds with friends and going to watch the St. Paul Open a couple of times, O'Donnell didn't know a great deal about pro golf—less about how the sport treated black golfers.

"Don't know about their rule, do you?" Flash said.

"Caucasians only," Louis spat out.

"The PGA boys have that damn rule for almost every tournament they sponsor," Flash said. "We're thinking of putting a stop to that."

"So, Johnny, tell you what we got up our sleeves," Louis said.

From what O'Donnell could gather, the two men meant to challenge the PGA's "whites only" policy at the St. Paul Open. Louis thought Minnesota had a reputation for being progressive on race issues, and the St. Paul Open, sponsored by the city's Jaycees, seemed a likely site to challenge segregation on the pro golf tour. Louis schooled O'Donnell about the Twin Cities' tight-knit, active civil rights community—the local NAACP, the black newspapers, and Whitney Young's group, the Urban League. Louis figured these groups could be counted on to help organize any actions.

"It won't do for whites hereabouts to cozy up to segregation in their own backyard," Louis said. "Especially after that speech your man Humphrey gave last week. You heard about that?"

"I heard about it," O'Donnell said.

According to the radio reports, Hubert H. Humphrey, the ex-mayor of Minneapolis, stirred up the delegates attending the 1948 Democratic National Convention in Philadelphia. He gave one hell of a speech on civil rights, and the Southern Democrats up and walked out of the convention hall. O'Donnell could understand why Humphrey's controversial speech made it seem like the time was right to challenge the PGA.

Flash said two black golfers had filed a lawsuit in the spring against the PGA for locking them out a California golf tournament. "I don't think the PGA wants much more trouble. We've got us a sharp St. Paul lawyer lined up. He'll pin their damn ears back. Already fixed me up with a place to stay, and been taking up the cause."

"Flash thinks you might help us out, Johnny," Louis said.

"Me?" O'Donnell wondered what the hell he was supposed to do?

"There's been some threats," Louis said. "Same old stuff, but it makes no sense to ignore them. If things get tough, we might be needing some help. You know, keep an eye out . . . sniff around to see who's up to no good."

"You don't throw the high hard one anymore, but people remember you. Hotshot local athlete, big war hero—that sort of thing." Flash pointed at the skin on O'Donnell's arm. "You understand, Massa Johnny? You can get around folks we can't."

Louis shook his head. "Jesus, man."

Flash tried his best to look confused.

Louis sighed. "Think about it, Johnny. We need all the help we can get."

"He'll do it, Champ." Flash gave O'Donnell a playful tap on the shoulder. "He owes me a favor or so."

"That's great to hear." Louis placed his plate and coffee cup on the porch railing. "Thanks for the breakfast, Johnny. I hate to do it, but I'd better go. The Zephyr leaves at noon."

Flash glanced at O'Donnell. "You play golf?"

"A bit."

"Okay. Meet me at that Como Park course. One o'clock sharp," Flash headed for the Buick without waiting for O'Donnell's answer. "I'll show you how the game is played."

"Saw you pitch against the Millers up here last year," Louis said, pausing on the porch steps. "You were good."

Louis pointed at Flash, sitting now behind the wheel of the Buick, looking anxious to get on the road. "He can tell you more about why we're doing this. I can't hang around to keep things right, so I'm hoping you'll keep an eye out for that young fool."

O'DONNELL RUSHED DOWN to the first tee from the Como Park clubhouse, golf clubs rattling like pots and pans in a scraggy leather golf bag. Flash Dawkins watched O'Donnell's approach, checking a fancy wristwatch with an exaggerated show of concern. He said something to a nearby foursome of black golfers, waiting none too patiently for their turn to tee off.

"We're up, O'Donnell," Flash said. "You go. No practice swings. No mulligans. No *nada*."

O'Donnell teed up a fairly unblemished golf ball, one of only four left in his bag. He let go with an unorthodox, but energetic swing. His drive zoomed down the right side of the fairway about twenty-five feet off the ground and drafted upward, ascending like no shot he could remember. When it landed, the ball bounced forward another twenty yards. O'Donnell guessed a short iron to the green might be the ticket. He stepped back from the tee and gave the foursome a nonchalant swagger. What he'd done to deserve such a drive he had no idea.

Sizing up the fairway, Flash ignored O'Donnell's show. A smooth shoulder turn, a strong coil of his upper body, and a pause at the top of his swing for a fraction of a second all primed the smooth, precise, but powerful downswing to come. Hardened persimmon collided with the dimpled cover of a brand new Spaulding "Air-Flite" ball. O'Donnell could imagine the ball's tiny airplane logo spinning madly, souring high above the fairway. Flash ended his swing with a flourish—weight balanced on his left foot, right toe pointed to the turf, belt buckle facing the flight of his shot. Just like the photos of Ben Hogan's swing in the latest *Sport Magazine*.

Flash's drive landed some seventy-five yards beyond O'Donnell's. The foursome near the tee stood motionless, mouths hanging open. Flash scooped up his golf bag and headed down the fairway at a quick pace, his eyes searching out the day's flag placement on the green.

As the two played through the front nine, Flash gave O'Donnell the story of his golfing career, making it sound like a mythic odyssey. He'd started as a teenager, caddying at a country club in L.A., earning two bits a round carrying the bags of the city's elite. The caddy master rescued a partial set of old clubs, and he sent Flash out to practice and play whenever the members weren't around. Flash proved to be a natural. He also had the advantage of learning to play on an excellent course. Most black golfers in L.A. played on a few scraggily municipal tracks. When they did play at a good course, those golfers were on foreign soil, unable to fit shot-making and putting to well-groomed fairways and greens. Flash didn't have that problem.

Before the war, Flash said he'd competed with great success in L.A. and California tournaments that would allow him to enter. When he returned from combat, he took up golf again in earnest. Within a year, he was a local legend, qualifying for the Los Angeles Open—the only major PGA tournament open to black golfers. He finished higher than some of the best white pros in the game. The next year he even led the tournament for a round. But his career remained restricted to the national events for black professional golfers held in cities like Detroit, Chicago, and Kansas City. The money wasn't much, but his playing success and Joe Louis' offer to be a traveling companion and personal golf professional opened up big opportunities.

O'Donnell lost any doubts about how well Flash could play golf after a couple of holes. Every one of his approach shots shadowed the pin, and putts dove into the cup like he had a secret formula.

At a par-three hole, with a long carry over a meandering creek, a twosome ahead attempted to hit out of a deep, greenside sand bunker. To O'Donnell's mind, they looked like Abbott and Costello cavorting in a movie short. Flash scowled as this Bud and Lou abruptly suspended their efforts, apparently for a serious conversation on the fine art of sand play.

"Pick the damn thing up," Flash yelled down from the tee. One of the golfers gave an embarrassed look over his shoulder, snatched his ball out of the sand, and flipped it on the green. Flash gave a cheer.

"Take it easy," O'Donnell advised, a bit shocked and worried at his playing companion's brash behavior.

Flash ignored the two golfers staring back at him from the green.

"The PGA picked a hell of way to welcome folk like me back from the war." Flash kicked at the turf, caught in silence for a time. The twosome ahead finished the hole, and slowly progressed to the next tee.

"I ended up in twelfth place in this year's L.A. Open, and that should have qualified me to play in the next tournament up near Oakland. So I went and paid my entry fee. That would have made me and Rags Rhodes the first black golfers ever playing up there."

"What happened?"

"Hell, I figured they wouldn't let me tee it up, but I wanted to put the PGA on the spot. I played practice rounds with a couple of white pros, and then the PGA boys came and escorted me off the course. What a laugh. I'll go out there next year and probably do the same thing." Flash set up for his shot and lofted a towering nine iron within three feet behind the pin. His ball stuck momentarily in the green, and then spun to within a foot of the hole. O'Donnell could only imagine making his golf ball do things like that.

They walked down the path to a quaint wooden bridge that straddled the creek. Flash said, "I'll bust up that PGA rule for good. Jackie Robinson, that's me."

O'Donnell didn't think Flash's bravado would go over well with the Twin Cities' locals or the press. He sure as hell hadn't been a hit with the twosome ahead, who now stood on the next tee glaring at their antagonist. Minnesotans didn't appreciate brashness and swagger, no matter what Hubert Humphrey might say in the national spotlight. Hell, his fellow Minnesotans thought seasoning their chili with ketchup was way too spicy. O'Donnell had to admit he didn't care much himself for Flash's self-centered, big talk. No wonder Joe Louis was worried.

"I'll be just like Jackie, except in the whitest game around. It's a perfect time for me." Flash pointed O'Donnell to where his ball had buried in the tall grass just beyond the creek. He kept talking as O'Donnell struggled to take a stance without falling into the muck of the creek bed. "The Champ's right, the good liberals in these Twin Cities are going to help. They won't let the PGA keep me from playing."

O'Donnell next shot had landed short of the green, falling into Bud and Lou's yawning sand bunker. He entered into the bunker and dug his feet in, ready he hoped for one hell of a recovery shot. The mud from the creek and the sand clung to his shoes like teenagers at a sock hop. His first attempt to get out of the bunker failed miserably, and the ball rolled back and past him. He could hear the snickers from the next tee.

"I've got the game to win. Sneed, Middlecoff, Demaret—I can take them all," Flash said, ignoring O'Donnell's sand trap woes. "And when I win, the gravy train will be a'rolling my way. Bet on it."

O'Donnell swung away, barely clearing the lip of the bunker, forced to watch his ball scooting across the green into a deep rough. O'Donnell's chagrin doubled as a cackling voice drifted down from the next tee box, "Wanna borrow my foot wedge, buddy?"

AT THE END OF THE FRONT NINE, O'Donnell and Flash headed for a beer at the snack shack. A group of black golfers clustered outside, sitting at a loop of wooden picnic tables, drinking beer in paper cups. O'Donnell knew most of the black golfers in St. Paul played at the Como Park course. It was public—one of few in the city where black golfers felt comfortable enough to play. The private clubs sure wouldn't let them in, and most of the other public links around served up an icy welcome, except perhaps for Hiawatha golf course across the river in Minneapolis. Black golfers certainly couldn't join the men's clubs at any of St. Paul's city courses, so they had to organize one for themselves at Como Park. The more he thought about it, the less O'Donnell felt confident people in the Twin Cities would jump to welcome Flash and his fight with the PGA.

As Flash and he approached the golfers lounging at the tables, O'Donnell spotted a familiar face from his high school baseball days.

"Hey, Flash. How you hitting 'em today?" "Butternut" Wilkins lounged on one of the wooden benches, drinking a bottle of Grain Belt beer, his mouth twisted in what passed for a smile. O'Donnell figured Flash hadn't wasted any time hitting some of St. Paul's low spots if he'd met up with Butternut.

"What'd you shoot out there, Flash?" One of the golfers called out. Several others demanded to know his score.

"Probably couldn't make a par." Butternut frowned at his mates.

From what O'Donnell could see, Butternut had gained thirty pounds since high school, with most of it hanging over his belt. That angry, suspicious expression hadn't changed though. The men near Butternut took note of his darkening mood and fell silent, nursing their beers.

"Flash, my man, who's the flunky tagging along today?" Butternut had re-gained the stage, so his buddies made up for their disloyalty and laughed along with him.

O'Donnell was used to the crap Butternut handed out. The two of them had played baseball and football together in high school, but "teammates" didn't seem the right word. As a catcher, Butternut never lost the opportunity to peg the ball back at O'Donnell as hard as he could, and encouraging visits to the mound were definitely not part of his repertoire. Still, O'Donnell had to admit Butternut was as good a catcher as any. Well . . . except for that time in their junior year. Butternut flubbed an easy pop fly behind the plate and screwed up a good chance for Wilson High to win the city championship. After that, some of the older baseball guys around the city started calling him "Butterfinger." Not that anyone dared say that to his face, of course. So "Butternut" it would be.

Butternut fell into trouble like raindrops into a barrel. He blew any shot at finishing high school when the police arrested him for busting the shop teacher in the nose. After a year at Red Wing Reformatory, O'Donnell heard Butternut came out meaner than ever, hating most anyone and anybody who got in his way—no matter what color, creed, or religion.

Butternut's father owned a bar in the Selby-Dale area, the black neighborhood in St. Paul. As rumor had it, "Daddy" Wilkins had connections with some black nationalist groups, and the word was Butternut's old man might have something going with the Communist Party from days gone by. As far as O'Donnell knew, Butternut didn't share his father's politics. Any politics Butternut had revolved around himself. He'd earned the reputation as a local hoodlum, but he hadn't slipped up enough to get arrested again. He worked the bar at Daddy Wilkins's during the day, and took the opportunity to run some numbers and sell things at a deep discount.

"Hey. L.A. man, how much you betting today?" Butternut glared at Flash.

"Whatever you want to pay me, pal." Flash declined to look in Butternut's direction.

"Well, how about you and your new buddy taking on Little Pete and me? High-low, a buck a hole."

Even with that fat gut, O'Donnell figured Butternut could bust a good one. Little Pete, who owed his nickname, of course, to the fact that he towered above everyone at six-foot-four, worked as the assistant caddy master at the River's Edge Country Club. He'd be the swingman in any match. O'Donnell wasn't eager to start placing bets.

"Get your clubs, pal," Flash ordered Butternut, who gave back his best scowl. "I'm grabbing me a brew first."

"COME ON. DON'T GO momma's boy here," Flash said, and glanced around the snack bar. "We'll go home with a the cash."

"You've seen me play. I won't be much help."

"Don't make any difference." Flash leaned back, downing the last swig of his Hamm's beer. "You're on my side."

From the tenth tee until the end of the match, Butternut yapped every chance he had, buzzing on non-stop, offering a running commentary on his shots and anything else to bug Flash and O'Donnell. He could play well enough, O'Donnell had to admit. Powerful through the arms and torso, thick catcher's legs, and meat hooks for hands, Butternut could put good distance on some of his shots. He lashed at the ball without much form, but showed an unlikely talent for getting up and down around the green.

Little Pete had an excellent game. He drove the ball a long way, and his iron shots had a nice, crisp sound. He'd already sunk a couple of long putts. But as well as Little Pete played, Flash was so good, he and O'Donnell won six of the eight holes played. Flash had three birdies and an eagle on a short par five. As the players walked up to the last tee, O'Donnell could guess Butternut's next move. A double-or-nothing bet. Flash wouldn't back away from that challenge, O'Donnell knew, no matter if it risked all they'd won.

As expected, Butternut announced, "Okay, suckers, double or nothing on this last hole."

O'Donnell glanced at his partner to see what he'd say.

"Accepted," Flash replied, all business. "You go first, O'Donnell."

The late afternoon sunshine poured over the fairway ahead, bestowing a brilliant sheen to its grasses. The tranquil setting in front of O'Donnell

17

should have calmed his nerves. He'd seldom felt this jumpy playing baseball, except in that final moment, standing on the mound, waiting to deliver the first pitch. Throwing a baseball for a strike seemed a hell of a lot easier than hitting a golf ball to the right spot.

O'Donnell swung away. His ball fell to the fairway well short of what he'd intended.

"Great pressure shot, O'Donnell," Butternut crowed. "Nerves of steel."

Flash stepped forward, pointing far down the fairway. "Gentlemen, if you would please direct your attention over here," he said, sounding like some docent at the Minneapolis Art Museum, "I'll demonstrate how to hit a drive you won't believe."

Butternut scowled at Flash, refusing to play along. Little Pete couldn't help but smile.

Flash continued his monologue. "After I birdie this hole, I'll collect every dime you lowlife, dog-butts owe us." He looked at Butternut without a trace of concern. "Any other bets?"

Butternut stared at Flash, at a loss for some sort of smartass reply.

Flash teed his ball, stepped behind, and took a couple of liquid, picture perfect swings. As he moved to address his ball, Butternut snaked out a question. "Hey. What're you doing for those pretty white boys so's they let you play in their golf tournament?"

Flash whirled around, stepping back to confront Butternut. Flash's driver vibrated like a divining rod in his hand, the veins on his arms and neck pulsed. The two men faced off like a pair of angry dogs.

O'Donnell tried to be a peacemaker. "Forget it," he said to Flash, and pointed down the fairway. "Let's see that drive."

Flash continued to stare down Butternut, not ready to back away. "Watch your mouth, my friend," Flash said. He jabbed a finger into the other man's chest before returning to his ball.

O'Donnell kept his eye on Butternut, expecting more gamesmanship. The crack of Flash's club sounded, and O'Donnell turned in time to track the ball soaring high into the growing darkness, well down the fairway as Flash had predicted. Flash scuffed his tee out of the ground in Butternut's direction. "How's that? Got an answer?"

"Luck, that's all," Butternut said.

Butternut and Little Pete both hit good drives, and the four men headed down the grassy knoll from the tee to the fairway without a word. When O'Donnell reached where his ball lay, Flash stood next to him, pointing down the left side of the fairway. "Swing easy. You've got more than enough club. Just set yourself up for a good shot to the green"

O'Donnell did as told. Flash grunted encouragement and headed for his own ball.

Each player ended on the green in regulation. Flash had stroked a perfect, high-flying wedge shot to within three feet of the hole. Butternut and Little Pete were on the green, but faced long putts. O'Donnell's third shot, a very lucky, screaming line drive that somehow cleared the pond protecting the green, left him with a difficult, twenty-five footer. He'd be first to putt.

Butternut made an elaborate ceremony of taking the pin out. "You're up," he said, pointing the flag at O'Donnell. "Don't choke, baby."

Thinking too much about a putt got in the way of doing it, O'Donnell figured, so he didn't wait long to send his on its way. About halfway to the hole, he knew it had a chance. His ball dunked into the cup, slick as a whistle. A birdie.

Butternut gave O'Donnell a long, acid look. "Lucky son-of-a-bitch," he muttered, preparing for his putt. His first attempt ran two feet by the hole. Little Pete lagged close, and tapped in for par. Flash unexpectedly missed his birdie putt by a cat's whisker. Butternut putted again, lipping out on the right side—a bogey. He slammed his putter into his golf bag, threw a wad of bills on the green, and headed straight away for the parking lot.

"Boys, I'm thinking you've just spoiled that man's evening." Little Pete gazed at the retreating figure, a hint of a grin on his face. "I'm thinking maybe you done pissed up his whole week."

"It'll still be light for a while," Flash informed O'Donnell. "I'm playing a few more holes."

"Go to it." O'Donnell said. "I'll see you around, I guess."

"You know that Blue Horse restaurant down on Snelling Avenue?"

"Sure."

"Meet me down there tonight? We'll talk some business then." Flash picked up the money lying on the green. "I think we can make do with this here cash."

"Works for me." O'Donnell could make it back home and take care of Cosmo in the meantime. "See you there."

Flash had already moved away toward the first tee. He gave O'Donnell an absent-minded wave over his shoulder.

THE BLUE HORSE BUZZED with dinner conversation, and waitresses picked their way through the crowded dining area like halfbacks in the broken-field. At the northwest corner of University Avenue and Dale Street, nearby a row of used car lots, across from a shady movie theater, and not too far from dancing at the Prom Ballroom, the Blue Horse served as a classy, step above alternative to a corner bar and grill. O'Donnell liked the mix, and made it his hot spot most Friday nights, especially because the Blue Horse manager booked some great jazz combos. Nothing really that fancy about the place, but the food was good, and the bartenders poured a strong drink. Guys from downtown crammed into the dining room and the bar, outnumbering the available women by a wide margin. They trolled for weekend dates . . . or something quicker. By the end of the evening, O'Donnell knew most of the hopeful horde left the Blue Horse looped and alone. He'd been one of them. Still, the cocktail glasses tinkled a happy tune, the lights were low, and a juicy Blue Horse prime rib dinner was hard to beat.

O'Donnell and Flash sat in a booth on the bar side of the restaurant, not saying much. Flash took a slow inventory of the clientele, meticulous in stirring the whiskey and soda he'd ordered. He stared at a table near the dance floor where two well-dressed couples and a beautiful black woman without an escort raised their drinks in a toast.

"The good thing is your restaurant here lets in folks like me," Flash said.

O'Donnell started to give a short lowdown on the Blue Horse and its clientele, but Flash cut in. "The bad thing is that gorgeous woman over there is going to be damn unhappy if she sees me."

"How's that?"

"You'll find out soon enough." Flash allowed a tight smile.

O'Donnell couldn't help stealing another look at the woman. A knockout. Dark hair pulled back on one side and secured with a red barrette, the same shade as her lipstick. Her eyes danced about the room as she half-listened to the conversation of her dinner companions. The small table candles gave her skin a tint much like the native Hawaiian women O'Donnell remembered from the Islands. A body-hugging, shimmering black dress showcased one hell of a figure.

"Eyes front, Marine." Flash waved a warning finger at O'Donnell. "Thinking about crossing the color line? That's way too much woman for you."

O'Donnell tried his best to swallow the irritation he felt at Flash's remarks, but it must have showed in his eyes.

"Don't get all bent out of shape, pal." Flash said, tracking the approach of their waitress.

"Are you the two hungry guys looking for their dinner orders?" The waitress looked from O'Donnell to Flash. She presented two large dinner plates laden with sizzling cuts of prime rib, asparagus, and baked potatoes. "You're ready for another round of drinks, too."

"I guess that's right," Flash said.

After polishing off their dinners, Flash took a long pull on his second cocktail and set it down, studying the remaining contents of his glass. "Whoever doesn't want me playing in the tournament been mighty busy," he said.

"How's that."

"Had someone on my tail from the golf course, and when I got back to the apartment, some other someone left a damn nasty note under my door."

O'Donnell could only offer a puzzled look.

"I think these local boys don't understand who they're screwing with," Flash said. "But I might have to watch my ass these next few days. Maybe they'll want to up the ante when they find out I don't scare easy."

Despite how he'd felt a few minutes before, what O'Donnell owed to the man across the table weighed heavy on his mind. It wasn't something to shove aside. He had a debt to square no matter what the ups and downs.

Flash leaned back in his chair, glancing up at the elaborate chandelier hanging over the dining area. He allowed the light to play through the glass and the few remaining chips of ice within it. His face relaxed. "Hell, I don't know. I just don't know."

"What?"

"Screw it. I'm going to enjoy myself tonight. Can't spend the rest of my life worrying about all the damn rednecks in this world. If someone is going to get me, they'll do it. Just like the war. But I'm going make it tough for them." Flash looked past O'Donnell, smiling. "Until then, the night is young."

Three young women occupied a table nearby. They stole glances at Flash, whispering behind their hands to each other. Flash gave the girls' table a burst of his smile. They turned their heads in an embarrassed sort of way. Flash grinned like some Hollywood director, casting for starlets. O'Donnell caught himself thinking about the "color line" remark Flash had made.

A silky voice slipped through the jangle of restaurant sounds. "Where you been hiding yourself, mister."

The woman in the black dress leaned into Flash's line of vision. "Let me try that again, Sugar," she said, a pout expanding on her glossy lips, her voice hard and edgy. "Where have you been, lover man?"

Flash stared her up and down. "You look nice, Gloria. Real nice."

The woman switched on a high kilowatt smile, but answered in a low, angry voice, "Don't you nice me. I'm expecting more than two-bit compliments from you."

"Why so mad, Gloria?"

O'Donnell had to concede Flash played a pretty good role as the innocent victim. He'd caught this beauty off-guard, and the young woman's toughness tank drained low. Her lower lip turned from pout to quiver.

Flash followed up quickly. "You're a knockout tonight, baby," he said, reaching out to grab her hand. "Come on, Gloria, sit down. Meet Johnny O'Donnell."

"Leave me be, Flash."

The girls at the table nearby looked at each other wide-eyed. Gloria gave them a withering glance before pulling out of Flash's grasp. She stumbled back slightly, bumping a waitress unfortunate to be passing by. Several orders of shrimp cocktail ended up on the carpet. Gloria exited by way of the mess she'd created, her high heels dissecting the fallen crustaceans.

"The girl has spirit," Flash said with respect, turning full around in his chair to watch Gloria negotiate a low stairway, "and one fine, wiggly ass."

No, Flash hadn't wasted a day since he'd turned up in the Cities, O'Donnell mused, unable to avoid appraising what Flash liked so much about Gloria's leave taking.

O'DONNELL SPOTTED THE WOMAN SITTING at the bar giving some salesman-type the cold shoulder. Thick red hair skimmed the white skin of her shoulder as she stretched to retrieve a new cocktail from an eager bartender. The classy, emerald-green dress she wore fit to perfection, with enough curves exposed to make any man dizzy as hell. He hadn't seen her for a couple of years, but O'Donnell's memories of Jill Gustafson hadn't dimmed much. Probably wouldn't for a long time.

They had first met in summer school, taking extra credits at the university. A class on Greek Mythology—Zeus, his babes, Gorgons, falling in love with statues, rolling rocks up a hill—things like that. O'Donnell's father, a history professor at the university, thought his son needed a keener appreciation of the classics. Jill's father apparently had the same idea, and he didn't want his high-spirited daughter up to nothing for a whole summer. That wouldn't do at all for one of St. Paul's most prominent lawyers.

In their shared class, Jill had sat in the front row of the lecture hall. O'Donnell slumped in the far back corner. He fell in love long distance, ignoring his professor and staring at Jill's beguiling profile. At the end of the first week, O'Donnell flunked a simple ten-point identification quiz. Who was the Goddess of the Hearth? Who cared? O'Donnell didn't have a hearth. Besides, his goddess sat in the front row, and he'd conjured a mythology about her enough to make Zeus blush. When the two got together at last, Jill more than lived up to O'Donnell's chimera—depending on how anyone wished to define it.

Few of the well-heeled families in St. Paul would let their daughters out with the likes of O'Donnell. But Jill had a bedroom in the back of the house with her own porch and set of steps handy for late-night escapes. O'Donnell would drive up the alley at midnight, turn his headlights quickly off and on, and Jill would climb out her bedroom window to a deck overlooking the pool, tiptoe down the steps to the back lawn, and sashay out the gate. Slick as a whistle. In a minute she'd be next to O'Donnell, pressing her body into his. They made love once—the night before she left home to attend Northwestern University. For O'Donnell, it was worth remembering. He convinced himself Jill Gustafson was like no other. He'd carried her picture all around the Pacific, from one island to the next. Other soldiers had Betty Grable or Rita Hayworth in their wallets. O'Donnell didn't need a movie star. He didn't need the "Dear Johnny" letter he received either.

Back in St. Paul after the war, he found out Jill had a serious relationship going with one of the local elites. O'Donnell felt sorry for himself for quite some time, but the Saints invitation to spring training camp took the edge off his misery. He was off to play baseball again, and lucky to be alive. In many ways, those summer nights before the war seemed a million years away. How ridiculous he'd been . . . imagining some cozy domestic future. Another foxhole fantasy. But seeing her again, O'Donnell admitted the fantasy had been a damn good one.

"I'm cruising," Flash announced abruptly, ending O'Donnell's reminiscence.

Flash left the table, and threaded his way through the crowd. After counting out a tip for the waitress, O'Donnell decided he might try to renew old acquaintances. On his way to the bar area, he glimpsed Butternut sitting at a table tucked into a nook near the front window. Butternut at the Blue Horse? Not his usual haunt, no matter the mixed crowd.

"How's it going, Butternut?"

The man in question offered O'Donnell a distracted wave.

"Rematch?" O'Donnell tried to sound playful. Butternut looked like he'd swallowed something awful as he realized exactly who stood next to his chair. His dark eyes filled like a storm drain of disgust.

"What the hell do you want?"

Butternut wore a pale yellow sports coat over flashy white pants. Under the sports coat was a Hawaiian shirt, blinking with a neon rainbow of lovely oranges, reds, and purples. Butternut had worked on the civilian side in Honolulu before the authorities sent him home on a suspected burglary charge. O'Donnell wondered if Butternut's leave-taking had anything to do with his wardrobe choices as well. The man in question sipped a fancy-looking rum drink—perhaps, O'Donnell conceded, a sentimental evocation of Butternut's island adventure.

"Enjoy the golf today?" O'Donnell couldn't hide his pleasure in asking.

Butternut shot out of his chair and into O'Donnell's face, but the long, muscular arm of the man sitting at the same table followed Butternut's ascent and restrained him. Not many had the quickness and muscle to do that. Under the brim of a gray fedora, the man's eyes had the look of someone who'd spent several years staring at things—maybe three gray walls and a door with bars on it. If he was an old chum of Butternut's from the Red Wing Reformatory, O'Donnell speculated, this one had stayed around for post-graduate study. He wore a bland gray suit, black tie, and a nasty scar down his neck. He allowed O'Donnell a peek at a special accessory—direct from Smith & Wesson. Butternut's business might not include sponsoring the local Cub Scouts, but what the hell was this? *Aloha* time?

O'Donnell headed to safe haven at the bar. There he pressed a finger lightly on the shoulder of a young lady sitting next to Jill's now unoccupied barstool. "Excuse me. Can I ask if that's Jill Gustafson sitting next to you?"

Strawberry-blond hair framed a well-scrubbed, fair-skinned face as the woman turned to look at O'Donnell. "Hi, Johnny. She'll be back in a minute."

The green of the young woman's eyes glittered and danced, reflecting the neon lights around the bar. "You don't remember me, do you? I'm Jill's younger sister." She cocked her head at O'Donnell like a puppy, and smiled. "I'm Abby. We met at a 'Y' sock hop once."

O'Donnell thought he might have remembered something like that.

"Don't look so apologetic," she said, touching O'Donnell's arm. "You were crashing a Central High party. I asked you to dance on a bet with my friends."

O'Donnell felt someone press close behind him, and twisted part way around to see. Smiling like a Miss America candidate, radiating all her charm, Jill Gustafson gave O'Donnell a well-choreographed hug, with plenty of body parts in action. Like a great running back, she had some nifty downfield moves.

"It seems like forever since I've seen you, Johnny." Jill stared up at O'Donnell, tiny lines of concern at the corners of her eyes. *It has been a long time*, O'Donnell thought, struggling to disguise the excitement he felt at seeing her again.

"You've met my sister, I gather?"

"Yeah. We were just reliving old times."

To O'Donnell's disappointment, Jill didn't seem much interested in what those old times might have been. She spoke to her sister. "I'm on my way out of here." Then, brushing her lips against O'Donnell's cheek, she told him, "It's so good to see you again."

He must have looked like a kid who'd lost his puppy dog, so Jill turned her Charm-o-Meter up a notch, pausing long enough to fuss over his tie. "You look handsome as ever. I wish I had time to talk." She followed that with a little pout of her lips, held his arm, moving in closer, gluing herself to O'Donnell's ribs. "Would you do me a big favor? Can you give Abby a ride home when you're ready to leave?"

Chaperone the kid sister? Just great. O'Donnell had dreamed about Jill from one end of the Pacific to the other. Didn't that count for anything?

"Jill, I can get a ride with one of the girls," Abby said.

The two siblings went a few rounds while O'Donnell considered beating his head on the bar. He wanted to talk with Jill. He wanted to take her home. He . . . was about to make a huge fool of himself.

He winked at Abby. "I can give you a ride, Abby. It'll give me a chance to remember our first dance."

O'Donnell watched Abby's eyes soften and her shoulders relax and figured he'd belted one over the centerfield fence. Jill dug into her purse for car keys, giving all concerned a knowing, indulgent smile. O'Donnell downgraded the four-bagger to an infield pop-up as far as Jill was concerned.

Flash had made his circuit and passed by the bar. He gave the two sisters a thorough once over, amping up the voltage on his smile. "It's Jill, isn't it," he crooned.

"Mr. Dawkins. Did you and Daddy have a good talk?" Jill asked.

"Yes, we did. Your father's a fine supporter of our fight, and we appreciate all the help."

What the hell was all this about? O'Donnell resented the intrusion, and felt like he'd really missed the boat.

Flash let go a theatrical sigh, smiling at Jill and Abby. "I hate to leave, but I see this cat has all the jive going." He tapped O'Donnell on the chest. "Where do I sign up for lessons?"

Flash left the bar area, weaving through the crowd like a movie star, waving at those who offered hellos. Walking near Butternut and the stranger on his way out the door, Flash cocked his fingers like a pistol and fired off a volley. Butternut flipped his hand, like he was brushing away a fly. He hunched forward, deep in conversation with the brim of the stranger's hat.

H ow do you know him?" Jill turned to the bar and retrieved the remains of her white wine.

"I wanted to ask you the same thing." O'Donnell watched Flash walk by the front window of the Blue Horse.

"What do you mean?" She took a sip, eyeing O'Donnell over the rim of her wine glass. He noticed the color of her eyes changing, glacial— like she wanted an apology.

"I only meant . . ."

"He and Daddy are involved in some civil rights thing," Abby interrupted, giving her sister a sideways look. "They had a big talk the other day with the editor of *The Spokesman* newspaper and someone from the country club."

"I don't think Daddy wants to spread this subject around," Jill said. She put her hand on the tip of O'Donnell's shoulder and moved closer. "But I think it's okay to tell if the two of you are good friends."

"I met him in the war," O'Donnell said. "All of sudden, he shows up out at the cabin today. I know he's planning to play in the St. Paul Open."

"And if they don't let him play, there's going to be *some* excitement," Abby said.

Jill gave her sister a cool glance. "Daddy said we shouldn't tell anyone about it."

"I think he's right about that," O'Donnell said.

Jill nursed her drink for a while, changing the subject, asking polite questions without much concern about O'Donnell's answers. Tough to admit, but O'Donnell knew she had it on her mind to leave the Blue Horse as soon as possible.

"I really have to leave now," Jill said, making it sound like she didn't want to go. "Give me a buzz sometime, Johnny."

O'Donnell watched her pivot to avoid a pair of drunks and slide past the hostess, leaving all to admire her style.

"Does she make you wonder what to do?" Abby asked.

"Yeah," O'Donnell muttered through his disappointment. "She does."

"I'm not so . . . complicated. Do you want to go somewhere else for a drink?"

Not a bad suggestion at all, O'Donnell thought. He wanted to know more about Jill. Besides, Abby seemed like she'd be a nice listener. He guessed that's all he wanted. "I'm about to head back to my place. We can listen to the loons."

Abby didn't hesitate. "Let's go. I haven't heard a good loon call in ages."

COSMO GREETED ABBY with a quick wag of the tail and an embarrassing sniff up her thigh. Courtesies disposed, the dog bulled past Abby and scuttled down the porch steps to the nearest patch of grass. Leg in the air, a hearty stream launched, he stared back at the humans, eyes glossed with canine satisfaction.

O'Donnell called for Cosmo to come sit. The dog leaped up on the porch, took several whiffs of the night air, made some small turn-arounds accompanied by the tick of his nails on the wooden planks, and with a pleasured sigh, stretched out at Abby's feet. Man, woman, and furry friend relaxed, spectators for a star-filled night sky, backed up by a full moon. The occasional, contented gurgles of under-dock-dwelling fish and crickets sawing their hearts out in tall grasses made for a quaint symphony. The poplar trees rustled, their leaves making that soft, clicking sound. O'Donnell and Abby sipped their beer and gloried in the night. Cosmo anointed his body parts.

"How did you end up living out here?" Abby asked. "It's lovely."

O'Donnell gave her the short version. "My Dad lets me rent it for keeping the place in good shape. He inherited the cabin when my grandparents passed away, but he spends most of his summertime in town at the university." O'Donnell's mother had died of pneumonia during

31

the winter before the war, and his father had since remarried. Professor O'Donnell's new wife didn't care much for the lake cabin life.

Abby placed her feet on the deck to stop the porch swing, and leaning forward, studied O'Donnell's face.

"What?"

"Nothing."

"You remind me of a high school guidance counselor. You're giving me the 'What are you going to do with your life?' look."

Abby was pretty in a different way from her sister, and O'Donnell thought most of what made her attractive had nothing to do with being a looker. Abby was nice . . . and easy to be with. With Jill, O'Donnell remembered, it was man and woman. Basic stuff.

"Is the job at Floyd's what you like to do?"

She'd had found a nice way of saying, "Johnny, why in the world do you work part time at Floyd's Pharmacy?" O'Donnell should have kept that piece of information under his hat during the drive out to the cabin.

"You don't think being a part-time jack-of-all-trades at the corner drugstore is my life's dream?"

"You know what I mean," Abby said. "I'll bet you had a good start on college between pitching baseballs and hitting homeruns, didn't you? You are a professor's son, right?"

O'Donnell let that subject drift past into the dark. She was right. He'd done well enough in college, but was so wild about playing ball he never did much thinking about an education to be something else. O'Donnell still thought he had a chance to play—no matter what his sore arm told him. But he didn't want to talk about stuff like that now.

"Miss Gustafson, you look radiant in the moonlight. And I like your pet mosquito."

Abby brushed away the insect, commonly known as a Minnesota Flying Fortress, but it lit on her wrist, intent on extracting a blood sample. Abby finished the bug's life cycle with a quick slap. She made a face, brushing the remaining mosquito parts off her fingers. "Sorry. I don't mean to pry. I always ask dumb questions like that."

O'Donnell wanted off the subject. "So tell me about yourself. What are you doing these days?"

She seemed eager to answer O'Donnell's question. He learned that after graduating college, she tried freelance journalism and really liked writing about art and theatre in the Twin Cities. But she couldn't make a living at it, so she'd taken a job as a part-time editorial assistant at Brentwood Publishing. She hated it. Abby lived at home, but wanted to get an apartment when she could afford one.

O'Donnell wanted to know more about Jill, so he worked some questions about her into the conversation, hoping he didn't seem too anxious about the information. Abby spoke reluctantly about her sister. "She's a real mystery lady. We don't see her much anymore. After she divorced that awful Brad Hoffman, she moved back to the house, but . . ."

"She married Brad Hoffman?" O'Donnell still couldn't believe it. He'd seen the guy's name in the newspapers every so often. Hoffman was a private school type from the upper-crust of St. Paul society.

"Let's not talk about him." Abby reached down and scratched Cosmo gently behind the ears. The dog watched her with loving eyes.

O'Donnell didn't want to press things, so he kept quiet, pretending to soak up the evening's peace.

"Something happened during the war," Abby spoke softly. "Jill quit college after her sophomore year."

"What for?"

"Are you ready for this? She joined the Marine Corps Women's Reserve with a friend of hers from college."

The Women's Reserves? That didn't fit the girl O'Donnell remembered at all. A contingent of the women Marines trained near Camp Lejuene when he was there. The guys dubbed the women "B.A.M. s"— short for "Broad-Assed Marines." The rednecks weighed in, too, with their special, ugly brand of humor. From what O'Donnell saw, the women trained hard and did what they were ordered to do.

"We couldn't get much out of her when she got home," Abby said. "Then, all of sudden, she married Brad. The rest isn't much fun to talk about." Abby sighed, murmuring something about "it's getting pretty late for me." O'Donnell understood she didn't care much for the way the conversation kept drifting to her sister's life.

Abby unexpectedly held O'Donnell's hand as they made their way down the darkened cabin steps. When they reached the car, she snaked an arm around his neck, and tugged him close. She kissed him on the cheek. Next thing O'Donnell knew, she'd moved around him and into the car. On the drive back, they didn't talk much, listening to late night radio songs to pass the time. When O'Donnell pulled up at her house, Abby scooted out of the car with a quick good-bye. He watched her unlock the front door and slide inside.

O'Donnell felt like maybe he'd missed something.

D INKYTOWN," A BITE-SIZED commercial village frequented by University of Minnesota college students and professors, lay at the northwest corner of the campus, separated from the academic goings-on by cross traffic whizzing down University Avenue. Dinkytown's abbreviated borders allowed for an ice cream parlor, a drugstore, a college guy's clothing store, the Varsity Movie Theater, an off-beat bookstore, a collection of tiny shops, student apartments, and for the breakfast cognoscenti, "Al's Breakfast." The diner beckoned hungry scholars and others to Dinkytown for a tasty start to their days. O'Donnell and Flash had agreed to meet for breakfast the evening before. Flash said he wanted to talk about plans for the St. Paul Open.

Al's reputation for good breakfasts at a cheap price far outstripped its seating accommodations, so Flash had exercised squatter's rights on two stools at the breakfast counter. He and O'Donnell, elbows pressed to their sides, squeezed in among several of the regulars. O'Donnell ordered coffee and his favorite on the menu, a stack of pancakes and sausage links. He fiddled with the syrup container before pouring a bunch on his pancakes.

Al's had a waiting line at the door now, and the hopefuls standing inside did their best to not drool on the seated customers' shoulders. Conversations filled the cramped space, and orders of eggs, pancakes, bacon, toast, and other breakfast goodies passed across the counter to willing hands. Flash took a gulp of his coffee and attacked his side order of waffles. He surfaced after consuming the delectable items, dabbing maple syrup off his upper lip. Without missing a beat, he aimed his fork at the main attraction—two scrambled eggs and bacon. Not long after, he snatched both checks and pushed back from the counter. "This one's on me."

"Can I finish what I've got left?" O'Donnell grabbed the last slice of bacon on his plate before it fell prey to his benefactor.

When they left the diner, the two men walked south past Gray's Drugs, across the wooden railway bridge above the four sets of railroad tracks, and then through decorative iron gates to the campus grounds. They settled on the lawn across from aging Pattee Hall. O'Donnell doubted the cafeteria food there had changed much for the better. Not far from where they sat loomed the statue of some past university notable. He looked hopeful despite the bronzing. O'Donnell and Flash reclined on the grass, silent, appreciating the morning's sunshine. After a time, O'Donnell sat up and brushed some newly mown blades of grass off his elbows. "What's the deal with these threats you're getting?"

"I didn't think our plans would get anyone so pissed-off, and I thought we'd been pretty careful about things." Flash eyed two college girls strolling through the columns that fronted Burton Hall, a building recalling the monuments of the ancient world. "All these nice young things walking around make me wonder if I should get some more schooling."

"Come on. What's going on?"

"Take it easy, man. Somebody's trying to scare me off. That's all."

"Seems like they're pretty serious."

"Don't know who it was," Flash said, "but lots of white folks in this country don't want any more Jackie Robinsons. And remember, the guys that run professional golf are the blue bloods, the country club dandies. Hell . . . they don't like most other white guys. Just about every one of those boys on the PGA tour grew up with a silver spoon, and they got more money than they know how to spend. The PGA is a playpen for rich white folks. It's a way to show off those nice private courses, and be some sort of hotshot. Folks like that don't want me spoiling their fun. I guess there's always exceptions. But a black man coming to tee it up on tour? Not welcome. No matter what."

"Who would want to make trouble around here?" O'Donnell asked.

"I don't know, but think of all that Jackie stirred up. The gutter is full of guys mean enough."

Flash watched a new group of coeds approaching. "I can't predict the future. But I'm not thinking it's the PGA going to get in the way of my playing in the St. Paul Open. They likely won't have much to say about it. Keller's a public course, and the Junior Chamber of Commerce boys are sponsoring." Flash smiled to himself, rubbing his hands together. "Think about me winning that tournament. It'll put the PGA up a long damn creek."

O'Donnell didn't have the whole picture framed, but he could see the possibilities.

"I'll sue the PGA for full membership, and they'll have to give it to me. I can be a golf professional and play in PGA events—anywhere. That Gustafson is paying most of the freight, mine included. He sort of sees himself as golf's Branch Rickey."

O'Donnell doubted things would work so easily. But according to Flash, Jill's father had convinced some lawyer friends and local civil rights leaders to join the action. Everything was ready to go.

"Damn it, I fought like everybody else." Flash prodded O'Donnell's shoulder. "I don't get a fair shake now that the war is over. It's time to get what I'm deserving."

O'Donnell wondered about Flash's impatience. He also wondered if the man next to him wasn't a bit too brash and cocky for the role of golf's Jackie Robinson. He could easily rub people the wrong way. *Hell*, thought O'Donnell, *he rubs me the wrong way*. O'Donnell had heard the stories about Branch Rickey and Jackie Robinson's first meeting. Mr. Rickey apparently play-acted what would happen at the major league ballparks, and screamed some pretty awful racial slurs in Jackie's face. "You want a ballplayer who's afraid to fight back?" Jackie asked. "I want a player with guts enough not to fight back," Rickey told him. O'Donnell didn't think Flash would accept that sort of restriction. As far as O'Donnell could see so far, Flash Dawkins didn't seem in quite the same league as Jackie Robinson.

"When did you start planning all this?" O'Donnell asked.

"Someone must have told Gustafson about me. He called this spring. Said he heard about my finish in the L.A. Open and what I tried to do up in Oakland."

"So, like you said, word about you probably got around town."

"Yeah. I guess so."

The more O'Donnell thought about it, the more he supposed Flash should reconsider how wide and deep support might run for him around the Cities. O'Donnell guessed it was a minority who supported Gustafson and his plans for Flash. A few more might say the right things but wouldn't lift a finger when push came to shove.

Another thing nagged at O'Donnell. Most folks around had not so rapidly and completely lost their prejudices, despite the principles and pride roused by nation's victory over the evils of fascism and totalitarianism. Many had jumped in with both feet now for the anti-Communist stuff. Some locals had already organized a rally at the university campus protesting the "pinko" professors. O'Donnell's father had lost a colleague in the History department on trumped-up charges. The way O'Donnell saw things, Gustafson and his friends were heading into dangerous waters.

O'Donnell and Flash joined a throng of students walking between classes, many filtering across University Avenue and back to Dinkytown for an early lunch. A rush of cars and delivery vehicles passed by, headed west toward Hennepin Avenue and downtown Minneapolis. An Oldsmobile convertible filled with young women sped by on the way to Sorority Row. Flash gave a low whistle.

"I gave up worrying about tomorrows a long time back," he said. The light changed to green and the men stepped off the curb. "No need to worry, Johnny-boy. I plan to look both ways before I cross the street and all that."

"Hey, you're the one who called this get-together. What am I supposed to be doing?"

"I'll think of something."

Flash had parked in front of Al's. He stood by the driver's side, sorting through his keys. He gave a quick wave, ducked into his car, and headed off down Fourteenth Street.

For all O'Donnell could tell, Flash had moved on from the threats he'd received. Was it the trick someone learned in combat—shrinking experience to its essentials and trading it for another day alive? Watching bodies stack up at a landing zone, O'Donnell figured a guy could do that. Not much choice really.

MINNESOTANS COULD SPEND seven months a year freezing their butts off, but give them a nice summer day in the embrace of reasonably warm weather and blue skies, and O'Donnell knew that hard lessons and years of experience counted for little as residents blotted out the memory of knee-knocking, back-hunching, skin-cracking winds, and below-zero temperatures that could freeze a car stiff as a cadaver. Rambling down Minnehaha Avenue, the Ford's windows open wide, O'Donnell had to think Minnesota wasn't such a bad place after all . . . until mid-October.

He pulled up in front of Floyd's Pharmacy. He had some money coming. The owner, Floyd Olson, was futzing around in the storeroom, sorting through a recently arrived batch of magazines. The latest issue of *Stag* in hand, Floyd's waved it in O'Donnell's direction. He always checked with O'Donnell about the few racy magazines allowed on the rack. As he said, "You've been around a bit, Johnny. See what you think." This month's issue had the usual snapshots of would-be Hollywood starlets with vacant looks and jutting, titanic breasts trapped in minuscule sweaters.

"It's a tough call." O'Donnell took a closer look-see. "My advice is to display this as a public service for young boys struggling with the challenges of puberty." He flipped through a few more pages for accuracy's sake. "Hide it up by *Popular Mechanics* and *Field and Stream*. That's where they'll expect to find it."

"My exact thoughts, Johnny."

Floyd dug in the pocket of the white lab coat he always wore and produced a stub of paper. "You had a phone call this morning."

Floyd had written down a number but no name. O'Donnell went downstairs and slipped behind the front counter where Floyd kept the phone. The phone number seemed familiar. He knew why the minute she answered.

"Hey, Jill. It's Johnny."

Jill hesitated, like she might be running O'Donnell's name through a mental Rolodex of those seldom remembered or easily forgotten.

"Did Abby call you?" Jill asked. "Let me see if she's around."

Silence, a click, and then an authoritative male voice on the line. "Gustafson, here."

"It's John O'Donnell, sir. I was just speaking with Jill."

"Fine, fine, Mr. O'Donnell," Gustafson said. "Actually, I'm the one who called you."

Jill came back on the line. "I can't find Abby anywhere . . ."

"Hang up, Jill dear. I need to talk with Mr. O'Donnell."

Curious now, Jill didn't hang up, instead asking for O'Donnell's number, saying she might call him later. Gustafson cleared his throat. His daughter hung up.

"John, I'm wondering if you could come by the house to discuss a matter with me. Bring along your swim suit if you want. It's a beautiful day and I'm infringing on your time. I'm sure Jill would like to see you after we're done talking." O'Donnell wondered about that, but agreed to be there in an hour. Gustafson hung up, his business concluded. No idle chit-chat. O'Donnell listened attentively to the dial tone.

EINAR GUSTAFSON HELD A SENIOR partner slot at one of St. Paul's top-notch law firms. Since the days when St. Paul's railroad and lumber barons built their empires and moved into splendid homes on Summit Avenue, they'd always had a need for sharp lawyers. Gustafson's father had attended to accounting and legal matters for the descendants of St. Paul's early captains of industry, and Einar picked up where his father had left off. He weathered the Great Depression, made a bundle during the war years representing St. Paul's munitions' factories, and by the post-war could pretty much do whatever he wanted. As O'Donnell recalled from a recent news feature in the *Pioneer Press*, Gustafson chose to take cases that involved high-level constitutional issues. He'd written a textbook on constitutional law, and a couple of years ago appeared before the Supreme Court to argue a public facilities civil rights case. Some said he had designs on running for the State Attorney General's office . . . or even higher.

Once O'Donnell turned off Marshall Avenue onto the River Road, an old feeling crept over him. He didn't belong in these neighborhoods. The further he drove toward the Mississippi River, the grander became the lawns and houses that fronted the street. The Gustafsons resided in a three-story Tudor mansion set back from the parkway. O'Donnell turned right and made his way up the private drive, curving by a colossal stand of oaks and a lawn design that looked like a French Impressionist landscape. He parked on a cobblestone area near the front entrance, stepped up to a massive wooden door, with ornately carved designs across the top and bottom. He drew back fancy doorknocker to deliver a polite couple of taps. Two hollow thuds rewarded his caution. The image of a lonely traveler in medieval Transylvania ran through his mind. He assumed visitors didn't peer through the triangular leaded window set in the door to see who might be home. He tried his best to look casual waiting on the doorstep for someone to open the stupid door.

"Johnny?" Jill's voice sounded to O'Donnell's right, near the side of the house. She wore a bright red, two-piece bathing suit, hair pulled back in a ponytail with a blue ribbon. O'Donnell thought she looked like a teenager masquerading in Rita Hayworth's body. A delicate, crooked finger motioned O'Donnell toward the wooden gate she stood behind.

"Thanks so much for bringing Abby home the other night. That was sweet of you."

"Not a problem. We had fun."

Jill gave O'Donnell a look like he'd admitted to a taste for some haute cuisine. "Really? Too bad she's gone today. I'm sure she'd like to say hi."

Jill took O"Donnell's hand, led him through the gate and down a walkway shaded by low trees. She stopped halfway and turned her face up, body attaching to O'Donnell's like a magnet. This was an invitation to kiss her if he didn't miss his guess. It was a long one. She broke it off finally, and smiled.

"Mmmm. That reminds me of high school days," she said, her breath like a feather in O'Donnell's ear.

High school? Had he not learned anything over the years? On the other hand, Jill's kiss seemed more like post-graduate level stuff to O'Donnell.

Jill smoothed out a wrinkle on O'Donnell's shirtfront where she'd plastered herself, ran her fingers down his forearm, and turned him toward the back yard.

"What is it Daddy wants to talk about?"

"He didn't say."

As they stepped into the pool area, Jill stopped abruptly. "You won't keep secrets from me, will you?"

Before O'Donnell could give her an answer, Jill stepped away to the edge of the pool, diving into the still water. She hardly made a ripple. O'Donnell watched her gliding under the surface, the red swimsuit glimmering through the water, legs kicking strongly, shapely hips moving in perfect synchronization. No wonder he liked Esther Williams movies.

"Mr. O'Donnell. Come on over here and sit."

Gustafson sat in a deck chair across the pool, watching his daughter's underwater progress. On a low, wrought iron table shielded from the sun by an ample green umbrella, Gustafson had spread books and papers within easy reach, and he had what looked to O'Donnell like a frosty glass of gin and tonic at his elbow. He didn't seem much older than how O'Donnell remembered from before the war. He still had a full, theatrical mane of hair that set him apart from the masses in matters of coiffure. Gustafson obviously didn't frequent Vince's Midway Barbershop where all the customers ended up with a buzz-cut. O'Donnell judged the older man to be in pretty good shape, with only a hint of belly poking over a pair of tartan plaid swim shorts.

"I'd get up to shake your hand, but I'm afraid I'll spill some Supreme Court business in the pool," Gustafson said.

"That's okay," O'Donnell said, reaching down to complete a handshake.

"Why don't you go change into your swim trunks?" Gustafson pointed over his shoulder to a substantial white cabana in the corner of the pool area.

When O'Donnell returned poolside in his faded blue swimsuit, Jill teased him with a low whistle. Her father acted as if he didn't hear, and directed O'Donnell to sit next to him on a lounge chair, hurrying through all the formalities and small talk. *Will you join me in a drink? Have some pretzels? Are you settled in yet? Going back to school anytime soon? Miss playing baseball? Is your father still teaching at the U? Where are you living these days?* . . . everything but O'Donnell's shoe size.

Sorting through papers balanced on his lap, Gustafson plucked out one of the sheets and held it up. "This is going to be quite a case."

Quick on cue, O'Donnell asked about it.

Gustafson pulled himself upright in his chair, warming to an opportunity to speak about his latest challenge. "This is a case from Kansas City that's going before the Court. Seems that the city fathers are refusing to share the new municipal pool with their Negro citizens, despite the fact that these good folks pay their fair share of taxes." He cocked his right eyebrow. O'Donnell countered with a left. He could play in this league.

Gustafson said, "The NAACP has asked me to work with their Legal Defense Fund lawyers."

"Is it a Fourteenth Amendment case?" O'Donnell hoped the question would establish his credentials as more than a ex-baseball player.

Gustafson rewarded O'Donnell with an approving look. No doubt, O'Donnell figured, the same one used for students in his Constitutional Law course at the university. The older man took a sip of his drink before launching into what promised to be a substantive intellectual journey through recent civil rights law. He didn't disappoint. In between nodding intelligently and looking intent, O'Donnell discovered Gustafson spent quite a bit of time working with the NAACP on their cases—especially equal access to public facilities. It was hard not to be impressed with Gustafson and what he did.

"What does equal access cover, sir?" O'Donnell asked.

"Oh, things like parks, theaters, swimming pools, and even golf courses. In fact, we've had more suits filed about golf courses than just about anything else." He chuckled a bit and said, "I bet you're going to ask why?"

"It had crossed my mind, sir."

"It's a couple of things. First, golf is a segregated sport," Gustafson said, pulling back and forth on one of his fingers. He frowned, and fell silent for a minute. "I think black men see the golf course as . . . yes, that's it. It's like a plantation."

O'Donnell watched the older man savor his analogy.

"Black citizens work on that modern plantation as caddies and groundskeepers, and even get into the 'big house' as cooks and servers," Gustafson said. "John, we see this sort of thing on public and private courses all over. So, breaking into that big house and bumping against all the prejudice surrounding it satisfies a lot of agendas for black folks across the country, particularly in terms of their psychological needs."

Gustafson paced in small steps by the water of the pool, stoking at his goatee. O'Donnell could see Gustafson had his professor's hat on now. Would there be an exam?

"It's quite funny, really," Gustafson said, smiling to himself. "Did you know most bringing these legal suits are dentists? They want to be like dentists everywhere. Fill a few cavities in the morning and play golf and drink cocktails in the afternoon. I guess that's progress, don't you think?"

O'Donnell laughed and said he guessed so.

"You know, don't you? Mr. Dawkins is going to be using my expertise soon."

"Is he filling cavities?"

"Very good, young man." Gustafson smiled, appraising O'Donnell as if he hadn't really thought much about him before that moment.

Score one for me, O'Donnell thought. *I'm a regular Jack Benny.*

"I'm going to put a tight squeeze on that damnable Caucasian Only exclusion clause the PGA holds so dear," Gustafson said.

Something in the way he explained things made O'Donnell wonder how much ego Gustafson had invested in his role. Gustafson clasped his hands behind him as he paced. "To think that in this day and age we have things such as that. I was in Germany with the Nuremberg group for a time after the war," he said. "I saw the camps. I spoke to the survivors."

Both men remained quiet for a moment. Gustafson lost in his thoughts. "No human beings should be treated without respect," Gustafson said, in a soft, distant voice. "Especially here . . . in this country."

"Segregation doesn't exactly help our world image," O'Donnell said. "I expect the Russians are licking their chops at the propaganda opportunities."

"Well put, John. Now let me tell you. If those dentists want to play golf in the afternoon," he said, measuring out each word, "they can count on me to help." He looked O'Donnell's way for confirmation.

"That's great, sir."

Gustafson motioned for O'Donnell to follow him to the shallow end of the pool, and stepped into the water about waist high. O'Donnell followed him in. The two men stood there, conversation suspended, Gustafson assessing the clouds passing overhead.

The cool water of the pool sluiced the undersides of O'Donnell's swim trunks, making it difficult to stand still. Jill now reclined at the other end of the pool on a blue mattress. O'Donnell tried not to notice as she shifted from one position to another, each suggestive of the starlets within the pages of Floyd's drugstore magazines. She caught O'Donnell staring at her, winked, rolled over on her tummy, and slowly unfastened her bathing suit top allowing the ends to slide down.

"I thought I would discuss a little matter with you." Gustafson stood near O'Donnell shoveling water over his arms and chest. "I trust you will be discrete," he said in a low, confidential tone. "Mr. Dawkins and Joe Louis have spoken of you, and I inquired around about your background. Most people seem to share a high opinion. I'd like you to keep an eye out for Flash Dawkins. He's a talented and strong-willed young man. In some ways perfect for our challenge."

"I've got a feeling Flash feels he can take care of himself just fine," O'Donnell said.

"That's not quite my judgment, and it's not that of Joe Louis," Gustafson said, leading O'Donnell to the pool ladder. "We have talked over the general situation, and both agree you're needed as a part of our team."

Things were beginning to sound like orientation at Marine boot camp, but O'Donnell could see the need for some way to keep Flash out of trouble. Gustafson climbed out of the pool and retrieved the remains of his drink, but set it down again. "We are ready to pay you a reasonable fee to closely chaperone Mr. Dawkins's activities leading up to and through the golf tournament. If you need any additional help, we'll cover that too."

"I don't know."

"It's no secret you could use the extra work, is it?" Gustafson looked to O'Donnell for some sign of confirmation. "I don't want to hire some seedy private detective. You can provide needed help in this situation, and I understand you two men have some history from the war. "

A phone rang in the distance, and Gustafson gathered up his drink and files. "I think that'll be it for me. I appreciate your coming by for this talk, John. Send me a reasonable bill for your fees and expenses you might incur."

As he watched Gustafson leave the pool and walk into his house, O'Donnell had to admit, the guy knew how to pull the right strings.

"Surprise, Johnny!"

A quick shove from behind sent O'Donnell splashing back into the pool. He hit the water at a bad angle, slapping his left side against the surface. It stung.

Jill was right there behind him, jumping on his back and trying to push his face under the water. He grabbed her wrists and yanked her up and over, sending her headfirst into the water. She surfaced with a nasty look. It changed quickly from the furious to mistreated child. She choked out some of the pool water, close to tears. "You didn't have to throw me like that." Another hurt look followed with a retreat to the pool ladder. O'Donnell watched her climb out to where her towel lay on the diving board. Her shoulders trembled. He felt like a bully. Just how she wanted him to feel.

O'Donnell hoisted himself out of the pool. He touched Jill's neck with his fingertips. She turned around, tears running down her face.

"Sorry. Are you okay?"

"Johnny," she whispered, pulling herself close to him. "I felt like you and Daddy were keeping secrets from me." She snuggled into O'Donnell's chest. He felt his heart melting like a Fudgsickle on a July sidewalk.

"We weren't plotting." O'Donnell didn't think he had to keep anything from her. "It's about Flash Dawkins."

"What about him?" Jill looked confused.

"From what I know, your father and Flash are working together on a civil rights protest, and I'm supposed to check around and make sure no one tries to interfere with their plans."

"What do you mean 'interfere'?"

"I'm not real sure yet," O'Donnell said. It seemed like Jill was in control of her emotions now, and she held O'Donnell's hand against the smooth skin of her cheek, smiling up at him.

"Thanks, Johnny. I feel left out of things around here. You know, don't you?" Jill stood on her tiptoes and offered O'Donnell a chance for a kiss. He remembered how she could change so quickly from one mood to another. The years hadn't changed that at all.

They spent most of the afternoon hanging around the pool. Jill suggested they should find something at a grocery store for a picnic at Highland Park. She went inside the house to change, leaving O'Donnell to ponder the remaining play of sunshine on the surface of the pool. After a few minutes, he changed out of his swimming trunks in the cabana, and walked around to the front of the house to stand by his car. Jill emerged out the front door seconds later. She wore white shorts, a blue sleeveless blouse, and a pair of spotless, white Keds. Her hair fell to her shoulders, thick and reddish-bronze.

"You have a sunburned nose. It looks cute, Johnny."

They drove to a market on Highland Parkway to look for some picnic stuff. As they approached the grocery store, Jill decided she didn't fancy that sort of adventure anymore. She wanted to eat an early dinner at O'Gara's Bar, a fun place with good steaks. That was okay with O'Donnell.

Arriving at O'Gara's, the couple slipped into a red leatherette booth with a gleaming, black formica tabletop. Each booth had a covered candle, and O'Donnell and Jill gave the menu a glance under its glow. The waitress stopped by for a drink order. Jill wanted a gin and tonic; O'Donnell ordered a beer. They talked about old friends and good times from before the war. The more Jill kept nuzzling against him, the more O'Donnell wanted to slide her down on the red leatherette. He ordered her a second gin and tonic instead. The waitress winked at O'Donnell as she hurried off to fill the order. Once finished with dinner, along with a half bottle of red wine, Jill suggested they forget the movie. "Why don't you show me your cabin?"

On the drive out to the cabin, O'Donnell's heart beat like a Buddy Rich drum solo. Jill seemed so relaxed. O'Donnell felt stretched tight as a piano wire.

He turned into his driveway at good speed, spewing gravel on the neighbor's property. He led Jill to the cabin porch, trying not to rush her.

Dragging her into the bedroom seemed poor form, although it's what he had in mind. He beat back Cosmo's assault at the screen door, turning him outside. Cosmo stood on the porch, panting, looking bewildered.

O'Donnell was out of beer and anything half sophisticated. He offered Jill the last shot from a bottle of peppermint Schnapps. She showed good sense and declined. He inquired if she was comfortable, and headed to the bathroom. He regretted saying, "be back in a second." Emptying a bladder thinking about what might be next on the program wasn't easy. The back and forth between future and present objectives posed a mechanical problem. He felt like a seventh grader at his first make-out party.

Jill had doused the lights in his absence. With a trail of moonlight gleaming through the windows to show the way, O'Donnell walked to the front room. Cosmo sat outside the screen door, wagging his tail.

"I'm in here," Jill called from the bedroom. O'Donnell liked a girl who made herself at home.

H E DROVE HER HOME some time around eleven o'clock. Jill told O'Donnell to stop halfway up the driveway. He struggled to think of something to say, but came up empty. Jill gave him a chaste peck on the cheek, and left him to contemplate their evening together. After O'Donnell heard the front door close, he shifted the Ford into reverse, backing out the driveway and turning down the River Road.

Jill had shown O'Donnell more than expected in their lovemaking. The thing was, she seemed to want to lead their dance. He didn't have anything to gripe about. He got what he'd been wanting for so long. Why start picking it apart? As his old friend Omar Khayyam might have said, "Ah, make the most of what we yet may spend. Before we too into the Dust descend." Omar always had a way with words.

At University and Snelling—"the Heart of the Midway"—O'Donnell recognized a Buick Roadmaster barreling across the intersection, heading west. He hung a left and followed.

The 427 Club perched on the second floor of a drab, two-story building at the corner of Prior and University. During the war, most of the workers at the big munitions plant made it their home away from home. A oak plank bar ran the length of one wall, and the drinkers could sit on wooden stools at the bar or cluster around a motley collection of tables and chairs spread throughout the room. The drinks were stout and didn't cost much, so peacetime hadn't dimmed the 427's appeal. The bar stayed open after hours to accommodate St. Paul's finest, and the policemen liked to drop in after patrol duty on Saturday nights.

O'Donnell's favorite bartender, Chuck Soderstrom, was a manic sports fan, well on his way to becoming a legend among his customers. There wasn't a batting average or a pitcher's career record he didn't know. Best of all, he could be cajoled into a free beer more often than not.

O'Donnell parked his car around the corner, across from the hulking YMCA building. He trekked up the 427 Club's two flights of stairs toward an aurora of neon lights and friendly noise beckoning at the top. Years of human traffic had worn the wooden stairs thin in their middles. At the doorway, a packed, smoky, noisy room welcomed O'Donnell. The customers stood almost two deep at the bar.

"Chuck, what's the occasion?" O'Donnell yelled over the din as he edged into a small break in the bar crowd near the waitress's serving station.

Chuck uncapped a couple of Hamm's beers at one of many metal bottle openers screwed into the bar. The glass bottles dripped from the heat, and Chuck sent one whizzing down the bar surface toward a heavy-set guy with forearms like a gorilla.

"Put the money on the bar, buddy," Chuck commanded, and jerked a thumb in O'Donnell's direction. "I got to talk with this late, great, right hander." He drew a bar towel across his forehead, swabbing off the heavy sweat he'd worked up tending his customers. "How's it going, Johnny? What are you drinking?"

"Give me a Hamm's and a schnapps, Chuck."

Chuck snaked one hand into the beer bin and grabbed a peppermint schnapps bottle with the other. In a matter of seconds, he had the drinks ready and his elbows on the bar, appraising O'Donnell. Dealing drinks at the 427 Club didn't require a degree in advanced mixology. Disregarding a beer gut and the asthma that kept him out of the war, Chuck was a jaguar behind the bar. The big Swede also was the most vocal, loyal, unquestioning cheerleader around—be it for Harry Truman, the Saints, Harold Stassen, or '48 Fords. A local welterweight and middleweight boxing brothers act, the Fighting Flynns, ranked high on Chuck's list of favorites. He loved this pair, and the Flynns made the 427 Club their hangout. O'Donnell spotted Donnie and Devin Flynn planted by the jukebox, surrounded by fight fans. O'Donnell figured the Flynns must have had a bout at the downtown St. Paul Auditorium—that's why the crowd tonight.

"Did you hear?" Chuck beamed like a proud papa. "Both of my boys won."

Chuck shadowboxed with the old man filling up the ice bins behind the bar. The guy gave O'Donnell a look, closed his eyes and shook his head, a weary, unwilling partner to Chuck's zingy pantomime.

"Devin bopped his guy in the second round," Chuck announced.

O'Donnell glanced at the Flynns. Not a scratch on Devin, but Donnie's face looked like pink cotton candy with specks of red peppermint mixed in.

"So how did Donnie do tonight?" Tact was important, O'Donnell reminded himself, especially since Chuck hadn't yet asked him to pay for the drinks.

Chuck frowned ever so slightly, but launched into a long-winded justification for why Donnie Flynn ended up his fight looking like Ireland's answer to Rudolph the Red Nosed Reindeer. O'Donnell listened until Chuck went to fill a customer's drink order, and escaped to other end of the bar. A nice guy, Chuck, but you didn't want to overload his circuits.

"O'Donnell, come on over here." Flash sat at a small table near a plate glass window facing University Avenue.

O'Donnell grabbed his drinks and headed over. "Counting streetcars?"

"The way this night is going, I might as well."

"What's the problem?"

"Actually, things couldn't be better." Flash reached over on the radiator behind him and passed over the sports section of the *Pioneer Press*. "Take a look at this."

Flash pointed to a short announcement on the last page of the sports' section. The header announced, "Negro Golfer to Play in St. Paul Open."

O'Donnell read the squib, re-folded the paper and handed it back. "I wonder how people are going to like all this attention you're getting?"

Flash nodded, and stared out the window again, his mood darkening. "That's why I'm not as excited about it as I ought to be. You know Horace Stone?"

"The editor and publisher of the *Spokesman* and the *Reporter*, isn't he?" Stone had been putting out newspapers focused on the Twin Cities black citizens for years. The politicians in both St. Paul and Minneapolis hated to be on his wrong side.

"He's been getting letters addressed to me at the newspaper since I came here. He had some new hate mail for me today."

"Care to elaborate on the contents?"

"The same old stuff." Flash swilled the remaining contents of his beer bottle.

O'Donnell told Flash about his meeting with Einar Gustafson. "You need to lie low and let me offer a bit of help."

"Who elected you the big boss."

The two fell silent, O'Donnell wondering why the man across the table from him had to be quite so stubborn. Across the room, the Flynn brothers still yakkety-yakked with their fans about their fights. Off-duty St. Paul cops had drifted into the bar area, grabbing drinks and gabbing with Chuck Soderstrom. The alarm clock Chuck used to signal closing time squealed its warning.

Nobody paid any attention, forcing Chuck to shoo out all but his closest cronies and the few cops remaining at a table. The noise level dropped to a murmur of voices. Chuck dimmed the lights and closed the entrance.

MAYBE YOU SHOULD SIGN UP the Fighting Flynns for protection," O'Donnell suggested, trying to get a rise out of Flash. "Neither one of them is getting rich in the ring. I bet they could use some real work. Think about it. Those boys are tough and know the street."

"Whoa, O'Donnell. Don't jive me," Flash said, looking at O'Donnell through narrowed eyes. "I'm not letting those two pugs near me. Can you imagine the Flynns be-bopping around on the golf course? Man alive."

O'Donnell did his best to keep from smiling. "You sure?"

"Damn sure," Flash drummed his fingers on the tabletop, "We need someone better than those two punks."

"I've got a friend who might help out." Bobby Borgstrom. He and O'Donnell had joined up in Mrs. Fancher's kindergarten class at Hancock grade school. They had stuck together as friends ever since. Nobody played games with Bobby. His dad had been a St. Paul cop—tough as nails. Bobby, too. A defensive end and offensive tackle in high school, Bobby made St. Paul All-City easy and went on to play for the Gophers.

"Why him?" Flash leaned back and took another sip of his drink.

"He still has friends at the Police Department from when his dad walked a beat. He's gone back to school on the GI bill, and he's looking for some extra money."

Flash nodded, waiting for more.

"His classes are in the morning, and he can spend the rest of the day playing bodyguard. Besides, I know him and trust him."

Flash shifted in his chair to look out the smudged window at the street below. The stoplights on the corner had turned to blinking amber for late night drivers going home. The University Avenue streetcar clattered by nearly empty—a lone passenger huddled up in the back row of seats. Flash followed the streetcar until it passed into the darkness beyond the corner. O'Donnell could tell Flash didn't much care at all for a shadow in his life, even for a few days.

"Guess I haven't much choice, do I?" Flash tipped his glass up and emptied his beer. "What a pain."

Flash's attitude about the whole thing was beginning to rankle O'Donnell. "People are trying to help you, right? Why don't you . . ." Maybe *show a little appreciation* was what O'Donnell couldn't help thinking at that moment, but he swallowed that thought.

"I know exactly what you want to say, man, and you can forget it. I got no time to give you a damn history lesson you folks already ought to know. Don't expect me to act like some black boy up here from the cotton fields."

O'Donnell downed the last of his beer, still angry, but confused about why Flash had to be . . . he didn't know which word fit best. "I'll have Bobby call you tomorrow morning, and the two of you can work out a schedule."

Flash groaned his agreement. "What about you?"

"I'll fill in the off-hours." The way he was feeling at that point about the man across from him, O'Donnell didn't have it in mind to sign on for more than necessary. Besides, he figured that some detective, ear-to-the-ground stuff might be more useful. "Bobby and I can double-team things during the Open."

Over by the door, Chuck shooed folks down the long flight of stairs and into the night. O'Donnell and Flash joined the exodus. Out on the sidewalk, small groups made their way to cars parked at the curb or across the way in the parking lot behind a dark and deserted Midway Restaurant. O'Donnell followed Flash to where he'd parked the Buick a few steps away in front of the Minnesota Driver's License building. Once Flash nosed the Buick into the street, O'Donnell headed around the corner to where he'd parked.

Some kids probably had thrown a rock at the streetlamp, dousing the lights on the west side of the building. Uneasy for some reason, O'Donnell glanced over his shoulder to check the shadows. Once behind the wheel, he slipped the keys into the ignition and reached to press the starter. That's when someone hiding in the back seat clamped a strong grip on O'Donnell's neck, fingers digging into pressure points. O'Donnell felt the energy drain from his brain like someone was slurping a soda. Before everything shut down, a deep, whiskey-flavored voice warned, "Keep your nose out of bad business, sleepy boy."

●●●●●

CHUCK SODERSTROM FOUND O'Donnell nose first in the steering wheel, arms and hands dangling down to the car floor. He dragged O'Donnell out of the driver's seat to the pavement. "What the hell happened?"

"I wish I knew." O'Donnell pulled himself up and sat on the sidewalk, back against a lamppost. He rubbed his neck and tried to clear his head. Chuck's suggestion for bacon, eggs, and coffee at the all-night restaurant up on Raymond and University didn't seem the ticket. O'Donnell couldn't help but conclude the breakfast invitation spoke volumes about Chuck's trains of thought: they rarely ran on time and towards a specific destination.

Once back at the cabin, O'Donnell stood on the porch steps, staring into pitch-black night. Cosmo raced back and forth near the lake, his nose an inch above the ground. Far out in the water, the loons broadcast calls to anyone still awake. An occasional fish broke the surface, plopped on its side, and slipped back into the murky water. Cosmo scared up an animal of some sort, and scampered around in hot pursuit. O'Donnell didn't know who the hell to chase.

H E SOAKED UP SOME of the next morning's warm sunshine on his sore neck and shoulders. Minutes before he'd finished a phone call to Bobby Borgstrom, recruiting his help and trying to explain what happened after the bar closed. He also mentioned the run-in with Butternut on the golf course and at the Blue Horse. Bobby didn't figure the police would be able to do much, but promised he'd make a few calls.

Sipping his first cup of coffee, O'Donnell spied Cosmo lying alongside a dilapidated blue rowboat that came with the cabin. The dog's eyes held a message for O'Donnell as usual.

Why not? O'Donnell dug up a can of worms from soft soil near the porch steps, and grabbed his bamboo fishing pole.

O'Donnell had long since decided that each and every purebred Minnesotan had the instinct to become positively avid about fishing. To draw a fishy analogy—it was like salmon swimming upstream. But, unlike most Minnesotans, piscatorial passions had no great hold on O'Donnell. He'd never warmed to the experience of some squirming, scaled creature swallowing a hook, wallowing in his hand, frothing bloody at the gills, pleading with a frantic fish eye for some sort of aquatic absolution. A *Field and Stream* guy O'Donnell was not, and proud of his dissent to the point he could miss the traditional Friday night fish fry at the Moose Hall without a hint of guilt. When he and Cosmo sallied forth on the waters of their lake, it was truly a rare occasion. It had to be good weather, and man and dog always headed to the sunniest spot, where the fish wouldn't think to bother them too much. As for others? This particular morning all the boats on the lake clustered within weedy areas, and armadas of fishermen, shoulders scrunched over their oars and hats pulled low, longed for a spot of rain so the fish would bite.

O'Donnell and his four-legged friend dropped anchor in a warm patch of sunshine and relaxed. O'Donnell nibbled on a couple of apples and threw down the cores for the dog. The gentle lolling of the water had the captain and first-mate fast asleep in no time. The snoozers posed no threat to perch, sunfish, or bluegill. But in the midst of his tranquil retreat from consciousness, O'Donnell felt a zingy vibration run through the boat. Fighting his way back awake, he discovered a frantic Cosmo wagging his tail, barking and yowling, and preparing for a dive into the water. That could mean only one thing, Bobby Borgstrom and his dog, Butch, had arrived.

"Be right there," O'Donnell yelled across the water at the familiar figure on the dock, who yanked against his black lab's efforts to dash away. Cosmo flew into the water, swimming toward his buddy, barking with joy as he paddled. Bobby waved and let Butch bolt into the lake as well. The two dogs met halfway, swam back to the little beach by the dock, and soon raced in circles at a dizzy pace on the lawn.

"Any luck, Captain Ahab? That bamboo rig should be good for at least a muskie."

"It's the little rubber worms that get them." O'Donnell clambered ashore and dodged a welcoming charge from Butch.

Bobby helped haul the rowboat up on the sand. He straightened and gave O'Donnell a long appraisal. "Captain Hornblower, you look like someone tossed you over the side."

"Thanks so much. What news?"

"I've been sticking my nose where it shouldn't be this morning, and I found out some things." Bobby eased down on the porch stairs, stretching out his long legs. Freckles spread from his nose across his cheeks, making him appear more youthful and puckish than someone the sports page writers had labeled "the meanest Golden Gopher lineman of the past half century." After that particular tribute, and with the offer of a free beer, Bobby could be counted on to extend his top two front teeth over his lower lip, followed by what he called biologically accurate rodent sounds. O'Donnell rarely failed to enjoy that particular stunt.

O'Donnell and Bobby watched as Cosmo, with all four paws back on *terra firma*, reverted to some aspect of his mixed ancestry, barking and nipping at Butch, trying to herd him somewhere. Butch screeched to a halt, and Cosmo's attempt to dig all fours into the sand for an emergency stop failed miserably. The dog slammed into the boat and careened into the lake. In time, Cosmo wobbled out of the water and shook himself dry, with a look that said, "I planned that . . . really!"

Bobby whistled for Cosmo and Butch to come and share a dog treat he produced from his pocket. O'Donnell asked what his friend might have learned from the St. Paul Police.

"So, Johnny. Nothing for sure, but you can bet Butternut's pal's no shrinking violet. You might check in with the police soon."

"Anything else?"

"If what you told me about the bad blood between Butternut and this Flash Dawkins is true, I wouldn't put it past our local hoodlum to get somebody to do his dirty work. Butternut's climbed up the pecking order of local crime lately."

"Can't he fight his own battles?"

"Doesn't need to, I guess. Your friend Dawkins should keep his eyes open, especially if he keeps pissing off the wrong people."

O'Donnell took that as a cue to outline plans for the St. Paul Open. Bobby had no objections about the body-guarding, but wanted details about how much time he'd have to spend and what he might expect as pay.

"If I have to spend all this time with this Flash Dawkins, what else can you tell me?" Bobby asked.

"Hard to figure," O'Donnell replied. "Not always the most pleasant fellow."

"That helps a load, Johnny."

"Just keep him out of sight as much as you can. He'll need to practice his golf game. But otherwise, make sure he doesn't go anywhere he doesn't have to for the next few days."

Bobby offered a hand, and he and O'Donnell shook on their agreement. Bobby was formal that way. O'Donnell figured Bobby would do the job as good as anyone.

O'DONNELL FOUND a parking spot across the street from Mickey's Diner in downtown St. Paul. A fried egg sandwich and a cup of strong coffee seemed right. As he reached to turn off the ignition, O'Donnell caught a glimpse of Butternut and his out-of-town associate exiting the diner. O'Donnell hunched down as the two men climbed into Butternut's sedan and rambled off. O'Donnell made a U-turn and followed.

Butternut gave it the gas and lurched down Cedar Street before taking a quick turn on Kellogg Boulevard. He and the mysterious stranger were on their way to the Union train station. O'Donnell parked around the corner and joined the crowd of rail passengers heading for the sweep of stone steps leading up to the neoclassical building. Massive doors, trimmed in lustrous copperplate sparkled ahead, sheltered under an impressive portico borne by ten granite columns. The columns mimicked some classical architectural style. Ionic? Doric? Corinthian? Yet another gap loomed in O'Donnell's general education.

People crowded inside the station, lining up at the ticket counters, talking in clusters, buying newspapers and magazines, lounging on the wooden benches. O'Donnell blended into the bustling mass of outbound passengers. Like a school of ocean fish, the rail patrons moved toward where the trains departed. Amidst the crowd, O'Donnell could make the long walk from the entrance to the train platforms undetected. Moving along a sloping walkway toward the trains, he spotted his quarry twenty-five yards ahead and to the right. Butternut strained to keep stride with the taller, long-legged black man. The stranger seemed irritated with his laggard companion, moving ahead like someone trying to rid himself of a pesky younger brother. The two angled left toward the entryway where the Hiawatha would depart soon for Milwaukee and Chicago. As they paused at the entrance to the train platform, Butternut eased an envelope from his jacket pocket. The stranger took the envelope, turned on his heel, and headed down the platform. Butternut looked like he wanted to say something more. The stranger swung up on the steps leading to the club car. He paused, and looked back past Butternut—directly at O'Donnell. The stranger smiled.

O'Donnell slipped behind a newsstand. He grabbed a copy of *Look Magazine*, busying myself with a full-page spread on Doris Day, a perky blond, one of Hollywood's latest heartthrobs. She looked great in one of those new-fangled, skimpy swimsuits. Butternut lumbered past seconds later.

It seemed a good time for O'Donnell to drop by the police department.

POLICE SERGEANT FRANCIS MCINERNY'S salmon-tinged skin floated underneath the bill of a police cap that seemed two sizes too small.

O'Donnell tapped his knuckles on the police blotter to get McInerny's attention. The sergeant had noticed O'Donnell's entry into the station, but pretended he didn't, never lifting his gaze from the comic pages of the newspaper spread before him.

McInerny finally snapped a pair of rheumy eyes up to meet O'Donnell's and righted his doughy body behind the high counter where he presided. He'd been O'Donnell's American Legion coach in high school, and he knew his baseball. Back then he weighed fifty pounds less and handled the fungo bat like a magician. These days, he couldn't have hit infield practice with a two-by-four.

"Bobby Borgstrom was in today. Seems like old times, Johnny." McInerny picked up a pencil, licked the tip, and wrote 11:20 a.m. on a large sheet of paper, not far below an entry that read, "Robert Borgstrom."

O'Donnell pointed at the entry. "Who did Bobby talk with?"

McInerny swiveled around on his stool, rotating his neck toward the open door behind him. "Hey, Ikola," he yelled, "got a customer for you." McInerny smiled like a cherub. "Detective Ikola will be out in a jiffy, young Master O'Donnell."

Detective Dan Ikola emerged from a door behind McInerny's post in seconds. The detective looked like a no-nonsense, straight-forward guy with a short fuse. He was a small and boxy type who cultivated bad taste in ties. A Lucky Strike hung from his lips. His puffy eyes and rumpled clothes revealed he hadn't much spare time outside the job. He crooked a nicotine-stained finger and motioned O'Donnell to follow him.

"Have a pleasant visit, Johnny," McInerny wheezed.

Fitting into Ikola's tiny office space required some skill. O'Donnell sat, legs-sideways, on a metal folding chair that had seen better days. Posed behind his desk, Ikola blended in with all the crap he had piled on it—case files, a huge ashtray, scraggly office lamp, rumpled evidence bag, and a tiny bowling trophy that teetered back and forth on the edge of all the mess. Ikola blew out a blue stream of smoke, his face expressionless. "Talk, O'Donnell."

O'Donnell leaned forward on his chair, searching for Ikola's eyes behind the smoke and the dim light. "Somebody's trying to scare off a citizen from playing in the St. Paul Open, and last night someone tried to get the message through to yours truly in a most painful way. In addition, I know an out-of-town bruiser has spent the weekend with our local bad guy, Butternut Wilkins. I'd like you to take a professional interest."

Ikola lit up another cigarette and let the smoke curl out his nose. "We are taking an interest."

"And?"

"Hold your horses. Are you willing to do us a favor? If you think you can, Detective McGee might have something to report."

"Depends on the favor, but I'm interested."

"Okay, let's get McGee in here."

Detective Pete McGee edged into the cramped office a few minutes later.

"Remind me what you've got so far, Pete," Ikola said. "Mr. Johnny O'Donnell wants to know who's trying to pinch his neck off."

"Your buddy was in here earlier and suggested we might have a look at Mr. Elrod "Butternut" Wilkins recent activity," McGee said. "Butternut has joined us here a number of times for little talks—the most recent of which, conveniently, was last week." McGee handed a sheet of paper to Ikola. "As per our custom, we had to ask Mr. Wilkins to trust us with the contents of his pockets while making himself at home in a holding cell. We chanced to see a scrap of paper in his wallet listing phone numbers. Among many, we found three quite interesting, especially for the likes of Butternut. Two are local. The other one turned out to be Chicago."

Ikola settled back behind his pile of desktop scramble, his gaze fixed on O'Donnell. "The local numbers are for the River's Edge Country Club and Mr. Jack Clancy."

O'Donnell nodded. He'd read about Jack Clancy organizing a special citizen's groups to fight the "world-wide Communist menace." Clancy owned a Ford dealership in the Midway, but spent a lot of time defending one and all from a Commie takeover. Apparently, he'd been with an OSS intelligence unit during the war. He struck O'Donnell as a real jerk.

Ikola unknotted his brown wool tie. He waggled a finger at O'Donnell. "You'll never guess about the third number."

O'Donnell didn't want to play guessing games at this point, so he waited for Ikola to continue.

"The Chicago number is some labor union headquarters." Ikola blew another cloud of smoke over the mess on his desk. It smelled like rubber tires burning at the dump. "Jack Clancy, River's Edge County Club, and a Chicago labor union." Ikola hunched forward, placing both elbows on the rutted surface of his desk, the ash from his cigarette threatening his case files. "An unlikely mix, right? You got a connection for me, O'Donnell?"

O'Donnell didn't. "So what's Butternut up to?" O'Donnell hoped someone knew the answer.

Ikola didn't; neither did McGee.

O'Donnell joined them a moment of silence, each man running the combinations and failing to hit the jackpot. Detective McGee shook his head and moved to the far wall. He didn't smoke, but being around his partner for any length of time made him an unwilling accessory. Ikola grunted and stood, hiking on his sport jacket and re-adjusting his tie. He motioned O'Donnell to follow him out past McInerny's desk to the front door. He clicked a silver Zippo lighter on and off a few times, contemplating another smoke.

"Do us a favor and make yourself useful, O'Donnell. Go check around the River's Edge Country Club. See if there's anything you can turn up for us. Can't hurt to try."

"Why me? Isn't that what police detectives are supposed to do?" Ikola's idea didn't seem the proper thing to do.

The detective only offered O'Donnell a pained look. "What I think is a guy like you may get more info at the Country Club. Me and Pete would stick out like a sore thumb." Ikola stepped back and spoofed a curtsy. "We ain't exactly the right types for sipping martinis by the pool."

O'Donnell couldn't argue with that.

"Give us a ring tomorrow morning, Sam Spade," Ikola said. "We'll compare notes."

HIGH ON A BLUFF not far from the Mississippi River gorge stood the River's Edge Country Club. O'Donnell could spot the clubhouse as he drove down Marshall Avenue past the south side of the golf course. The first private golf club in the city, River's Edge had played host to St. Paul's powerful elites since the 1890s. These movers and shakers had made their club a prestigious membership. It boasted a formidable eighteen holes with trees and hills enough to make most of it a tough test for the best golfers. According to one of O'Donnell's better-heeled college friends, the River's Edge clubhouse and swimming pool were not anywhere near so grand as some other clubs in the Twin Cities. Still, the wealth, position, and clout of its membership lent River's Edge enough of the requisite atmosphere. It was a place where the best families of St. Paul could mix genteelly, and while they were at it, the parental elites could train their children to be just like themselves.

As foursomes tracked their shots up fairways close to the lower-middle-class neighborhood that bounded the course on three sides, O'Donnell imagined the young and old of River's Edge membership passed by the common folk like aristocracy. Those outside the fence mowing their lawns, planting flowers, and washing their cars could catch a glimpse of someone important, or many times more prosperous—a someone who wouldn't be much affected by the recent dip in the economy and a lack of good-paying jobs. At times, an errant golf ball would sail across the fence, bounce high off the pavement, and skitter into a yard—a benevolence the neighbors could collect and later sell at a garage sale. O'Donnell supposed that no rancor, no class warfare shadowed the encounters between the gaily clad foursomes of golfers and their weekend neighbors across the roads. Those wielding the lawn mowers and hoses probably hoped they might someday trade up for a set of clubs and a relaxing afternoon on the course. "Folks over there had to start somewhere—just like us," O'Donnell imagined people to say. Despite the Summit Avenue mansions, the private schools and prestigious colleges in far off places, and the screened invitation lists for their parties at the St. Paul Hotel and the Downtown Athletic Club, the River's Edge membership excited little resentment. O'Donnell couldn't help but think the American dream was alive and well, even standing on the wrong side of the fence.

To O'Donnell, the funny thing about River's Edge was its membership selection. He'd heard that for a short time after the war, money and connections served to blur theological preferences. As things had evolved over the years, a coterie of members at River's Edge had come to accept tolerance as a principle they wore like a well-tailored, understated business suit. It all made good sense. The social universe of the elite and powerful at River's Edge would spin quite nicely even with a few outsiders, whoever they were and wherever they came from. Besides, in the days after the war, with the discovery of what the Nazis had done in the concentration camps, visible intolerance and prejudice would have been in poor taste. O'Donnell imagined that for many at River's Edge, it felt better to be tolerant and extend a welcome invitation to a chosen few. Of course, warm milk and cookies might be taken too much to heart. As most at River's Edge might think, or whisper to a kindred spirit, "We have to draw the line somewhere." While Gustafson had joined the club and played in foursomes with the O'Hanlins, Hansons, and Hellers . . . a Flash Dawkins and any like him would never color that mix.

O'Donnell knew his best shot at information would be at the nineteenth hole. Sitting amongst like-minded pals, sipping gin and tonics in the cozy atmosphere of the men's grille would be the regulars. The growing anxieties about communism, liberalism, labor radicalism, and civil rights, to name a few troubling issues, had likely touched off conversations aplenty among these boys. O'Donnell wanted to know if they'd gone beyond talking.

O'Donnell turned right and motored down the boulevard leading to the River's Edge clubhouse, coasting past golfers hitting practice shots on a narrow but adequate driving range. He could see the first tee on the east side of the clubhouse, with foursomes swinging away in preparation for their rounds.

It was a busy day at River's Edge, and a good thing for O'Donnell. No matter what Ikola thought, he didn't qualify to hang around without a reason even though he knew several of the younger members from college days. He parked his car at the far end of the lot and walked the path toward the clubhouse entrance. He cut through an opening in a large, trimmed hedge surrounding a practice putting green. On the club's veranda adjacent to where he now stood, Abby Gustafson sat alone under a sun umbrella, looking to the world like a magazine model in a white tennis dress that made ample way for legs like Betty Grable. Beyond the table, sister Jill leaned over the rail of the terrace, talking with her father as he and members of his foursome waited for the call to tee off. Jill's red shorts rode up the back of her legs, revealing pale skin not yet tanned from the sun. A number of older men, reclining around the terrace, cocktail glasses suspended for the moment, had their eyes glued to the same spot as O'Donnell's. In answer to a common prayer, Jill leaned over further.

"Something catch your eye, Johnny?" Abby dipped her head in Jill's direction. Abby crossed one beautiful leg over the other, laughing at having caught O'Donnell. He pulled up a wrought iron chair next to her and tried to keep from further inspection of Jill's backside.

"Big tournament day for the members," said Abby. "Do you want to watch them tee off?"

"I don't think so," O'Donnell said. "The 'ohhs' and 'ahhs' will be enough for me."

Abby slid out of her chair. "I'm going to watch this. Daddy needs some support."

She squeezed in next to her sister at the rail, and looked over her shoulder at O'Donnell, an impish grin on her lips. She leaned out on tiptoes, and her tennis skirt pulling up like an opening curtain at the theater. O'Donnell couldn't help but compare the two sisters.

After a few minutes, the spectators traipsed back to the tables. Jill lingered at the rail, staring off into the distance. Abby stopped briefly to say hello to a group of older folks sitting nearby. She stepped in front of O'Donnell, placing her hands on her hips, and thrusting a thigh toward him in a movie starlet pose. "Well?"

"You're terrible," O'Donnell groaned. "I stand guilty of all charges."

Abby gathered up her tennis racket and her handbag.

"Where are you going?" O'Donnell didn't want her to leave so soon.

Abby tilted her head in Jill's direction. "Three's a crowd," she said, and walked toward the terrace doors, but hesitated, reversed direction, and came back to where O'Donnell sat watching her. She put her hands on his shoulders and bent down to whisper, "I'd like to see you again." She tousled O'Donnell's hair and turned to go. O'Donnell watched her glide away. She glided well.

Jill gave up her place at the rail, and moved toward the outdoor bar the club had set up for the event. Their time together the other night spun through O'Donnell's head. Jill noticed O'Donnell and switched direction, but the 100-watt smile failed to switch on.

"How did your dad's tee shot go?"

"Not so well." She regarded her nails at close range.

"Do you want to go to the ball game," O'Donnell asked. "Saints and Millers at 1:30."

She touched his arm. "I'm sorry, Johnny. I'd love to go with you, but . . . I really don't feel well." She rubbed her temples and turned her face away, sun brightened tresses falling forward, masking her deceit. "I have the worst headache."

O'Donnell eased back in his chair, a spectator for her performance.

"I get these every once in awhile. They just knock me out." Jill touched her fingertips on the back of O'Donnell's hand. "Besides, I'd rather watch you play ball than watch a bunch I don't know."

Not much chance of that, thought O'Donnell.

"Sorry, Johnny, but I've got to get along." Rising halfway from her chair, Jill pursed her lips, looking at O'Donnell like he was a puppy in the dog pound. "Call me." She gave him a quick buzz on the cheek. "What are you doing here today anyway?"

"Just nosing around."

"Oh?" Jill sat down on the edge of the chair next to O'Donnell's. He'd hooked her interest.

"Nothing to tell. It's not a big deal," he said.

"Sure, Johnny. Thank you so much." Jill grabbed her purse off the table and left without a backward glance.

O'DONNELL TOOK THE STEPS leading down to the Members' Grille. Most of those inside had already completed their rounds of golf for the day, and they'd scattered about, sitting at a well-polished mahogany bar and around a number of hefty wooden tables. At one of the tables, some guys playing gin had attracted several onlookers, and O'Donnell figured the stakes were at a level well beyond his imagination. This group spent more money on a day at the club than most working slobs ever saw in a week's paycheck.

"Johnny O'Donnell. What brings you here?" Little Pete stood behind the bar, polishing cocktail glasses.

"And what the hell are you in here for?" O'Donnell asked, so only Little Pete could hear.

Pete smiled and shrugged his broad shoulders underneath the starched white serving coat he wore. "I'm sure the members wanted to keep me safe from golf balls flying all over." He appraised his River's Edge bartender's outfit. "Maybe they wanted me to stretch the damn seams on this here silly looking thing. I feel like something out of *Gone with the Wind.*"

Little Pete wiped the bar clean, centering a round paper coaster in front of O'Donnell. "What'll it be? I owe you one after that golf exhibition the other day?"

"I got lucky."

Someone bumped his way near the bar, pressing O'Donnell to the side. "Give me another whisky sour." The "sour" sounded like "souser" to O'Donnell.

"I'll be with you in a second, Mr. Hoffman." Little Pete shifted his attention back to O'Donnell. "A draft beer, Johnny? It's ice cold and tasty."

Brad Hoffman, Jill's ex-husband, wasn't smiling like he did for all his publicity photos.

"You take member's orders first around here," he said to Little Pete, adding a quick, belligerent glance at O'Donnell. He had a well-fed, pampered quality to his face and an outfit to match—a chocolate-colored golf sweater and spiffy white pants. Something like an ice cream cone to O'Donnell's way of thinking. All he lacked was some pistachios. He gave O'Donnell the once over.

"Go ahead with the gentleman's order," O'Donnell said to Little Pete, trying to defuse the situation. "I'm not sure what I want yet."

Hoffman had his dark-brown hair in a longish brush cut, with a stylish set of sideburns added. His eyes were dark and small, swimming a bit with what he had drunk so far. He wasn't unpleasant looking, O'Donnell judged, just unpleasant. Of course, O'Donnell didn't exactly qualify as an unbiased observer. The word "dickhead" kept repeating in his mind as Hoffman made Little Pete dainty up a whisky sour. O'Donnell was damn tired of being nice to people.

Hoffman wrapped a hand around his drink and turned to leave. O'Donnell caught his arm.

"What the hell do you want?" Hoffman twisted out of O'Donnell's grip.

"Sorry. But you forgot something."

Hoffman shifted to stand toe to toe. He pushed O'Donnell back a step with a surprisingly sturdy forearm, making a challenge. "What did I forget, huh?'

"The little pink umbrella." O'Donnell could hear Little Pete trying his best to contain a laugh. Hoffman didn't think it was so funny, and he pushed against O'Donnell's chest.

"I know who you are, O'Donnell. A washed-up jock asshole." Hoffman stepped back a pace, setting himself. "Nothing but a has-been loser."

Several of the club members nearby stopped their conversations. They looked uncomfortable, expecting something to give. O'Donnell smiled at Hoffman, and turned back to the bar. Little Pete slid a draft beer in front of him with a flourish.

"Tell your buddy Dawkins he'd better watch out, too," Hoffman snarled from behind O'Donnell.

"What?"

"You hear me good, O'Donnell." He leaned in closer. "Your hotshot friend and you watch your step. Not everybody around here favors what all those people and their white buddies are doing these days."

Some of the members laughed, mumbling their agreement. Little Pete worked his jaw back and forth, his eyes dark with anger. Hoffman moved closer so only O'Donnell could hear. A mix of whiskey and barbershop cologne stuck in the air. "And keep the hell away from my wife."

"I think the correct term is 'ex-wife.'"

Hoffman pulled back. Ready to throw a punch. Before he could, an older member stepped between the pair. He barked an order for Hoffman to move away, and held O'Donnell back with an open hand on his chest. Hoffman gave one last glare, and aimed himself in the direction of a table where a couple of guys gave him an encouraging pat on the back.

"Now . . . you are?" the gentlemen asked.

"John O'Donnell. I don't believe we've met."

A hint of amusement flickered in the older gentleman's eyes. "I'm Charles Nelson, and I hate to ask, but are you here with one of the members?" He lingered on the last word for emphasis.

"I'm waiting here for one of them. Einar Gustafson? He's out on the course right now."

"Gustafson. Yes, well, club rules do allow guests to be in the Grille if accompanied by a member."

O'Donnell put on his special stupid look. In grade school, he'd found it most effective in the presence of authority. Nelson appraised O'Donnell without sympathy for the obvious disability.

"If you don't mind, I'll finish my beer and be on my way," O'Donnell said.

"You do that." Nelson smiled, and returned to the table of gin rummy players. Little Pete busied himself at the far end of the bar, washing glasses and tidying up. O'Donnell felt about as welcome as one of the members' wives. Bullying and embarrassment never went well over with him, especially when it came from a bunch of rich folks. He couldn't see backing down, and his worst instincts surfaced, drawing him to where Hoffman lolled at the table with his buddies. O'Donnell pinched a chunk of Hoffman's neck. Hoffman's eyes bulged in pain.

"I enjoyed our conversation." O'Donnell increased the pressure, leaning close to Hoffman's ear. "How about we finish it sometime soon?"

Hoffman sputtered something, his eyes searching for help from the others. O'Donnell let go his grip, and walked out before Mr. Charles Nelson decided to reprise his role as clubhouse diplomat.

THE GROWL IN O'DONNELL's stomach signaled he'd missed lunch by far more than he liked. All he'd had to eat were a few handfuls of peanuts at the bar. A short ride over to the Saints game at Lexington Park would fix things. He could grab a couple of hotdogs, sit in the sun, and enjoy the old ballgame. If the fans remembered him, there might be a few free beers.

O'Donnell picked his way around the Lincolns and Caddies packed into the River's Edge parking lot on the way to where he left the Ford. Ahead, near a white '47 Chevy, he spotted what looked to be a very unhappy Abby Gustafson.

"You modeling for the car show?"

"Oh, thanks a bunch," Abby said. "Just what I'd like to do with my life."

Had he not delivered a compliment? O'Donnell leaned an elbow on the car's hood. Abby's hair reflected the sunshine, like a "Breck Girl" shampoo ad. She stared straight ahead, obviously angered about something. O'Donnell half-expected her to apologize for being so grouchy, but she didn't say a thing.

"What's wrong?"

Abby stared at O'Donnell for a few seconds with a look that he could best characterize as exasperation. He didn't like making her feel that way.

"First of all, I'm not some stupid bimbo model, and I don't want you thinking about me like that." She slid off the car hood and stomped her foot near O'Donnell's toe. "I'm not some helpless bleach-bottle-blond waiting for someone like you to rescue me. Furthermore," she said with a short hitch, "this damned car won't start, and I don't know anything about the intricacies of the internal combustion engine. I hate feeling like some ninny who can't even get home by herself."

O'Donnell worked hard not to smile, but by the way Abby's brow unfurled and her eyes brightened, he knew the storm clouds had passed. The pair burst out laughing. O'Donnell slipped his arm around Abby's shoulders and gave a squeeze. She nudged him away, but the smile remained.

"Let's go to the Saints' ballgame, eat hotdogs, and drink beer," O'Donnell suggested.

Abby kicked the side panel of the Chevy. "Can you get this darn thing started first?"

"It's probably flooded." O'Donnell patted the hood—Mr. Ace Mechanic. "Leave it and we can come back after the game. It'll start."

"Let's go then. Can I have a Baby Ruth if I eat my hotdog?"

"Only if you drink all your beer with it."

The couple drove north from River's Edge on Cretin Avenue, slipping through a neighborhood of storage facilities, tool and die shops, car garages, and itty-bitty frame houses with neat, postage-stamp lawns. Abby fiddled with the radio until she found a station playing a Gene Autry tune. *"I'm back in the saddle again,"* Gene sang, and Abby harmonized with the radio cowboy. When the song ended, Abby tuned to another station. A ballad came on that O'Donnell remembered from well before the war. Abby knew all the lyrics, singing along with a pleasing voice. O'Donnell stole a glance at her. She sat forward in the seat, giving the song her own special phrasing. O'Donnell's top female vocalist, Jo Stafford, had nothing on the skylark beside him. Abby caught O'Donnell looking, and a slight blush rose on her cheeks. She smiled, but kept singing.

As they neared the ballpark, a kid waving a sign that said "Parking 10¢" stood on the curb, motioning O'Donnell to pull into a private driveway by a small house. He took up the offer. Abby and O'Donnell walked hand in hand, joining a parade of fans on the sidewalk heading for the ticket booths.

"Do you get free tickets if you played for the Saints?" Abby asked.

"Not really."

O'Donnell supposed he could drop in the locker room and beg tickets from his former teammates, but he didn't want to remind himself about the old days. He felt like a major league pitcher still lurked inside him. No big fastball like Bob Feller's, his curve didn't cripple a hitter in the batter's box, and most of all, O'Donnell didn't have that third pitch to keep the hitters guessing. He was good, but maybe not quite good enough. Then he blew out his arm. Today, he'd buy a couple of tickets and watch the game just like everyone else.

O'Donnell found great seats about five rows up from the Saints' dugout. He and Abby could enjoy the sunshine, and O'Donnell could cheer on the guys he still knew on the team. He'd followed most of the Saint's games on WMIN radio, listening to Marty O'Neill do the play-by-play. Marty could make the away games with the Toledo Mudhens, the Milwaukee Brewers, or the Louisville Colonels sound like the real thing—unless, of course, he forgot to move the teletype machine far enough away from the microphone. The Saints had good players left from last year, and they'd signed some promising youngsters who'd soon be up with the Dodgers in September. Most of the Saints' fans thought their boys might bring home the American Association pennant.

"Are you a fan?" O'Donnell asked Abby.

"I will be if you grab the hotdog guy."

"Any favorite players?"

"Well, if you must know, Bobby Addis is a real dream."

For some reason, O'Donnell wished she had seen him pitch. "I don't know, I think he's got a hitch in his swing."

"Just get the hotdogs," Abby said, "I'll decide about any hitch in his giddy-up."

The Saints poured out of their dugout and took the field in the bottom of the first. Their uniforms were copies of the parent club—crisp white with royal blue script across the chest reading "Saints." The Millers, the team all St. Paul loved to hate, sported their New York Giant's motif, with the black-and-orange team colors.

The Saints' infield threw it around the horn. They hollered encouragement at their pitcher as the Miller's leadoff batter stepped up to the plate.

He swung at the first pitch and sent it rocketing into the alley in right center. By the time the relay man turned to throw, the batter had made it to third with a stand-up triple. The Saint's shortstop yelled toward the mound, "Keep your dauber up, babe."

"What's this 'dauber' they're always yelling about?" Abby asked loud enough the man sitting in front of her overheard. He half-turned in his seat, waiting to hear O'Donnell's explanation.

"Sorry, Abby, but that's one of the mysteries of this game," O'Donnell said. "I'd be breaking the ballplayers' code if I told you."

"Good answer," the man in front added.

Abby wasn't ready to let it go. "I suppose it means keeping your spirits up. But a 'dauber'?"

The first five innings of the game sped by. Both pitchers had their best stuff, and the Saints had managed one run on a triple by Earl Naylor and a long sacrifice fly to left by the Saints leftfielder, Eric "Old Reliable" Tipton. Eric averaged a hundred RBIs every year, and usually won the fans' favorite player award. Problem was he never quite made the next step up the ladder to the major leagues.

Every so often between innings a fan would drop by and say hello to O'Donnell. He guessed his brief pitching career with the Saints hadn't been all that bad. Abby gave him a funny look after one guy came by and gushed a bit. He bought O'Donnell a beer and sat in the isle jabbering away for half an inning.

"Gee, just imagine," Abby said, after the fan had returned to his seat, "me sitting next to such a fan favorite."

As O'Donnell struck a heroic profile, someone took it as an opportunity to bean him with some salted peanuts. O'Donnell and Abby turned to see where it came from. Five rows back, along with two other giggling fools, sat Brad Hoffman.

"Abby. How're you doing?" Hoffman yelled down. "You must be hard up, sitting with a loser like that?" He hadn't sobered up much from before, and one of his buddies signaled for another round from the nearby beer vendor.

Abby stared out at the diamond, sinking lower in her seat. "He is such an ass."

O'Donnell patted her hand. "I agree. What's his problem? Today he warned me to stay away from your sister."

"He did?" Abby cocked her head, smiling. "Maybe he isn't such an ass after all."

Another peanut sailed by and struck the middle-aged lady sitting in front of Abby. She turned around and glared at O'Donnell, red-faced, with a look that said, "Are you going to let him get away with that?"

O'Donnell hoped the errant toss would mark the end of the kiddy games. The woman glanced up again to where Hoffman and friends sat. "You need to stand up for yourself, young man." Abby earned a sympathetic look from the woman, as if she had picked a real loser for a date.

"Right." O'Donnell stood up.

"Johnny, don't."

The lady in front reached back and patted Abby's knee. "About time, dear. Those boys need a word about deportment."

O'Donnell took his time moving up the stadium aisle toward Hoffman and his two friends. As he passed up the steps, the fans craned their heads back toward his quarry. Hoffman sat nearest the aisle in the row of seats. One of his friends struggled up to intervene, stepping by Hoffman to meet O'Donnell in the aisle, but losing his balance in the attempt. O'Donnell caught him by the arm before the bozo went sprawling. He pushed Hoffman's friend upright and sent him back hard towards his seat.

"Whaddya think you're doing?" Hoffman slurred his words—very drunk after a good head start at River's Edge. He'd be more of a challenge sober, O'Donnell thought.

"I'm going to tell you something, Hoffman."

"Yeah, what's that?" Hoffman didn't make much effort when he tried to throw a punch. O'Donnell grabbed him by the wrist, drew his hand to the side, and whipped it back across his face. It was the adult version of a kid's game, "Stop hitting yourself." O'Donnell kept a lock on Hoffman's wrist, and told him matter-of-factly, "I'll say it once. Cut the bullshit." Another turn of the wrist, and Hoffman collapsed into his seat.

O'Donnell retraced the steps, and the fans let out a round of applause. The beer vendor stood next to Abby, a smile creasing his face. He poured a cup of Schmidt's Beer with great ceremony. *Johnny O'Donnell, the people's choice.*

After a brief silence, Hoffman and friends turned to making loud complaints about anything and everything. The beer vendor refused to acknowledge their requests for more cups of brew, and one of the Saints' security officials appeared at this point. On their forced retreat from the stands, Hoffman yelled back, "I'm not done with you, O'Donnell."

The fans booed him and his departing colleagues. O'Donnell settled back to enjoy the game. Abby slipped her hand over his. The lady in front appraised O'Donnell like a potential son-in-law. "I guess he's a keeper after all," she confided to Abby.

Once the lady turned back to watch the ballgame, O'Donnell whispered to Abby. "What am I? A rainbow trout?"

The Saints put two more runs on the scoreboard in the bottom of the eighth, and Abby celebrated with a Baby Ruth candy bar. O'Donnell asked if she wanted to drop by at the lake after the ballgame, even offering to make his special meatloaf recipe. Abby kept her eye on the game.

Top of the ninth, the first two Miller batters tapped routine groundouts to the Saints' second baseman. The Saints' starter sizzled a good one over the outside corner, knee-high. The kid pitcher looked like he'd toss a complete game, with plenty of gas left in his tank. Abby applauded the next offering—a good curve ball that had the batter flinching, bailing out. The fans clapped in rhythm now, rooting on the kid for a final strikeout. He came up the ladder on the 0 to 2 count, putting all he had on a rising fastball. The Miller's batter took a good cut, but his bat fanned the air six inches below the ball as it slapped into the catcher's mitt. Game over. Abby beamed. " I don't think this kid's going to be around here long."

As they walked up the ramp to leave the ballpark, jostling through the exit, O'Donnell looked back on the field, thinking about his lost chances.

"Come on, Johnny," Abby said, pulling him down the ramp toward the exit. "Don't look so glum."

"How about my place for that dinner?" he asked again. Better than going home and sulking with the dog.

"I appreciate the offer, Johnny, but I think I'll take a rain check."

"Why?"

"I've already thrown myself at you enough for one day. You need time to rest up."

What could he say? Jill still played around the edges of O'Donnell's mind, and as much as he liked being around her kid sister, it didn't seem to feel the same. Maybe that's what Abby was telling him.

"Come on, Abby. Let's find a place to eat around here." Cosmo knew how to butt open the back door when he had to go, and the dog could have a late supper. Most times O'Donnell found Cosmo over at the neighbor's getting all the treats he could stomach. O'Donnell promised himself he'd take his canine buddy for a good run later.

Abby squeezed O'Donnell's arm. "Okay, slick talker, I'll give you a break."

O'DONNELL KNEW OF A CAFETERIA over on Snelling Avenue that fit his budget with good home cooking. The "Quality Cafe"— a neighborhood spot where O'Donnell's parents used to go every once in awhile—seemed the right ticket. In those years past, the cafe had a sign hanging over the sidewalk that included some sort of bird no one could identify, so his father dubbed it the "House of the Puking Buzzard." The new owners had replaced the sign.

O'Donnell and Abby heaped their plates with cuts of meatloaf and mounds of mashed potatoes. The vegetables had been steamed to death, looking much like they'd been on a forced march through Burma, so the hungry pair gathered up some salads instead. Abby insisted on the three basic food groups. "We wouldn't want to forget what we learned in home economics, would we?" she teased, making like an old biddy teacher.

O'Donnell couldn't resist a couple of home baked ginger cookies. Abby went for what looked to be a piece of Almond cake. Both decided that a glass of milk would be the right thing, and ferried their trays to a small table in front of the substantial plate glass window looking out on the street. Laughs came easy. They played at guessing the occupations and personal histories of the couples who came in to eat. They talked awhile about books they'd been reading. Around 6:00, they left and drove back to Abby's house. When they pulled up the drive, Abby said, "Come on in for a minute, let's see how Daddy's golf match went."

"I don't know, Abby."

Abby caught O'Donnell's hand and pulled him towards her. She put her face next to him, her soft skin warm on his check. "Pretty please?"

Einar Gustafson sat in the front room, looking through the windows at the sunset. He sipped from a leaded crystal glass, filled with what looked like a stiff shot of whiskey. Abby went over and kissed his forehead, settling down next to him on the arm of his chair.

"Hi, Daddy. We went to the Saints game."

"That's nice," Gustafson said in a small voice, maintaining his gaze out the window.

O'Donnell sat on the piano bench. Abby talked about the game, every once in a while stroking her father's hair, looking at O'Donnell with worry in her eyes.

"How did the golf go today, Mr. Gustafson," O'Donnell asked.

"Oh, so-so." He finished up his drink, and headed for a cabinet at the other end of the room that held several bottles of liquor and more of the fancy glassware. He selected a bottle of imported scotch, and poured about half a glass of the amber liquid. He looked drawn and unsteady.

"Daddy, what on earth is wrong," Abby hugged her father.

"She's gone again." Gustafson shook off his daughter's embrace, leaning forward in his chair, staring at the contents of his glass. "Your sister promised to accompany Mother and me to the Minneapolis Symphony Orchestra concert tonight."

"I'm sure she had a good reason," O'Donnell said.

Abby gave him a warning look.

"Do not patronize me." Gustafson narrowed his eyes, anger and frustration mixed in his expression.

O'Donnell thought Gustafson ought to remember that his daughter wasn't still in high school. A grown woman, right?

"Sorry," O'Donnell offered.

Gustafson dismissed him with a backward wave of his hand. O'Donnell excused himself and retreated toward the front entrance like a bad dog, leaving the gentleman to whatever he wanted to brood about.

Abby called from behind as O'Donnell pushed open the front door. "Wait, Johnny. Where are you going?" She looked back toward the room where her father still sat. "Johnny, she's my sister. I love her, and I worry about her. But she can be trouble."

"Any other advice?" O'Donnell asked, with a sarcasm he didn't mean to let slip.

Abby didn't back off. "I hope you wake up soon," she said, and flicked on the front entry light.

"What's that supposed to mean?" O'Donnell asked, pausing on the doorstep.

He never got an answer. Abby closed the door and flipped the latch.

THREE BLOCKS INTO AN ANGRY EXIT from the Gustafson's house, O'Donnell's car stalled. Maybe too much excitement for the elves under the hood? As he coasted to a stop at the curb, it dawned on him that Abby had forgotten to pick up her car at the River's Edge. He waited a few minutes, trying to cool his anger at Gustafson's icy attitude and Abby's parting words. He tried the ignition again, and the engine caught—spewing a cloud of blue exhaust into the overhanging trees along the road. Abby could go start her own damn car. His was trouble enough. But O'Donnell's conscience soon caught up with him, and it sat like an elephant on his shoulders. Abby hadn't done anything wrong. She had his weakness pegged. He needed to do some clear thinking about all that.

O'Donnell pulled into a Texaco gas station on Grand and Fairview. A young kid sat behind the counter, a pack of cigarettes rolled up in his tee shirt over a pathetic, skinny bicep. He allowed O'Donnell to use the phone, adding any call would require at least a couple of nickels. O'Donnell knew that any payment would end up in the kid's pocket–capital for a next pack of Chesterfields. A lecture on cigarettes stunting the kid's growth came to mind, but O'Donnell doubted the gas jockey's vocabulary folder had the word "stunt" in it.

Abby answered the Gustafson's phone, which was good, because O'Donnell wasn't in the mood for any more conversation with her father. He reminded Abby about her car. At first she didn't answer, but then laughed and promised she'd be watching for him. O'Donnell said he had to find a babysitter for Cosmo, but he'd be there in five minutes. He called the Andersons out at the lake. Sheldon and Elva, a good-hearted elderly couple, lived a couple of cabins down and liked dogs. Elva informed

O'Donnell that Cosmo was already there, lying by the fireplace—which could only mean the dog had once again pushed through the bottom screen on the back door. Elva allowed that Sheldon would walk the "puppy" and he could stay overnight. O'Donnell told her thanks, but he planned to be home in an hour or so.

O'Donnell left the kid at the gas station his nickels and doubled back to the Gustafson's house. The sky had turned dark and cloudy. A few streetlights clicked on. Spaced at wide intervals, the lights left most of the curb line shrouded in darkness. From a distance, O'Donnell could make out a car pulled halfway up Gustafson's driveway. O'Donnell continued down the street, took a U-turn and coasted back toward the driveway along the curb of the street. Without warning, the other car flared out in front of O'Donnell, without headlights. The car sped away before he could catch a glimpse of the driver. When he pulled up to Gustafson's front door, Abby came out and slipped into the passenger seat.

"Still mad at me?" she asked.

O'Donnell wasn't mad, but ignored her question in favor of the one on his mind. "Did you notice a car come out your driveway just before I got here?"

Abby shifted in the seat and looked out her window. "No."

The way she answered, O'Donnell assumed she had seen the car. "Did Jill just get home?"

"Do you want to listen to something on the radio?" Abby reached for the dial.

"Was that her coming home?"

"Oh, all right," Abby said, exasperated, refusing to look at O'Donnell. "She walked in the door just before you came."

O'Donnell's thoughts jumbled like confetti. Not long before, Jill was in his bed. Then she hardly gives him the time of day and begs off doing anything with a fake headache. Now she's been out with someone. O'Donnell imagined the worst, and felt stupid . . . betrayed. A damn sight embarrassed, too. He didn't like being played for a fool. He liked it even less that Jill took him for exactly that. Why would he want to keep coming back for more?

Abby slid over next to O'Donnell. They had arrived in the River's Edge parking lot, and idled to a stop by her Chevrolet. "Tell me what you're thinking."

O'Donnell didn't know what he was thinking. He stared straight ahead, seeing nothing but the night dimming the parking lot.

"If we were truly friends, you'd let me know." Abby moved even closer, leaning her head on O'Donnell's shoulder. He had no idea what to do or say to that. Abby confused him as much as her sister did. At least it was a more pleasant confusion.

A night watchman entered the drama by flashing his light around the parking lot and focusing it on O'Donnell's car.

"He thinks we're a couple of teenagers necking," Abby said. She giggled and reached over to turn O'Donnell's face, pulling him into a kiss. He tried not to be too enthusiastic, but allowed time enough to enjoy the opportunity.

The watchman yelled something from across the parking lot. He waved the flashlight beam at the O'Donnell's car windows.

"Oh, darn," Abby said, "I haven't parked with a guy for years." She opened her door. "Will you wait a minute while I see if my car will start?"

"Of course."

"Shine that thing over here," Abby yelled at the watchman, still defending his parking lot. Her car started, but with an uncertain idle. "It looks like it'll work now. I'll let it run a bit."

She yelled thanks to the watchman, and turned her high beams on him. He threw his hands up to ward off the glare, and crab-walked backward, retreating up the path toward the clubhouse. Once again, O'Donnell had to admire Abby's style.

"I had a good time today," she called over to him from her car. "Don't be too unhappy, Johnny. It doesn't suit you."

Maybe she wanted to say it wasn't worth it. O'Donnell smiled as she drove by and out the parking lot. He sat for a minute in his car before following. This was supposed to be his night to take it easy, sitting on the porch with a bowl of popcorn and a beer, listening to something like *The*

Shadow on the radio. But here he sat like a dumb cluck in a dark parking lot, a half-hour from home, and mad at the world. Finally, he stuck the car in gear and rolled out of the River's Edge parking lot.

A BACK ROAD FROM THE CLUB ran about a fourth of a mile before it turned into a main avenue along the river. About half way down the road, a car churned out from behind an equipment building, cutting O'Donnell off, forcing him to brake hard or crash. He laid on the horn and yelled at the driver.

The driver came flying out of his car, sidestepping the glare of O'Donnell's headlights, and arriving at O'Donnell's partially open door fast and furious. Halfway out his door, O'Donnell found himself face to face with the business end of a pistol.

The gunman had packaged his cranium in a nylon stocking, and the nylon smirked at O'Donnell. The gun barrel pressed into O'Donnell's forehead, and a fist thumped into his chest. Then cold metal slammed into the side of O'Donnell's head. He went down like one of Primo Carnera's nosedives against Max Baer. Out for the count. Again.

O'DONNELL CAME TO LYING on the pavement next to the front wheel of his car. He struggled to his knees and gently probed the lump growing on his skull. Sore ribs confirmed Mr. Nylonhead had kicked him a good one while he lay on the pavement. O'Donnell managed to drape himself into position behind the wheel and pulled the car door closed. He turned on the ignition and flicked on the radio. Strains of the opening theme for *The Shadow* filtered throughout the car interior. O'Donnell knew all about the Shadow's "unique power to cloud men's minds," and considered the possibility that Lamont Cranston might have an evil twin who liked to wear nylon stockings.

Did Nylonhead have other items on his agenda for the evening? In the scheme of things, O'Donnell figured he ranked second to Flash as a prime candidate for a head bashing, so he searched his glove compartment for the Summit Avenue address Flash had given him the other day. It was only a five-minute drive if O'Donnell kicked it in gear.

Flash's digs turned out to be the second floor of a sprawling, three story, late nineteenth century house. O'Donnell guessed the house had been divided into two or even three apartments when the original owners hit hard times before the war. The place looked deserted. No lights showing to the street from any of the windows.

O'Donnell hobbled up the stone steps and across a wide veranda to a double door that served as the main entrance. The inside door stood wide open. It led to a long hallway and a set of stairs to the second floor. An umbrella hung desolate on a coat rack. O'Donnell thought about taking it with him. He could always threaten to poke an eye out if he met up with trouble. The steps going up creaked and echoed loudly, making his ascent sound nothing at all like the Shadow.

He paused at the landing, and scanned the second floor hallway. A slender beam of light emerged from where a door stood ajar. Only the distant sound of a radio broke the silence. O'Donnell covered the last fifteen feet to the apartment door, hugging the wall. Through the opening, he could see most of the living room. A chair upended, a lamp leaning against a bookcase, and a splintered, wooden end-table made for an unpromising panorama. O'Donnell strained to hear any movement beyond the open door.

A car started on the street, but no sounds from inside the apartment.

O'Donnell shouldered open the door, and charged into the room, crouching and weaving to avoid whatever danger awaited. Nothing happened . . . no bad guys . . . only the scattered remains of a shredded houseplant, it's long stems and leaves ripped and torn. The bright-yellow-and-periwinkle pot that held the plant now broken in half, muddy water staining the throw rug beneath it.

O'Donnell ventured deeper into the apartment, toward a back hall. A narrow trail of blood, still bright red and liquid on the wooden floor, led him to a bathroom. Flash lay on his stomach, his face turned toward the door, blood leaking from the side of his mouth. His breathing came in short gasps. His eyes flickered open, looking nowhere in particular. His right arm had twisted under his chest.

O'Donnell sorted Flash out so he lay on his left side, propped up his head with a couple of towels, and bathed some of the blood away from his mouth and from a nasty gash behind his ear.

"I'm doing okay," Flash said.

"Looks like it's worse than you might think. Keep still." O'Donnell went after a phone.

The receiver lay on the living room floor. The phone cord had been ripped from the wall. O'Donnell ran back downstairs to bang on the door of the other building resident.

"Anyone in there?" O'Donnell slapped the wood panel. "Open up! It's an emergency."

No answer. O'Donnell tried again.

Finally the door opened a crack. "Hey, I've got to call the police. Let me use your phone."

"Just a minute," a small voice cautioned, and O'Donnell could see a crabbed hand struggling with a chain lock. "I always have trouble with this silly thing."

The door swung open, and an elderly lady dressed in a flower print, Hawaiian muumuu and a white wool sweater stood tottering back and forth on a cane. She motioned O'Donnell inside with her free hand.

"Ma'am, I need to use your phone. Emergency."

"My Lord! What's happened?"

"We've had an accident upstairs."

"Well, come in . . . come in." The woman beckoned O'Donnell into her apartment. Apparently, details didn't matter much to her.

"Where's your phone?"

She lifted her cane up, pointing it toward a dark corner of the living room near a heavily curtained window. "I don't have much use for a phone. My son's just around the corner. My daughter lives over by Macalester, but she's always busy. Year-old twins, you know."

O'Donnell nodded in time to the lady's prattle, struggling to see the phone's location in the dim light. He located the phone under a crocheted cover, and dialed the operator. The lady kept talking, something about her sister's arthritis. O'Donnell reached the operator, and gave her the details so she could send an ambulance.

The old lady tugged on his arm. "Would you like some tea, young man. You look like you could use a nice cup." She peered up at O'Donnell, examining the side of his head. "You could use some ice on that, too."

She looked disappointed when O'Donnell declined the beverage offer, so he winked and said, "Thanks, anyway. Next time."

O'Donnell made a quick call to Bobby Borgstrom. Bobby said he'd be right over. "But I better call the police, Johnny."

"Did you see or hear anything unusual tonight," O'Donnell asked the old woman after he put the receiver down.

"What?" She put her hand up to her ear. "I don't hear so well anymore."

"I have to get back upstairs," O'Donnell said.

The lady patted him on the arm. "That's nice."

He found Flash sitting on a couch in the living room, busy pressing a bathroom towel on the cut behind his ear, looking sick and uncertain about what had happened to him. Blood still leaked from a corner of his mouth.

"I'll get some ice and aspirin," O'Donnell said, heading for the kitchen. "The ambulance will be here in a jiffy."

Flash held his head still, as if afraid he might dislodge something. O'Donnell rummaged through an electric refrigerator and found a tray of ice cubes. He spotted an aspirin bottle on the kitchen windowsill and carried it and the ice cubes back to the living room. He wrapped the ice up in one of the towels. "Put this on that cut. I'll grab a glass of water for the aspirin."

"You're like a regular nurse, man." Flash said as O'Donnell returned. He washed down the aspirins. O'Donnell took the water glass, and set it on the tile floor.

"Can you tell me anything about what happened?"

Flash looked at O'Donnell, his head wavering back and forth as he tried to focus. He rotated his neck, wincing at the pain. "All I can tell you is it's a good thing you got here. I think the guy wailing on me went out the back steps. Must have heard you coming. He wasn't near ready to call it a night."

BOBBY BORGSTROM PULLED UP at the curb five minutes after the St. Paul ambulance crew left with Flash in tow, heading downtown to St. Joseph's Hospital.

"Hop in, Johnny." Bobby said. "I called the police, and one of the detectives is going to meet us at the hospital. I guess they'll send someone by here soon."

O'Donnell squeezed into the front seat of Bobby's aging Plymouth. He had a hard time finding a place to sit with all the textbooks and junk littering the seat and piled on the floor.

"What happened to you?" Bobby stared at O'Donnell.

"I think I ran into the same Mack truck as Flash."

O'Donnell described what he could remember about his meeting with the mysterious Mr. Nylonhead earlier that evening. Bobby started the car and spun the wheel to turn away from the curb. Rolling down the Grand Avenue hill toward the flats, O'Donnell and Bobby tried to piece together the evening's events.

Bobby drummed his fingers on the steering wheel as they waited out a red light on West Seventh Street. "I left Flash here at six after he was done practicing. He told me he wasn't going out, but he must have gone somewhere. That's how whoever worked him over got into the apartment."

"Makes sense," O'Donnell said. Most anyone with the requisite tools and experience could jimmy the lock on Flash's door.

"I told him not to go out." Bobby took a hard left, the Plymouth's aging frame creaking with the effort. "Why take a chance?"

When they arrived at St. Joseph's, the ambulance stood at the entry port to the hospital, lights still blinking. Detective Ikola waited nearby, watching Bobby maneuver into a parking spot. He flicked his cigarette into the driveway, and pushed open the emergency room doors, a trail of smoke behind him.

"Let's go find out what evil lurks in the heart and mind of my favorite police detective," O'Donnell said.

They caught up to Ikola at the elevator, near the nurses' station. He crossed his arms and watched with surly amusement as the two approached. Bobby stepped close to Ikola, peering down at him, saying nothing. The two had met before. No words needed, O'Donnell guessed. The elevator door opened and Ikola barged past, punching the third floor button. When the doors opened again, Ikola put a restraining hand on O'Donnell's chest. "You go sit in the lounge. I'll get to you two later."

O'Donnell watched as Ikola spoke to the nurse on duty. She pointed down the hall, staring at the detective as he left to follow her directions. She fanned her hand in front of her nose. The blend of cigarette smoke, and a suit that needed some serious dry-cleaning had worked its magic.

The waiting lounge sported a well-scrubbed linoleum floor of alternating light-green and cream-white blocks—standard decor for most hospitals. A pair of stiff looking, well worn yellow couches faced each other, separated by a low wooden table that held a supply of month-old magazines—the *Saturday Evening Post, Life, Reader's Digest*, and *Good Housekeeping*. After scanning a few pages, Bobby threw down his *Reader's Digest*, regarding its tattered cover like a rattlesnake. "What time did you get punched out over at River's Edge?"

"Well, it was already dark."

"When did you get over to Flash's apartment?" Bobby asked.

"I'd say about 9:15."

Bobby raised his bulk off the low couch. He paced the waiting room pulling his hands together behind his back, attempting a stretch. Football stayed with you a long time, O'Donnell knew, no matter how much punishment you dished out.

"I don't think it's one guy," Bobby said. "He wouldn't've had time for all that action. It's two bad guys." Bobby readied to sit down again, but thought better of it. He paced back and forth rather than contort himself

93

to sit again on the yellow couch. He stopped in front of O'Donnell. "How are you feeling anyway?"

"Like a punching bag."

Ikola entered the room, agitated, searching for something other than O'Donnell and Bobby. His eyes fixed on a metal stand supporting a glass ashtray. He grunted with satisfaction as he plucked out a two-inch cigarette stub someone had left among the debris. Ikola substituted an empty, crumbled Lucky Strikes package for it. He smoothed out the cigarette and lit up. After a long drag, Ikola focused on O'Donnell with a deprecating look. "You got anything to tell me?"

Before O'Donnell progressed very far in his recollection of the evening, Ikola cut him off. "I need Pete in on this thing. Be in my office tomorrow morning, O'Donnell."

Ikola tossed his cigarette stub into the ashtray, looking at the butts for another one he could salvage. Failing to find another free smoke, he exited the room without a backward glance. Bobby studied the ceiling, shaking his head. O'Donnell signaled his friend to follow, and headed down the hall to find Flash.

Flash lay on his back, a bandage covering the left side of his mouth and chin. His eyes looked clear now.

"So what's the damage report?" O'Donnell asked.

Flash shifted in the hospital bed, trying to find a comfortable position. He spoke with some effort and a rasp in his voice. "Maybe a slight concussion, bruised ribs, and a report yet to come on my spleen or something. All other parts are in working order."

O'Donnell passed him a cup of water from the hospital tray next to his bed. The cup had one of those curved glass straws, and Flash sucked down three-quarters of the water as best he could. He nodded and handed the glass back.

"Can you fill us in about tonight?" Bobby asked. "I thought I'd left you safe and sound."

In a meandering fashion, Flash related what he remembered. He'd left the apartment to drive over to Highland Park about 7:30 p.m. "Thought

I'd go to Lee's takeout and get something to bring home." He estimated he'd been gone about thirty minutes, no longer. When he walked into his place, intending to grab a beer from the kitchen before eating his food, the attack took place. "Next thing I know, someone hits me hard in the ribs and whacks me over the head. I tried to get away . . . made it as far as the bathroom." Flash moved his head back and forth on the pillow, as if he might erase some of the pain doing so.

Resting on his elbows, he said, "Look, I made a big mistake. I should have stayed at home." He worked his neck back and forth, flinching with pain. He looked tired now, and if O'Donnell didn't miss his bet, Flash's chances for playing in the St. Paul Open qualifying round didn't seem such a sure thing. O'Donnell had more questions, but they could wait. He told Flash to expect him back in the late morning. The patient closed his eyes, and waved a weak good-bye.

On the drive home, O'Donnell tried to puzzle out what had happened. He didn't reach any case cracking conclusions. More questions than answers. Most troubling was O'Donnell had seen no evidence in Flash's apartment of a visit to the take-out restaurant. Maybe the mystery guest couldn't resist stealing a juicy Lee's hamburger and a bunch of fries.

APELTING RAINSTORM brought O'Donnell awake. Bleary eyed and aching, he curled under the blanket and tried to fall back to sleep. The temperature had dropped sizably, and wet cold from the lake crept under the covers and seized his legs. He grappled for the rest of the blanket, but couldn't budge it from the bottom of the bed. Cosmo had made one of his rare ventures off the floor. In the half-light, O'Donnell could make out the dog's bulk. He lay snuggled on the lower half of the bed without guilt or shame. O'Donnell tried to nudge him off the blanket. Cosmo rejected the effort with a faint, unexpected growl.

The alarm sounded minutes later, and O'Donnell swung his feet to a linoleum floor that felt like a Lake Superior ice flow. He had to do some decorating—a couple of rugs at least. At the worst, he could buy some mukluks. Hell, everyone else in Minnesota had a pair of those stupid-looking sock things. Why not join the crowd?

A quick inventory told O'Donnell he'd pretty well survived the damage Nylonhead had laid on him the night before. A slight headache, a knot on his skull, and ribs with a purple and yellow tinge, but he'd be okay.

Cosmo padded into the kitchen and sat in the middle of the room at full attention. He looked rested. Anxious for his breakfast, the dog slipped into his role as man's best friend like a Broadway theatre star. His tail pulsed back and forth across the floor. Eyes sparkled with innocence and anticipation. Like most dogs living closely with humans, he knew pretty much what to expect on any given day . . . and how to get it. He wanted a real breakfast. No canned dog food. No sir.

O'Donnell lined up the eggs, butter, and a half loaf of Wonder Bread. The bacon smelled reasonable, so he rescued that from his icebox. Cosmo liked bacon. The rain drizzled outside the cabin. A *noir* Monday. O'Donnell liked things sunny side up, so he flipped on the radio to *Don McNeill and the Breakfast Club* out of Chicago. He declined the radio host's invite to march around the kitchen table.

After gulping down his share of breakfast, Cosmo posed at the door, staring into the mist, wagging his tail again. O'Donnell let him out and tuned up the WCCO weather report on the radio. Joyce Lamont, the nice weather lady, only confirmed the obvious. He puttered around the cabin a bit, trying to forestall leaving for downtown and his appointment with the St. Paul Police. He thought ahead about the day. After meeting with Ikola, a visit with Flash at the hospital would be in order. That visit might result in some answers to match up with questions O'Donnell wanted to ask. A final item to consider: Jill Gustafson.

● ● ● ● ●

DONUT CRUMBS AND POWDERED SUGAR traced the outline of Sergeant McInerny's lips, and coffee spills adorned the front panel of his starched police shirt, though he couldn't see the mess. The way his cheeks puffed out below his eyes, O'Donnell doubted the man knew much about what happened below.

"Hey, Sergeant, how goes it for you this morning?" O'Donnell looked past McInerny to the detective's room. "Is he in?"

His eyes never leaving O'Donnell's, a big grin on his mug, McInerny called loudly for Ikola. The sergeant got so tickled at himself his cheeks vibrated. O'Donnell gave the sergeant a playful tap on the arm, and marched in the direction of Ikola's office.

"McInerny, you got a damn intercom . . . use it or shove it." Ikola yelled out his threat from behind the increasing pile of trash littering his desktop.

McInerny didn't answer, but O'Donnell could imagine his fatty neck, billowing over his shirt collar, quivering with delight. Ikola pointed to the folding chair for O'Donnell to sit. He lit up what looked like one of many morning cigarettes, and exhaled a smoky stream across his desk.

"Here's what we have so far," Ikola said. "Last time you were here, some unknown thug had waylaid you outside of the 427 Club. Last night it's somebody in a nylon stocking." O'Donnell had no doubt Ikola was enjoying his recitation. "To top it off, someone tries to make a meatloaf out of your buddy, Mr. Flash Dawkins."

Ikola pretended to give the file intense study, his lips moving in time to his reading. "You find out anything over at the River's Edge?"

"Nothing concrete. It looks as though not everybody over there is on the same cheering squad. I got the impression some of the members would be just as happy down in Alabama wearing sheets over their heads," O'Donnell said. "Look Ikola, most of the River's Edge boys aren't anywhere near ready to walk arm and arm with Gustafson waving a big banner for racial equality, and they don't want a Negro playing their golf course, even as a guest."

"You can't blame them. It's a private club, for crissakes."

Detective McGee walked in as Ikola and O'Donnell glared back and forth.

"Johnny, how's it going?" McGee asked, trying to cut the chill.

"Slow," O'Donnell answered.

Ikola broke off the eyeball-to-eyeball combat and stubbed out his butt. He turned to McGee. "Our ex-jock here was just telling me about a difference of opinion over at River's Edge. I guess a 'fair deal' means different things to different people over there."

"Sort of confirms what we found out from Jack Clancy, doesn't it?" McGee said.

"How's that?" O'Donnell guessed the detectives had something.

McGee moved around Ikola's desk to a wooden cabinet to retrieve a coffee mug. He looked at its contents and frowned, replacing it on a file folder. "We talked to Clancy out at his house yesterday morning. He's an original. I'll grant him that."

"What does that have to do with anything?" O'Donnell asked.

"Go on, Pete, tell our friend how Jack Clancy sees the world these days," Ikola said.

McGee assembled himself in a chair near Ikola's desk, careful not to bang his knees. "Well, for one thing, Clancy is not a man to keep his opinions to himself. No sooner do we have the handshakes and hellos done than we get a lecture on the worldwide communist threat, pinko labor unions, free enterprise, uppity Negroes, and the decline of American motherhood."

"Yeah, but the guy had it right about a lot of things," Ikola chimed in. "Especially on what's been going on with the women. My old lady ain't been the same since I went into the service, and she started working part time at the munitions plant. Stupid broad won't quit now."

Having added this high note to the conversation, Ikola stared at O'Donnell, looking for some sign of agreement. The detective's wife wasn't anybody's fool, O'Donnell thought.

"So what did Clancy say about Butternut having his telephone number?" O'Donnell hoped to move the conversation on.

"I'm getting there," McGee said. "After he finishes his lecture, he asks us why we're bugging him. So I told him . . . real polite . . . that we had his telephone number from Butternut."

"Clancy doesn't bat an eyelash," Ikola added. "Tells us right out he 'might' place a bet every once in a while. Says he couldn't see much harm in that since most of his friends do the same thing. The guy didn't worry one second about admitting it."

"So Clancy's in on all this?" O'Donnell asked the question, but didn't think the answer would be yes. It was common knowledge that the heavy rollers like Clancy did a little gambling and procuring every once in a while with St. Paul's lowlifes. The police reasoned no one got hurt, and they didn't want to step on the toes of "civic leadership" if they didn't have to.

"Clancy's okay. He's clean." Ikola said.

"What do you think?" O'Donnell asked McGee.

"I guess he's okay." McGee's answer didn't sound like a ringing endorsement of Ikola's conclusions.

"What about Butternut?" O'Donnell asked.

"That fine young man has been pretty scarce since you last saw him. We talked to Daddy Wilkins out at the bar yesterday, and he claimed his sonny boy was down visiting the homefolks in Alabama. No luck yet turning him up for a talk."

"We'll snag him soon enough," McGee said.

O'Donnell felt the irritation creeping into his voice. "So what the hell do we know?"

Ikola pushed a pile of paper to the side of his desk, and tapped it lightly with his pencil. Then he surprised O'Donnell. "The FBI guys told us something worthwhile."

"Such as?"

"Butternut's mystery friend," Ikola said.

"Who is he?"

"He's an ex-con from Chicago who spent two years in Joliet for assault and battery," McGee said. "He seems to be making a living these days as a union organizer and tough guy for some CIO affiliate. Hoover's boys think he's worth watching."

"This whole thing doesn't make much more sense now than before we started talking." O'Donnell felt like he did in Geometry class when everyone understood a hypotenuse except him.

Ikola gave O'Donnell a counterfeit smile. "It's a puzzlement, isn't it?"

"It's giving me a hell of a headache."

McGee reached into his jacket pocket and pulled out a sheet of teletype paper. "To be specific, the Hoover boys in Washington identify your mystery man as Marcus Sanford. Born in Scottsboro, Alabama. 1912. Grew up fast. Too fast, maybe. Got himself involved in some things down South in the early '30s before he disappears for a couple of years. Then he turns up in Spain with the Abraham Lincoln Brigade." McGee's brow furrowed at that. He traced his finger along the report sheet. "Looks like he was a combat pilot."

"Flying a damn airplane?" Ikola looked puzzled.

McGee gave Ikola a brief once over, struggling to disguise his irritation. "You never heard of the Negro air units that flew cover for us in Europe? Those suckers got my vote. I was a tail gunner on the B52s. I tell you, we could always count on those guys to keep the Krauts off us."

"How the hell would I know," Ikola said, losing himself behind a cloud of his smoky exhaust. "I wasn't flying any damn airplanes from my foxhole.

Ikola drummed his fingers on the desktop. "So, what's this Lincoln Brigade?" he asked.

McGee explained what he knew about the Abraham Lincoln Brigade. Ikola pretended to ignore the explanation. The way O'Donnell remembered it, fighting broke out in the late 1930s between the Spanish Republican forces and the Fascists, a nasty bunch with support from Hitler and Mussolini. Although the U.S. stayed neutral, along with the British and the French, a small group of leftists from the United States, calling themselves the Abraham Lincoln Brigade, went over to fight against General Franco and his army. The Brigade included several black volunteers. The FBI had them all tagged as Communists or fellow travelers.

McGee made some notes on the margin of the FBI report. "After Spain, Marcus came back to the states and started working on the presses at the *Chicago Defender*."

Ikola jumped back into the conversation. "That's some Commie newspaper isn't it?"

O'Donnell corrected him. "It's a black newspaper in Chicago. They own it and publish it."

"Yeah, yeah. Same damn thing," Ikola said.

McGee went back to reading the FBI sheet. "Before you can say 'Pearl Harbor,' Marcus Sanford is writing editorials. But it says what he's writing about is Roosevelt ought to declare war on the Axis, and that black men should be ready to fight."

"So I guess the FBI gave him a gold star for that, huh?" Ikola glared at his partner.

McGee turned the FBI paper over and scanned the other side, like he was studying for a test or something. "So why would the FBI keep him under observation during the war?"

Neither Ikola nor O'Donnell had a good answer to that.

"What else does it say about this guy?" Ikola asked, his interest piqued somehow.

McGee savored the moment. "Well, he never makes it to the fighting. He spends most of it down South doing some kind of Army maintenance work." McGee looked puzzled. "Hell's bells. If the guy had combat experience in Spain, you'd think they'd at least send him to fight. Anyway, he's discharged in '45, knocks the bejesus out of some Army lieutenant at a Chicago nightclub, and spends until last September incarcerated. The FBI's tagged him as a A-Number One security risk."

"Now the thing is," McGee continued, "he had a reason for coming out here, and we know he's been busy in one way or another. So we need to find the guy and ask some questions."

That pretty much finished the meeting. Ikola informed O'Donnell he'd let him know if they needed to talk again. As O'Donnell walked to the front entrance, McGee hustled up from behind. He steered O'Donnell through the door and over to the side of the steps.

"I got a hunch . . . and I can't pin it down for a fact, but this Jack Clancy is bigger in all this than Ikola thinks." McGee looked over his shoulder over at the front door, as if he wanted to get back in before anyone missed him. "All this Clancy talk isn't just off-the-wall conversation. I think he means it. And if he does, then I doubt he has a soft spot for somebody like Dawkins."

O'DONNELL'S MIND FELT LIKE a jumble of disconnected threads. He drove west down University Avenue from downtown, wondering what to do next. The sun had come out, and it looked like a nice day ahead after the rainy morning. At the corner of Lexington and University stood the Saints's ballpark. It was a gem. A quiet seat under the grandstand roof seemed the ticket right now. O'Donnell needed a place to think.

He parked across the street, and entered the ballpark through the main gate. A wooden ramp led him up to a walkway overlooking the stands and the field. From that vantage point, he spotted the Saints's groundskeeper, Jimmy Hansen, hard at work on the pitching mound. Jimmy had been with the Saints for quite a stint. He'd grown up on a farm in near Stillwater, and in the mid-thirties, Jimmy moved to a 160-acre plot of land in New Brighton where he started a landscaping and Christmas tree business, barely making a living. Driven by necessity to find a paying job, he'd convinced the Saints's owners he could grow grass and tend dirt like no one else around. They hired him on as the groundskeeper, and he didn't disappoint. With Jimmy in control, the Saints had one of the best infields in the American Association.

O'Donnell called down to Jimmy and descended the grandstand steps toward the field. Jimmy trotted over to the wire mesh gate where O'Donnell stood.

All the time Jimmy spent outdoors had deeply tanned and creased his face. His thick eyebrows made his eyes, deep set in their sockets, look smaller than normal. He wore a beat up Dodger cap from the parent club bestowed on him from some ex-Saints's ballplayer. Jimmy pumped O'Donnell's hand. "What brings you back to the ballpark? I thought we were done with you." He stepped back and appraised O'Donnell like some critter on display at a 4H exhibit. "You look strong as a bull."

"I'm keeping in pretty good shape, and you're looking like a racehorse yourself."

Jimmy laughed and motioned for O'Donnell to follow him on the field where he pulled part of the tarp off the mound. He stepped back and gave his handiwork the once over. "Looks like it came through the rainstorm okay. It'll do with a bit of grooming, though." He grabbed a tapping tool he kept under the tarp and firmed up areas where the dirt had taken on some wetness.

"You mind if I just sit in the stands for a while?" O'Donnell asked. "I've got some thinking to do."

"Fine with me," Jimmy said, giving him a quick glance. "But you ain't got but thirty minutes of quiet before the boys come out for batting practice."

"That'll do."

O'Donnell retraced his steps to the grandstand. The grass felt good under his shoes. Being on the field again filled him with bittersweet memories. He'd brought along a pencil and a small notebook from his car, and he settled into a row of seats behind the visitor's dugout. He let his legs hang over the seat in front. On a clean sheet of paper, he attempted to put everything he knew in an outline of sorts, like he did studying for an exam in college. By the time some of the Saints ballplayers began filtering out to the field, packing the air with the taunts and horseplay of batting practice, O'Donnell had a short list of places to go and people to see.

"Hey! Johnny O'Donnell," a voice boomed up from the playing field. "Y'all get your butt down here and pitch some batting practice."

Clay Hopper, now the manager for the Montreal Royals, stood just inside the first base line. Hopper managed Jackie Robinson the previous year, and he knew about everyone in the Dodgers organization. Many a player had passed through his clubhouse some place or another. O'Donnell thought Hopper must have taken a couple of days off from managing the Royals to do some scouting. Probably looking over a few

Saints's players to bring to Montreal for the pennant race. Hopper hailed from the Deep South . . . Mississippi. After a bad start, made worse by Hopper's Mississippi background and bigotry, he'd proven fair in handling Robinson. At the end of that first season in '47, the manager apparently had told Robinson, "Jackie, you're a great ballplayer and a fine gentleman. It's been wonderful having you on the team."

"I don't know about throwing, Skipper." Besides, O'Donnell muttered to himself, I just got stomped by a guy in a nylon stocking last night.

"Bull. Go on in and find yourself some shoes and a glove. I need a look-see at a couple of these prospects they're trying to pass off on me. Ain't none of the lazy-assed pitchers showed up yet."

O'Donnell did have spikes and a glove in the car . . . a perfect baseball morning, too. He couldn't resist the offer, no matter his bangs and bruises. To hell with his arm. "Let me run get my stuff. I'll give it a whirl."

Hopper gave him a broad smile. "Well, get on it, son. I'll get a catcher's mitt and warm you up."

O'Donnell's spikes and glove lay in the back corner of the trunk where he'd tossed them two months before. His Saints's cap had survived its excile, so he grabbed it along with a beat up tee-shirt. On the way back into the ballpark, he did some stretches and windmills to try and loosen up his arm. O'Donnell laced up his spikes, kneeling on the infield grass. Hopper tossed him a baseball and motioned toward the pitching mound. A couple of baby-faced players lolled near the batting cage, swinging their lumber and sizing up O'Donnell.

O'Donnell lobbed in a few throws from the front of the mound. He could hear cracking noises in his shoulder, reminders of why he'd quit pitching. No twinges of pain in his elbow for the time being. But the sun warmed him, and soon he'd worked up a good sweat, easing the pains his body carried from past and not so distant injuries. Every couple of throws, he stepped back a few paces toward the pitching rubber. His pitches had leveled off some, and O'Donnell welcomed the sound of the ball smacking into a catcher's mitt.

Hopper relinquished his mitt to a younger player. O'Donnell didn't remember him from the spring. The kid squatted easily behind the plate and his size made for a great target. O'Donnell couldn't generate any heat in his pitches, though, and now each time he threw, the same, familiar twinge of pain registered from the top of his shoulder down to his forearm. The idea of throwing any harder or breaking off a curveball made his elbow ache in anticipation.

"Johnny, let me show you something here."

Hopper stood behind the mound now. He stepped up on the rubber, taking the ball from O'Donnell. "That old wing of yours ain't going to carry you very far the way you're using it now. Try going like this."

Hopper wound up and brought his hands together down on the right side of his body, about belt high. He turned his left shoulder down and back, rotating his left leg around his right, which now supported his pirouette. A batter would only see the back of his body, all scrunched up and covering the ball. As Hopper began his motion toward the plate, thrusting off his right foot, he let his pitching arm drop loosely toward the ground. Planting his left foot on the down slope in front of him, his right arm came whipping out from behind, delivering the ball toward the plate in sidearm, almost underhand motion. About ten feet in front of the plate, the ball changed direction and dipped back to the inside corner. His pitch fooled the catcher, the ball passing under the mitt and digging into the dirt.

"Might look like some sort of weird snake, but it sure don't put pressure on my arm." Hopper dug in his pocket and pulled out another baseball, tossing it to O'Donnell. "Give it a try."

O'Donnell damn near fell off the mound on his first couple of attempts. The next few tries had the boys by the cage laughing and covering their heads. Hopper gave him a few pointers, and succeeded having O'Donnell place his left foot in a better line with the plate as he released the ball. Pretty soon, the poor catcher could relax in his crouch and not have to chase errant pitches all over the cage. After five minutes, O'Donnell developed a good rhythm, and his pitches now plunked into the catcher's mitt with some authority.

"Now, when you release that ball, let it roll off your middle finger." Hopper demonstrated what he meant. O'Donnell gave it a try, and his pitch had a nice, sinking break to it. Hopper motioned for one of the players to take a few swings, and the catcher pulled down his mask, setting up behind the plate. For the next fifteen minutes, O'Donnell threw batting practice, feeling like his old self again. It wasn't proper batting practice manners for a pitcher, but every few pitches, he'd try experimenting with different releases off the sidearm motion. A couple of times, he had the batters wailing away at nothing but sticky air. Most of the time, he put the ball over the plate at decent speed and with surprising movement. Even if the batters tagged the ball up the middle or hit ropes to the fence, it felt great to O'Donnell.

Hopper ambled over to the side of the mound, motioning for O'Donnell to stop. "That's enough, Johnny-boy. If you don't quit now, we'll have that arm in traction. "

The sweat O'Donnell earned for his pitching labors soaked through the legs of his trousers, and his tee-shirt looked like he'd been running through a garden hose. "Thanks, Clay. That was fun. Think I'm ripe for a comeback?"

Hopper didn't laugh as expected. "Go see if they'll let you have a towel in the locker room and come on back here." He turned his attention back to the young prospects, calling over to one of the Saints's coaches who'd come up through the dugout to pitch some more batting practice. O'Donnell headed down to the locker room. He guessed Hopper didn't plan on taking him back to Montreal for a comeback.

26

O'DONNELL PLUCKED A FRESH TOWEL from a pile in the Saints's locker room. Several of the regular players he knew sat around on benches, playing cards and drinking sodas, killing time before practice. Eric Tipton, a long-time Saints veteran, asked some friendly questions, and O'Donnell put up with a few wisecracks from the others. When he returned to the field, Hopper motioned him over to the dugout. Players now swarmed all over—throwing back and forth, stretching, shagging fly balls, and playing pepper up against the grandstand.

Hopper leaned back against the dugout wall, eyeing the action. He pushed up the brim of his ball cap and rubbed a hand across his forehead, wiping away the sweat. He said a few hellos to players who ambled toward the water cooler. After the frosty early morning, the weather had switched gears completely. It must have been pushing eighty degrees, and the humidity covered the field like a wet washcloth.

"How are things with the big club, Clay?"

"We can always use pitching, but we'll be in the thick of it come the end of the season."

Hopper reached over and pushed up O'Donnell's cap. "What's that purple and yellow thing you've got on the side of your noggin there? Been fighting in the bar?"

"It's pretty complicated." O'Donnell stood up and pushed his hands up against the edge of the dugout roof.

"Does it have anything to do with the report in this morning's paper about this Flash Dawkins?" Hopper asked. "The article mentioned you as the one who found him."

Some beat reporter must have been on the ball at the Police Station last night. O'Donnell hadn't seen a morning paper.

"Isn't this Dawkins the one who's playing in the Open qualifier?" Hopper reached down and retrieved an errant baseball and rolled it back on the diamond. "Any connection?"

"Why do you say that?"

"Jackie Robinson." Hopper leaned over and fiddled with the laces on his spikes. "I've seen things like this before."

O'Donnell related what he knew about Flash and what had happened in the past few days.

Hopper shook his head and spat into the dirt of the dugout floor. "Let me tell you a little story that might help. I was born and bred in Mississippi, and I don't make apologies for it. I ain't telling you nothing you don't know, but down South every white boy grows up with a certain way of thinking and living. It may not be the way it ought to be, but it's the way most all of us live.

"Thing is, when baseball got me out of the South, and up in Montreal . . . I had to face all the things I'd taken as gospel in Mississippi. Jackie Robinson made me think." Hopper took off his hat, and ran his hand through a thatch of gray hair, now plastered to his scalp with sweat.

"He's made a lot of us think twice about things," O'Donnell said.

The sun no longer reached into the dugout, and the shadows helped cool the humid air. The players had finished batting practice, and moved with practiced skill through their infield and outfield drills. The pitchers had repaired to the right field foul line and commenced the drudgery of running from there to the left field fence and back again. That part of baseball O'Donnell didn't miss a bit.

"Even after I'd come to peace with the changes, my old life didn't go away easy," Hopper said. "Every time I'd go home, there'd be the good ol' boys waiting for me . . . and even those I'd thought were a cut above it all looked at me real different than before. Got so I didn't like seeing folks, so as I didn't have to talk about it and feel like I had to defend myself."

O'Donnell wondered where Hopper was going with his recollections, and hoped he'd have a point worth all the listening.

"Next thing I know, I'm getting letters from all over the States, not just the South," Hopper said. "Most of these letters are telling me I shouldn't help Mr. Rickey ruin the country by mixing the races. I still have some of those letters. Helps to remind me of how hateful we can be."

Hopper held his baseball cap, turning it from side to side, appraising its condition. "Then I started getting some stuff that was different from all the peckerwoods' scribbling. It was all about fighting the Communists." He slapped his cap on the wooden dugout bench. "I didn't have much quarrel with that, but these letters said the Communists planned to use the blacks against us."

"I take it you didn't agree."

"Well, I think the Communists have been trying to do that for a long time. We've got proof of their sneaking around in the unions . . . and what about all that spying in the government? But what I couldn't buy was that Jackie Robinson was some Commie agent, that he could bury the 'American way of life' just by hitting and fielding a damn baseball. I'm as loyal to this country as the next guy, but I couldn't pick up the spin on that pitch. No, sir."

"So what happened?" O'Donnell asked.

"Those particular letters kept coming, and they started reading more like threats."

"What kind of threats?"

"Nothing like, 'You play Robinson and we'll get you.' Different stuff. Threats about exposing things that happened long time past . . . things that would hurt me and my family."

"How did they find out?"

"That's the scary part. It must have taken a lot of digging. I thought I'd buried it real deep." Hopper rose up from the bench and stretched. "I'm getting stiff sitting here. Let's ramble around a bit."

Climbing out of the dugout into the bright sunlight, O'Donnell couldn't escape the twinge of pain in his ribs. At least his arm didn't hurt like it used to. Maybe the sidearm thing was the ticket. He and Hopper walked down the right field line, toward the fence. Some of the players came over, and Hopper exchanged a few words with them. The new Saints's manager, Walter Alston, had come out of the dugout and signaled for the players to gather round. O'Donnell thought how nice it would be to join them.

O'Donnell and Hopper eventually sat on the grassy slope leading up to the right field wall. Across the whole outfield, from right to center, the fielders had to scamper up that crazy slope if they were chasing a long fly.

"I told Mr. Rickey about the letters," Hopper said, "but he couldn't find out much. He pulled out all the stops trying to see who was behind most of the serious threats Jackie or I got."

O'Donnell thought about Jackie Robinson. Did Flash have any idea how much trouble he was taking on? Jackie Robinson hadn't exhausted all the haters.

"I never feared for my life like Jackie," Hopper broke the silence. "That young man is going through hell. It'll mark him for the rest of his life." He stood up and brushed off the seat of his baseball pants, ready to go back to the action on the field. Hopper put a hand on O'Donnell's shoulder. "I do recall one thing . . . a lot of those Commie conspiracy letters were postmarked from up here."

"St. Paul?"

"Minneapolis, too." Hopper cocked his head O'Donnell's way. "I always thought that was sort of odd. Thought you folks were a bit more sympathetic to black folks in these parts." He walked back toward the infield, leaving O'Donnell to wonder. He had Communists and anti-Communists rubbing against each other now. It wasn't much, but at least it pointed somewhere.

THE WAR ENDED IN 1945, but a strange, new one started soon enough. It had been brewing for a long time.

According to the foreign policy experts, the defeat of Hitler and the Axis powers cleared the stage for a battle between the United States and the Soviet Union. "Inevitable" was a word often heard, and O'Donnell noticed the newspapers and airwaves were clogged with alarms about the threat of a Communist takeover from Berlin to Shanghai. According to the radio newscasts, "the Reds" weren't, of course, a ball team O'Donnell knew from Cincinnati. They were Communists in the Kremlin, playing a deadly game without rules. Americans faced a "Red Menace" inside the nation with a bunch of Communist agents and sympathizers subverting the common folks, and a bunch of spies sneaking around stealing military secrets. O'Donnell guessed most of the returning vets didn't want to hear any of this stuff at first. They'd been at war too long. But after the A-bomb, it was a new ballgame no matter what anyone wanted.

Every day, O'Donnell heard more and more about the Communist threat, and he could agree with President Truman, who told Americans there wasn't any difference between totalitarian states. "I don't care what you call them," Harry said, " Nazi, Communist, or Fascist."

O'Donnell knew politicians and pundits might exaggerate, but they didn't just imagine what Stalin and his boys were doing behind the Iron Curtain. Still, O'Donnell found it hard to buy the idea that agents of the Kremlin had Americans standing one step from disaster at home. From what he could tell, more than a few politicians had started using the anti-Communist line to get elected and smear anything and anybody they didn't like. So, belong to a labor union, believe that Negroes had civil rights, or raise any doubts about the good life in the U.S. of A., and a man better think twice before spouting off. Increasingly, it seemed, given the anti-Communist's worldview, anything that might change the lives of black folks, union workers, and alter the "march of free enterprise" constituted a fearsome threat. Funny how many of the rip-roaring, anti-Communists business leaders safeguarded their profit margins by crying "Reds" at any unions demanding higher wages. Branding civil rights advocates as subversives worked just as well. O'Donnell suspected the anti-Communist vanguards had fashioned a political two-for-one sale, and they were always on the lookout for add-ons.

A bunch of pea brains in the Congress, flinging accusations wherever they might have a chance of sticking it to someone they didn't like, soon had their "fellow Americans" on the lookout for "Pinkos" and "Fellow Travelers." The House Un-American Activities Committee now yapped about Hollywood being infested with Communists. They wanted to spend a wad of taxpayers' money to make sure moviegoers wouldn't be fooled by Bugs Bunny and his Hollywood pals. *Heavens to Elmer Fudd!* O'Donnell wanted to know what the hell that Wicked Wabbit was trying to do?

The Commies were everywhere—at least that's what O'Donnell gathered from the news. They were in the factories, banks, butcher shops, on the street corners—and who the hell knew where else? It made a guy worry about getting a haircut.

Thinking usually gave O'Donnell an appetite. Given the subject of the worldwide Communist menace, it was dicey choice, but O'Donnell drove north on Lexington from the Saints's ballpark over to Nick's Lebanese Restaurant on Grand Avenue.

Nicky Awada was an old high school buddy, and he ran the restaurant that carried his name. He pumped O'Donnell's hand in greeting and guided him to a small booth near the kitchen. They caught up on his family and some of their old friends from high school. All the while, Nicky orchestrated the waiters and yelled through the door at the kitchen help. He ordered O'Donnell's lunch as well. "You have little or no taste, Johnny."

Crunching his way through a salad of romaine lettuce, feta cheese, grapes, some sort of tiny nuts, and topped with a wonderful cucumber dressing, O'Donnell consulted his note taking from the Saints's grandstand. He considered connections between current events and what all he'd learned that morning from the St. Paul police detectives and Clay Hopper. Marcus Sanford sure seemed like the logical choice for a first-rate troublemaker, as well as someone who could easily be responsible for beating up both O'Donnell and Flash. But why? And what about Butternut? What was that penny-ante gangster up to? What's more, Butternut and Sanford didn't match at all with how O'Donnell remembered Mr. Nylonhead.

Nicky brought O'Donnell a beer and served up what looked to be thin slices of lamb, fragrant with fresh garlic, served on flat bread with lettuce, tomato, and sour cream. Nicky poured some sort of sauce over the lamb, and waited for O'Donnell to taste his order. "It's great," O'Donnell offered, grabbing another forkful of the lamb.

"You don't deserve it, but the beer's on the house," Nicky said, and glided off through the packed dining room to greet some new arrivals.

O'Donnell returned to his mental puzzle. If this Jack Clancy was anything like the anti-Communists who'd sprouted up over the past couple of years, O'Donnell could easily imagine him as a determined foe of Flash, Gustafson, and their supporters. Given what Clay Hopper remembered about Jackie Robinson's trials and tribulations, Jack Clancy had earned a star by his name on O'Donnell's list.

O'Donnell thanked Nicky for lunch, and grabbed some mints from a bowl by the cash register to battle the garlic.

O'DONNELL CLOSED THE DOOR to Flash's hospital room. "I like the Teddy Bears."

Flash pulled the arm of his hospital gown forward to examine it. All he found were small, blue and tan polka dots. "Very funny. Tell me what's going on."

O'Donnell pulled up a straight chair with a red plastic cover over the seat. He'd checked with a nurse on the way in about Flash's condition.

"The nurse seems to think you're ready for a pasture and the nearest mare," O'Donnell said.

"If that's the report, I might want to hang around awhile." Flash looked out through the open door to his room and down the hall toward the nurses' station. "But I'm going home this afternoon."

"Let me know what time. I'll have Bobby come by and baby-sit you."

"I don't think so."

"What do you mean?"

"I take care of myself. No need for someone hanging around all the time."

O'Donnell could tell, once again, any further argument would lead nowhere on this issue. "At least let Bobby hang around when you go out to practice?"

"Forget it." Flash unraveled himself from the bed and walked over to the window. "Any new ideas about what's been going on?"

"I have a few things I need to follow up."

"Like what?"

O'Donnell related what he'd come up with so far in his talks with the police and Clay Hopper.

"What Clay Hopper told you fits with the crap I've had in the mail since deciding to play in the Open," Flash said. "Gustafson's had some of the same."

Flash took a long drink of water from the glass on the bed tray, watching O'Donnell's reaction. His face was a bit swollen under the bandages and tape, and O'Donnell could tell he was stiff and sore. O'Donnell fingered the bruise running along the side of his head. They were quite a pair, but he didn't feel much of a bond. He doubted Flash did, either. O'Donnell hoped the whole thing would go away soon.

Flash took another thirsty swig of water. "The letters have been postmarked from around here."

Flash described the letters as intelligently written, in a warped sort of way. Subtle threats about what might happen to him if he played in the

Open. Flash smiled to himself. "Whoever's writing this stuff doesn't quite get it, though."

"Why?"

"He doesn't understand what it's like to be in my shoes. If you live on the borderline of what's supposed to be proper in this country, you get to the point where it doesn't scare you anymore. Just makes you madder and bolder, wanting to do something big." Flash removed the glass straw and blew a soft stream of air through it. "That's why I can't wait for the Open. Jackie did baseball. I'm the next step."

"Tell me more about the letters." O'Donnell had heard enough about Flash and Jackie Robinson.

"I can do better than that." Flash struggled out of bed and motioned at the hallway. "You get that Doc Martin to release me now, and I'll show you."

FLASH TRACKED THROUGH the length of the apartment, passing by the bathroom where O'Donnell had found him the night before—rust-colored bloodstains on a green throw rug a prominent marker of the violence. He paused to look at the stains, shrugged off his thoughts, and completed the couple of steps it took to reach his bedroom. In the corner stood a wooden, three-drawer desk, a study lamp, and an old wooden chair with a red, white, and black plaid cushion on the seat. The room had one large window to the left of the desk. It faced out on Summit Avenue, allowing a nice view of the mansion across the street.

Flash sorted through some papers and letters. He pulled out a few envelopes already opened and studied their postmarks, shuffled them into order, stacked them neatly, and signaled for O'Donnell to look.

"Take them into the living room and make yourself comfortable. I'm going to make a sandwich," Flash said. "You want one?"

O'Donnell didn't. Lunch at Nicky's had been quite sufficient.

Each of the letters to Flash played on similar themes–wrongheaded to O'Donnell's point of view, but written with intensity and an obvious, but irritating display of intelligence. The thought and style of each letter matched.

"Clearly, we were fighting the wrong enemy in the war," O'Donnell said.

Flash nodded his agreement.

"Let's see if I have the thinking straight." O'Donnell waved the packet of letters at Flash. "The Kremlin plans to mastermind a worldwide Marxist revolution. A critical part is establishing a Fifth Column in the United States to bore from within." O'Donnell thought he was beginning to sound like one of his father's undergraduate lectures. "The internal subversion proceeds by disguising and glamorizing Moscow's revolutionary agenda as progressive and democratic."

Flash considered his pickle slice before taking a bite. He took a drink of what looked to be orange Kool-Aid, and caught O'Donnell staring at the contents of his glass. "Want some?" he asked.

When O'Donnell declined, Flash looked at him as if he'd turned down a glass of twelve-year old Scotch.

"As we all know," O'Donnell continued, "these Commie bastards spend years of study figuring how to bamboozle us. If they bamboozle enough people, we'll soon have their odious propaganda dripping from our radios, magazines, and newspapers."

Flash continued the spiel. "They'll control those new-fangled television sets. You name it. These ruthless, fanatic swine will bamboozle the nation."

"Our letter writer thinks the NAACP and those in favor of civil rights are part of this vast network of conspiracy," O'Donnell said. "Makes your blood run cold, doesn't it?"

"Oh, right you are, Comrade. Those Commie bastards adopt the good things us black folks desire and pervert them to their evil design." Flash slipped into a country cousin vernacular, "Folks like me is being used and abused by those bad boys. They pushing us so hard and fast to things we just ain't ready for. You know we poor souls couldn't think up this civil rights stuff for ourselves. It's them Ivans stirring up a mess of trouble, putting ideas in our woolly heads."

Flash drained his drink. "Tastes good," he said, and headed to the kitchen for a refill. When he returned, he set down a glass of the orange stuff next to O'Donnell.

"This guy's also worried sick about the rest of the world finding out about our dirty laundry," O'Donnell interrupted.

Flash frowned. "What are you getting at?"

"I mean, he doesn't want any bad publicity about what's going on here at home to spoil our international image."

"So, this crackpot is a bundle of motives, but it's all making good sense to him." Flash tapped his fingers on the pile of letters. "And we know he's damn serious enough to carry out his threats."

"I'd say you fit his enemy list to a 'T.'"

Flash got up and walked over to the window. He let out a long breath, rubbing his forehead.

"If you play in the Open and win," O'Donnell said, "it'll be something he doesn't want to see. It'll be a national news story, and you and the NAACP will get all the press you can handle. The PGA will fight you, and they'll look like a bunch of Ku Klux Klan boys with golf knickers instead of white sheets." O'Donnell pointed to Flash. "You might capture the public's heart. Who knows? But this guy can't let that happen. If he's so worried about the Commies and protecting all that's dear to his American heart, you'll be like the biggest, bad fox in the hen house."

Flash didn't seem to like the analogy. He took one of the letters and looked at it for a long time, then slapped it down on the table. "I can still play, and I can win it."

"Things might get tougher than you've seen already."

"I can handle my end of this thing," he said, his voice soft. He started to say something else, but didn't.

29

I T WAS ORANGE KOOL-AID.

O'Donnell stopped at a small gas station on Grand Avenue to fill-up, taking the occasion to buy a pack of Wrigley's Spearmint for the bad taste in his mouth. While he waited for the attendant to check the oil and wash the windows, O'Donnell paged through the telephone directory, looking for Jack Clancy's number. He shoved a nickel in the pay phone and dialed.

After a couple of rings, a voice mumbled something like, "Mishta Clanshees."

O'Donnell pretended to be from a local insurance company. The scam didn't seem to impress the guy on the other end of the line.

"Aininow," the voice said.

"Excuse me?"

After a brief pause, the receiver clattered down, and all O'Donnell had to remind him of the precious moments of conversation was a dial tone. Was a house call in order? Time was moving fast toward Flash's tee time at the St. Paul open.

The address listed in the phone book made sense for a big wheel businessman and a country-club member like Clancy. Once again, a house set near the Mississippi River at one of the best addresses on the River Road.

Once O'Donnell turned into Clancy's neighborhood, he felt a little less confident about his plan. When the body attached to the voice that answered Clancy's phone loomed in the front doorway, O'Donnell knew he was in for it. The guy was like a wrestler, with thick shoulders, well-muscled arms, but a tiny head perched on a neck as wide around as a tree trunk. Diminished reasoning capacity or not, the freak at the door had about fifty pounds on O'Donnell just in the neck alone, and the guy's hands looked like they could crush moose skulls. The incongruity of his cranium compared to the rest of him left O'Donnell more than somewhat astonished. The guy had no hair, and his lips, nose, and eyebrows allowed his face no description except that of an unfinished wax mold. His eyes were set back so far under the shelf-like forehead he had the look of some primordial lizard. When he spoke, his lips hardly moved, and O'Donnell half-expected a long, split tongue to probe his face.

O'Donnell furnished his best and most sincere insurance salesmen's smile. "Hi, I called a while back. I think we were disconnected."

The thing in the doorway clamped a hand on O'Donnell's shirtfront. His lips cracked open, revealing a wall of yellow, pointy teeth. He jerked O'Donnell toward him, then pushed him backward off the steps. He obviously didn't like insurance men.

"Gi-loss," the words gargled in his throat.

O'Donnell made like a bird with a broken wing to divert attention, and snuck a quick look at the bozo looming in front of him. The hulk had his hands at his sides.

Bad move.

O'Donnell threw a quick, solid punch to the midsection. The lunkhead staggered back into the doorway, stupefied. O'Donnell faked a right and planted a nice left cross up against nasal cartilage. Joe Louis probably could have done it better, but not by much.

"Hold it," a loud voice boomed from the doorway. "That's enough, dammit."

O'Donnell wanted to finish what he'd started, but a little voice in the back of his head said to back off. He let the guy crumple on the front steps.

Another wave of anger swept over O'Donnell. It felt good.

"Put a stop to it, mister," the voice commanded.

A broad-bodied man in his early fifties stood over O'Donnell at the front door. A thin, tightly drawn mouth served as a median between a long, sharp nose and a small, but defiant chin. He swept his dark-brown hair straight back from his forehead, elongating his face and emphasizing the intensity of his eyes. He wore a sharp, double-breasted suit and a starched white shirt, split by a blue and gold regimental striped tie. He'd lost his trim long ago, and his suit coat puffed against its buttons.

"You've made a mess of poor Arnold." Jack Clancy looked down on the body sprawled in front of him with disgust. "It's usually the other way around."

Arnold lay quiet, massaging his nose.

"Arnold, get your fat behind off the ground and go fix yourself up," Clancy chided. "You become less tolerable everyday. You can't fight anymore, and next thing we'll find is you can't carry on with your usual eloquence."

Clancy smiled O'Donnell's way. O'Donnell didn't return the favor.

Arnold labored up, wiping some blood off his nostril with the back of his hand. He made a poor attempt at a tough guy look. His heart wasn't in it.

Clancy gave O'Donnell the once over. "No introduction is necessary here, Mr. O'Donnell. I know quite well who you are and why you think you should pursue this visit. The police detectives have already been around for an interview. But I suppose you know that, too."

Clancy motioned for O'Donnell to follow him into the house. They trekked down a long, wood-paneled entryway and into a spacious, oak-paneled room that served as an office. Clancy stood behind a wide desk, devoid of any paperwork, and lowered himself into a plush, black leather chair. He swiveled around so that he could retrieve a file folder from a low table behind him. O'Donnell took a seat in a wingback chair, covered in nubby, dark-green fabric. He sat at a low angle to Clancy. He supposed that was on purpose.

Clancy opened a file and reviewed it, his lips pursing. Behind his desk, several framed photographs of what looked to be politicians and business types graced the wall. To the left, near two, floor length windows that looked out into a garden, a simple wood stand held a large bible, opened and marked with a red velvet cord.

O'Donnell scanned the floor-to-ceiling bookcases that took up an entire wall near the door to Clancy's study. Most of the titles appeared to be about world affairs and religious subjects. He also had a section of the titles screaming things like *Subversion in the Schools, The Truth About Zionism and Communism,* and *Negroes in a Soviet America.* Bedtime reading for fanatics?

He leaned back in his chair, fixing O'Donnell with an ill-tempered glare. "I'm far too busy for these interruptions, so I don't regret that Arnold tried to dissuade your visit. But since you've made it this far, I'll give you a few minutes for whatever questions you'd like to ask."

"You didn't want any insurance, then?"

"Get on with it. Don't waste what little time I'm willing to permit you." Clancy smoothed the front of his suit coat and gave the knot of his tie a little tug.

O'Donnell tried a change-up. "What keeps you so busy?"

Clancy looked surprised. "I assumed you would find out things like that before you embarked on this interview."

O'Donnell tried to look like an eager schoolboy, and asked his question again.

"If you must inquire," Clancy said, still insulted by O'Donnell's obvious disregard of his current newsworthiness, "I'm scheduled to deliver an important speech in Detroit next week. From there I'll journey to Cincinnati for their 'Save America' rally. After that, I'll be working on a nation-wide radio broadcast." He seemed impressed by what he had to do. O'Donnell tried to look impressed with him.

"That's quite a schedule," O'Donnell said, sitting at attention. Clancy seemed to like that. O'Donnell could hear the man's ego thumping.

"As you suggest, I'm a busy public figure," Clancy said. "However, I haven't always sought the limelight."

He intertwined his fingers and leaned forward in the chair. The creak of his leather chair sounded expensive to O'Donnell, as it should. Clancy struck a reflective profile.

"Not until after the war did I find time for an appeal to the public mind." Clancy straightened a green blotter on his desk just so. "Following graduation from Yale, I decided to devote my life to the nation's service. I took advanced training in Washington, and then it was time to apply my skills. Until these last two years I've lived, shall we say, 'in the shadows,' where I've served my country and the United States armed forces in what might be termed . . . 'backdoor' operations." He clasped his hands and stared at O'Donnell, indicating a new question would be appropriate at this point.

"I didn't know all that." O'Donnell thought it best to keep stoking the fires.

"Perhaps some future historian will." Clancy placed his elbows on the desktop, and knit his fingers together, his eyes fixed on O'Donnell. "One thing I will say, though. I learned enough about our real enemy to keep me busy until the end of my days."

"Our real enemy?"

"The Nazis and the Japanese were formidable enemies of this nation, but hardly the ultimate threat represented by the Communists and their worldwide revolutionary movement. You can't imagine, Mr. O'Donnell, how sophisticated this plan of the Kremlin is. Agents are being trained by the Soviets who will soon infiltrate every major free world government. These agents will spend years preparing for their roles. As I instructed the delegates of the American Legion convention in Chicago last week, 'the diabolic Communists' plan will be . . .' Now how did I phrase it? Ah, yes. '. . . one aimed at world domination and brought into play with exceptional cunning and dedication.'"

Apparently, Clancy found himself eminently quotable. O'Donnell couldn't help wondering how such a blowhard had succeeded at highest levels of responsibility. He also noted the echoes between Clancy's thinking and that expressed in the letters Flash had received.

"As you well know," Clancy continued, "the Reds have battalions of agents, spies, and saboteurs plotting the overthrow of our system." He rose and walked to the window, drawing aside the curtain a few inches. He retraced his steps to the desk and sat casually on the edge of it.

"It's not only the military threat posed by the Russians and their allies that should concern us," Clancy continued, his words urgent, passionate. "There is a cancer spreading within our Republic that will rot our resolve. Hating the Communists will not be enough. We must use every means to root them out and crush their vile schemes."

He bolted off the desk, paced to the window and back, continuing to lecture O'Donnell on the Communist threat. The man loved oratory, even if confined to an audience of one.

Clancy returned in his chair, and again picked up the threads of his autobiography—this time apparently not worried a bit about any future historian and obviously pleased to recite his life's accomplishments. Clancy had graduated Annapolis back in the early '30s, and turned up in Washington as an aide to one of the admirals, soon advancing within the growing intelligence community. As Hitler and Stalin joined hands on their Non-Aggression Pact in '38, Clancy apparently went under cover, running spy networks in Europe until the end of the war. He emerged from his clandestine operations into the national limelight within a matter of months, appearing on J. Edgar Hoover's arm at the American Legion's national convention, rising quickly as a leading anti-Communist spokesman, joining the ranks of national political firebrands like Gerald L.K. Smith and J. Parnell Thomas. O'Donnell suspected those boys didn't care much for the competition.

"Might your concern about this internal conspiracy be a bit . . . overstated?" O'Donnell couldn't resist asking.

"Overstated?" Clancy looked at O'Donnell like he'd told him the world was flat. His chest puffed up as he launched into another civics lesson.

"I cannot emphasize enough the real threats to this nation that you characterize as overstated conspiracies. I don't have time to go into an extended dissertation in response to your question, but I can assure you I'm not without proof of what I say."

He reached into a drawer and emerged with a fistful of brightly colored pamphlets. Waving them in O'Donnell's face, he said, "Let me suggest you take along some of the literature I've published."

O'Donnell glanced at the first page of one pamphlet. Had Clancy selected it on purpose?

Clancy's writing gravitated toward words in capital letters, lots of underlining, and more exclamation points than you could count—all sticking out like fence posts at the end of sentences. O'Donnell wondered if the man signed his name with one.

"Do you think the NAACP is controlled by the Communist Party and ultimately plans to . . . 'mongrelize' the white race through intermarriage?" O'Donnell asked, attempting his best to keep the cynicism from his voice. The pamphlet also suggested that blacks asking for civil rights were being manipulated by a Jewish conspiracy, not just Commies. What amazed O'Donnell was how so many fellow Americans turned out to hear what Clancy and the others had to say—and believed what they heard.

"The civil rights movement is a fraud," Clancy roared. "I have something else for you to read."

He snatched a thin volume off the bookcase shelf behind his desk, sliding it across the desk. The book's title read, *American Negro Problems*. "It's written by a Hungarian Jew and avowed Communist, and published in this country in 1928," Clancy said. "This book is a veritable blueprint for an internal revolution to establish a 'Negro Soviet Republic' in the South."

Clancy waited for his information to sink in. O'Donnell's expression obviously didn't register the right way.

"Do you really believe that?"

Clancy smirked, relaxing the military bearing he'd mustered. His smirk changed to a conspiratorial smile. "I may not believe all I say, but in a fight such as this . . . I'll say whatever I must. Besides, Mr. O'Donnell, are you in favor of allowing intermarriage?"

"I doubt that's an issue on which the fate of the free world will revolve."

Clancy smirked once again. "It's always been part of what the Communists use to recruit the unsuspecting to their civil rights conspiracies," he said with perfect conviction. "I wouldn't be so smug about your liberal opinions, O'Donnell. You might find cause to regret them one day. From what I can tell, you're a reasonably intelligent young man. Let me give you a hint. The Communists threaten our capitalist system on a worldwide basis. Their combination of subversion and military maneuver leads the fragile nations of the world toward revolution. Such instability and revolution is a terribly threatening outlook for our future economic health and for the re-birth of prosperity here in our nation. I trust you haven't forgotten the depression years?"

O'Donnell indicated he hadn't. Where was the man going with this dissertation? It seemed so much at odds with Clancy's earlier, more flamboyant rhetoric?

Clancy stared at O'Donnell with amusement, not venom. "Aside from restoring control in our world marketplace, we must make sure our economy is well-organized, efficient, and able to produce trade goods as well as domestic products at the lowest cost of manufacture. Do you follow me?"

O'Donnell could guess where he was heading.

"We do not need a continued growth of government and its interference with the economy. A 'New Deal' welfare state will cut us off at the knees, devouring profits for tax monies to finance big government devoted to the spending schemes of the Jewish Liberal Establishment, the leftists, Communist unions, and all those bleeding heart groups looking for a hand out."

Any other conspiracies, O'Donnell thought, and Clancy might need a librarian to catalog them all.

"I'm out to destroy these internal threats to this great nation." Clancy settled back in his chair.

"You don't really believe half of what you preach, do you?" O'Donnell asked, attempting to deflate Clancy's ego a bit.

Clancy's eyes narrowed, and bored into O'Donnell's. "Don't misunderstand me, O'Donnell. While an internal Communist threat is less than what I'd admit in public . . . it *is* there, and has the potential to grow through the damn foolishness of those traitorous groups who do all the thinking for it. Soften up our nation long enough . . . and the Communists will have a cakewalk in twenty years."

"So what makes you any less manipulative than the Communists?"

"Nothing, young man," Clancy glared at O'Donnell. "Except . . . I fight dirty for the right ends."

Somehow O'Donnell didn't suppose Clancy's reasoning would pass muster in a college ethics course.

"Does your defense against the evils you've conjured here allow you to beat up people who get in your way?" O'Donnell caught Clancy off guard, proving once again the benefits of a good, hard fastball under the chin.

"If you are referring to what happened to that Negro friend of yours, who thinks of himself as golf's Jackie Robinson, I don't bother with that sort of thing as, no doubt, you'll find out." Clancy allowed O'Donnell a moment to ponder his response, and walked to a low cabinet near the window, pouring himself some water from a crystal pitcher into an equally impressive, finely etched goblet. Clancy gazed out the window, slowly revolving the goblet he held. "I trust you fully understand my position now and that you've learned something important to your 'well-being' as it were. Please show yourself out, Mr. O'Donnell."

At the doorway of Clancy's study, O'Donnell paused. "You never fought on a battlefront during your illustrious career, did you? You're a behind-the-scenes type. Right? Spies . . . assassinations . . . that sort of thing."

"What is your point?" Clancy sighed, tapping his nails on the desk blotter. "You really have become quite tiresome, O'Donnell."

"People on the front lines don't back off so easy. Try to remember that."

O'Donnell had tried his best to throw a scare into Clancy. No luck, it seemed. This was a dog with a lot of bite.

On his way out, O'Donnell passed by Arnold, sitting in the front hall on a colonial bench under an impressive gilt mirror. Clancy's henchman looked more than a little worse for the wear. He worked hard again at his tough guy glare, nevertheless.

CLANCY SURE AS HELL didn't want Flash playing in the St. Paul Open, and O'Donnell wondered how far the man had gone already. Surely Clancy didn't hire someone like Sanford for the rough stuff. Those two started out in quite opposite corners, to say the least. That piece of the puzzle didn't fit at all.

On the road home, O'Donnell bought a six-pack to go from Harry's Tap, a 3.2 joint across from the fairgrounds off of Snelling Avenue. It wouldn't be long until the gates would open for the Minnesota State Fair. O'Donnell mouth watered at the thought of Mrs. Hopkins' pork and baked beans at the Hamline Methodist church tent. The corn dogs and coleslaw at the Knights of Columbus hall were darn tasty, too. And the strawberry short cake and homemade vanilla ice cream the Lutheran ladies always offered for dessert? It was enough to make a man take religion seriously.

A late model Lincoln sat in the middle of his driveway. Jill stood next to it, staring at the lake, wearing a snug bandana top and skimpy shorts. She wiggled around to wave hello, getting every penny's worth of effect from her abbreviated outfit.

"I hope you don't mind me chasing you out here," she said.

O'Donnell told her he didn't mind. "You look beautiful."

"I need all the compliments I can get today." Jill slid off the hood and walked by O'Donnell, trailing her fingers across his shoulder. She sat on the porch steps, once again looking out at the lake.

O'Donnell opened the door for Cosmo, who after allowing brief petting session, took off towards the neighbor's hedge to re-mark his turf. A glance back at the porch sitters, a hasty wag of his tail, and he set off for the Anderson's cabin again. O'Donnell figured he needed to buy more doggie treats.

"Anything wrong?" O'Donnell asked. "You look sad."

"I'm so sorry the way I've treated you, Johnny. You don't deserve it."

O'Donnell moved close to her, and held her hand in his. They sat beside each other on the porch steps.

"I want to apologize to you for treating you the way I have," she said in a small, determined voice. "I haven't been myself lately."

O'Donnell waited for her to say more. She traced the palm of his hand with her fingers. "Do you know what I did during the war?"

He already knew about the Women's Reserves, though still found it hard to believe.

"I joined the Women's Reserves." Her eyes brightened at the memory, and she looked for a reaction. He could tell this had been an important time for her. "I'm really missing those days," she said.

Jill told O'Donnell she'd joined up with a college friend on the spur of the moment. They dropped out of classes at Northwestern, and traveled to the Hunter College campus in New York City to train with the first group of Women's Reserves. They waited until the enlistment papers were sealed and delivered before informing their parents.

"Daddy came around a little after he recovered from the shock," Jill laughed, "but Mother couldn't imagine how I could do such a thing. We were in the middle of a world war, and she's worried what her friends would say. The only thing she ever said was a proper young woman 'simply does not do things like that.' Can you believe it?"

Yes, O'Donnell could believe it.

"I couldn't wait to send her a picture of me in my uniform," Jill straightened her back, as if readying to assert her independence all over again. "Joining the 'WRs' was the best thing I've done in my life."

As she talked about her experiences, she seemed at the moment a long way from a fragile, spoiled woman-child. He prompted her to continue, and she pulled on her memories of that time. She talked about the encampment at New River, recalling the same barren landscape of scrub pines and sand flats O'Donnell remembered.

"We moved from Hunter College to Camp Lejeune in April of '43. Holly and I had only been training for a couple of weeks. We were so wet behind the ears. They put us in the men's barracks and we had an honest to goodness Drill Instructor. He was so scary."

"Nothing new there," O'Donnell told her.

"He was from some horrible place in Louisiana and had been a D.I. forever. All of us hated him at the beginning. But then we started working together as a team. It was such a wonderful time once we came to know each other."

"Why so wonderful?" O'Donnell asked.

Jill thought for a minute. "I guess it was the fact that nobody was expecting us to succeed, and we wanted to show we could. No matter what they called us or made us do for those first few weeks, we didn't quit. There were plenty of tears, and just about every one of us broke down at one time or another. But when one of the girls would get down, the rest of us would help her out."

She squeezed O'Donnell's hand. "I don't mean to hurt your feelings, but for the first time in our lives, it seemed like we didn't need a man do things for us. We did just fine without daddies or brothers or boyfriends."

O'Donnell hoped that was only a wartime exigency. "Did you train to be anything in particular?"

"I trained how to tell my left foot from my right and how to get rid of fleas and ticks." She gave a husky laugh, "Did you see the roaches they grow down there?"

O'Donnell remembered them well, especially the ones that would hitch a ride in a pants' pocket.

"Actually," she said, drawing out each syllable, "In boot camp I excelled in the scullery arts. At least that's where I spent most of my effort. What a laugh, the slogan was 'free a Marine to fight,' and it was more like 'free a Marine to eat!' I swear I spent most of my waking hours knee deep in potato peals and dirty dishes. Of course, I couldn't tell my folks about all that."

O'Donnell had trouble picturing Jill as one of the "gung ho" gals he'd seen in the Women's Reserve, much less peeling potatoes. He heard more than a few of the WRs packed it in after the first few days and tried to run home as fast as they could. The Marines acted as if every WR was a cheap whore or some sort of slut begging for a quick roll in the hay. Not an easy life for someone as pampered and sheltered as he imagined Jill. Maybe he was being too cynical.

"Where did you end up after boot camp?"

Jill hesitated before answering, tracing a small circle around the setting of a jade ring she wore. "I went to San Diego on duty."

O'Donnell spent a week or so hanging out on Coronado Island after returning from duty in the Pacific, and had doubts about ever leaving. He told Jill where he'd stayed and what he liked so much about the city. She seemed far away. When he asked about her experience in San Diego, it wasn't what O'Donnell wanted to hear.

"I was with a wonderful man there." She brushed at a tear starting a free fall down her cheek, "and I fell in love. We were different in some ways, but we really just clicked." She glanced at O'Donnell. "It wasn't one of those wartime romances."

O'Donnell's heart sunk imagining Jill with another man. He didn't need to hear this particular story.

Another tear made its descent from the corner of Jill's eye, sliding past her lips to the edge of her chin. "We saw each other every chance we had before he left for duty." She nibbled at her lower lip. "We had some problems . . . our relationship wasn't easy."

She smiled once again at what might have been a better memory, but the tears continued. O'Donnell didn't know quite what to think. He wondered if this was simply another one of those tragic love stories from the war. The couple falls madly in love, the guy ships out to combat, and a month later the gal finds out he's K.I.A. It happened all the time. Either that, or the guy ships out, and three months later his sweetheart has hooked up with the boy at home in Fergus Falls. He hadn't forgotten his own such letter penned by the woman next to him.

"After the war was over, I waited for him in Los Angeles," Jill said. "I rented a little place to stay, and I took a hospital job. Abby came to visit once."

"What happened when he came back?" O'Donnell could tell by how her shoulders slumped that the story would be an unhappy one.

"At first, everything was so wonderful. I'd waited so long to see him." Jill smiled brightly at the memory.

The exact sort of detail O'Donnell didn't care to hear. Jill seemed oblivious to that affect.

"Then . . . I guess the excitement of being back from the war and being together again wore out. He started going off on his own, saying he needed some time to himself. He'd go out early in the morning, and come back late at night. One night he didn't come home at all. I left a note in the morning when I went out." She spoke as if each word were weighted down with hurt. "I told him I loved him. I asked him to come back to me when he was ready. I told him we could work things out no matter how big the problems. And I guess I made it clear I wanted him any way I could have him, even if he didn't love me as much as before." Jill shrugged, and her voice cracked as she spoke again. "When I got back to the apartment that day, the note was gone . . . and so was he."

Jill stared out at the night sky, her face set and drawn tight.

"I felt so stupid about loving him so much," she said. "I don't care. I wonder if he ever truly loved me."

O'Donnell thought she spoke in the way of an unexpected discovery, as if she couldn't imagine any man not being crazy for her. Jill hadn't much experience on that front.

"I wish I could hate him, but I can't. But I suppose it could never work out for us."

O'Donnell and Jill remained silent for what seemed a long time, sitting close together, each lost in thought. O'Donnell thought about the differences between the two Gustafson sisters. It was clear who made a better match, but he couldn't quite break the hold Jill had on him.

Jill laid her head on O'Donnell's knee and hugged his leg like a child. He smoothed her hair and moved a hand across her shoulders like he imagined a father might with a daughter. After a time, her breathing calmed and the tears stopped falling.

Before she left, Jill rapped her arms around O'Donnell and held on for a long moment. He knew she did so without the promise of anything.

THE NEXT MORNING, O'Donnell affixed the only tie he owned—a red one—to a clean, but infrequently worn, white shirt. A reasonably presentable pair of light wool trousers hung in the closet, waiting to be of service, lonely on a wire hanger. Wool in July? A bit out of season, O'Donnell had to admit, even in Minnesota. But what the heck, most of the professors at the Faculty Club only had but one season represented in their clothes' closets. O'Donnell wouldn't feel out of place . . . just itchy.

No way around today's dress-up exercise. He'd been invited for lunch. "We need a chat," his father said. O'Donnell had heard that line many times as a kid—usually when he'd done something stupid.

Around noon, O'Donnell found a parking spot behind the Coffman Student Union and took the elevator to the Faculty Club on the top floor. Professor Thomas O'Donnell had picked a table by a window overlooking the Mississippi River, and a student waiter in a starched white jacket led the way to it.

O'Donnell's father had been at the university since the early 1920s. With a Ph.D. in history from the University of Michigan, he'd risen to prominence in academic circles before the war as an historian and archeologist. His classes were sellouts with the students. O'Donnell would sneak in to hear his lectures every once in a while, and his friends all took Professor O'Donnell's survey course on Greece and Rome. At close to fifty, he looked ten years younger—darkly handsome, with thick, wavy black hair, only slightly tinged with gray. He kept trim playing handball a couple of times a week at the courts underneath the football stadium.

The coeds loved him. O'Donnell remembered sitting in a required humanities class in front of three sorority girls. One of them cooed, "Wasn't Professor O'Donnell dreamy today?" Between sighs and giggles, the girls continued their catalog of Professor O'Donnell's sex appeal. When the professor walked across campus to and from his classes, a trail of students, usually coeds, followed in his wake. Of course, life as his son had predictable results. When people discovered the younger O'Donnell lacked the old man's brainpower and his intellectual interests, the result was clucking tongues and wonderment at the vagaries of genetic inheritance. O'Donnell did well enough in his short, pre-war study at the university, but the tongue clucking and head shaking made his student days less than jolly. The war gave him an excuse to say good-bye to the books and hello to a much deeper learning experience.

O'Donnell took a seat facing his father across a white linen tablecloth, embroidered in the middle with the university's academic motto and seal. A large row of windows beyond where his father waited at a reserved table offered a panoramic view of the quadrangle across Washington Avenue. On the walkways, coeds strolled towards their classes, arms laden with books and purses. Couples sat close together on the lawn and the steps of buildings, pretending to study. It all seemed a far away world to O'Donnell. Every so often, he could spot veterans like himself walking with purpose up the library steps. Thousands had come to the U after the war—a great many joined by their wives and children, clustered in Quonset huts near the St. Paul agricultural campus off Como Avenue.

The vets spent their days taking courses on everything from philosophy to business accounting. The G.I. Bill helped pay for their training and intellectual growth. They sat in classes with men like O'Donnell's father, who'd often been their commanding officers a few short years before. Now, instead of saluting, the vets marked the right answers on multiple-choice tests and memorized the circulatory systems of frogs. Once they had their degrees, and it didn't matter much what in, they'd be off to jobs they could do probably without ever being on a campus. At least that's what O'Donnell's father sometimes would argue after a poor performance by students on an exam.

The U.S. Navy had recruited Professor O'Donnell in 1941 to serve as an intelligence expert. From the small hints he'd dropped, O'Donnell assumed his father was one of the Navy code breakers. He picked up languages like candy bars in a grocery store, and he'd been an honor student in mathematics as an undergraduate. Before the war he'd made tremendous progress deciphering the ancient Minoan language. His reputation had soared. That's when the Navy nabbed him for its intelligence operations against Japan. He landed in the middle of all the big shots already down from Yale and Harvard. Professor O'Donnell bragged uncharacteristically that in no time flat he'd shown up all "the Ivy League boys."

Father and son sat munching tuna fish sandwiches and drinking iced tea, talking about the Gopher football team's chances in the coming season. O'Donnell's father poured himself another glass of iced tea, taking time to stir in a bit of sugar. "Okay John, let's get down to business. I have a grad student seminar this afternoon."

He re-folded the maroon table napkin he used and laid it beside his plate. "I had a call yesterday from a friend in Washington. I think you may have stepped into something more serious than you might think."

It only took a second for O'Donnell to figure out which way the conversation would be heading. "Jack Clancy. Right?"

"Exactly."

"I can take care of myself."

O'Donnell's father frowned. "Give a listen, young man. Then you can decide how well you can handle things."

His father hadn't said that to him since high school, so O'Donnell listened.

"We are now at a time in which the rules of fair play and the laws of the land can be bent far past the breaking point," O'Donnell's father said. "It's happened before, and it'll happen again. This new crowd in Washington plays a high stakes game in foreign policy, and they're of the mind that what goes on in St. Paul is as important as Moscow, Berlin, or Shanghai."

"I guess I don't see how I fit into all of this." O'Donnell did know, but he wanted to hear his father's version.

"Clancy is one of the anti-Communist up and comers. He's well-connected with all the big boys in the intelligence outfits and even beyond. I'm told he may end up running a special initiative. You push Jack Clancy too hard, and you'll have no defense against what he can do. Be very careful. My friend wanted me to emphasize that."

"What do you think I ought to do?"

"What you and this golfer friend of yours are doing is the right thing, of course, and I'd hate to think that social reform has to stop in its tracks for Clancy and his ilk. Clancy sees himself as protecting the future of the nation, but that's not the sort of future most reasonable people want. Just be very careful whose toes you're stepping on. Use some common sense."

O'Donnell's father rose from the table and collected his briefcase from the chair next to him. As he turned to leave, he again warned his son to be alert for trouble and granted him a fatherly noogie on the skull. O'Donnell felt like he was a ten-year-old again. Not a bad feeling.

32

YOUNG WOMEN IN SWEATERS and slacks parading by the intersection near Memorial Stadium caused O'Donnell once again to regret his short residence as a full-time undergraduate. But once he'd driven past the water tower at Prospect Park, the lure of the sweater-set sirens on campus had worn off. He was free to entertain more immediate objectives.

He headed straight down University Avenue to the Saints's ballpark again. No game today, but the team took batting practice at 2:00 p.m. He had all his baseball stuff stowed in the trunk now. Maybe he could work out with the Saints, and then drive over to Midway YMCA for a nice steam and shower.

At the ballpark, the Saints's players clustered around the batting cage. They'd been through infield, and now relished the chance to take their cuts.

"Come on old man," one of them yelled, "get that soup bone warmed up and throw a few." Exactly what O'Donnell had in mind.

"Get out there on the mound, O'Donnell," said Walter Alston, the Saints manager. "Clay said you'd figured how to throw the ball over the plate again."

As he warmed up, O'Donnell kept to the sidearm delivery Clay Hopper had suggested. He had the ball diving and coming in at a pretty good speed after about five minutes. It felt damn good. It felt like he'd been pitching this way all his career.

"Looking sharp, O'Donnell," said Spider Jorgensen, a reserve third baseman, as he trotted past the mound on his way to the dugout.

"Just call me the Comeback Kid." O'Donnell realized he wasn't kidding.

Alston pawed the ground with the end of his fungo bat, looking serious as always. "If we're going to win this league, we'll need some pitching help in a couple of weeks. You know the Dodgers will call up one of my kids." He scratched around the dirt some more. "If you think you can make a comeback, let's set up something regular."

"What are you thinking?"

"Well, hold on a minute. I want to see you throw off the mound before I jump into anything."

To O'Donnell, Alston's easygoing personality made him seem more like a friendly bank clerk than a baseball manager. But he knew his business.

"Let's do it," O'Donnell said, "You send up some of your sluggers and give me a decent set of infielders."

"You don't need an outfield, hotshot?"

"What'll I need them for?"

O'Donnell busied himself gardening around the mound while Alston called the Saints over and sent the reserve infielders out on the diamond . . . as well as the outfielders. By the looks of it, he planned to use his best hitters at the plate. The Saints's players laughed along the sidelines, a few of them pantomiming the new pitching delivery.

Just you boys wait, O'Donnell thought. Maybe his confidence had outrun his talent, but he felt good. Even the butterflies in his stomach felt good, too. Like old times.

The Saints regular catcher, "Andy" Anderson, strolled out to the mound for a conference. Andy had caught a few ballgames for O'Donnell the season before. He called a good game, and with his strong peg to second, Andy could throw out a gazelle trying to steal. He put his mitt up by his mouth, intending a private chat between catcher and pitcher. "So what have we got for pitches, Johnny?"

"To tell the truth," O'Donnell said, "I'm not sure. I'm not throwing like a normal human being these days."

Andy grinned up at O'Donnell. "So throw me what you've got, and we'll pick out some fingers."

Andy trotted back behind the plate and O'Donnell threw him some fastballs and a couple of curves. He tried a change-up, but it was meat.

"Hey, Andy, let's stick with number one and number two." The change-up would have to wait for a finger.

"You got it." Andy called out. "Your fastball looks like a change anyway."

"Whose side are you on?"

Andy whizzed the ball past O'Donnell's left ear to the second baseman. He threw with almost as much velocity to second base as O'Donnell did from the mound to home. Maybe O'Donnell had let his ego get in the way of reality.

Alston stood behind the mound, intending to call balls and strikes. O'Donnell checked his fielders, looked in for the sign, concentrating on the match-up between pitcher and hitter. Andy called for a curveball. O'Donnell shook him off. He wanted to start off with a reliable pitch. The sinking fastball had some pretty good juice on it, O'Donnell thought. But everything turned bad as the batter lashed out at the pitch, catching it on the fat part of the bat and sending it sailing down the left field line. Home run. One pitch and one run circling the bases.

Andy pulled off his mask and stepped in front of the plate. "That's why the catcher calls signals, Meathead."

O'Donnell could only nod his head in agreement. Still, it wasn't that bad a pitch.

The next batter and the on-deck guy laughed it up at O'Donnell's expense. Even the guys on his side joined in on the catcalls. That did it. O'Donnell drilled the next batter in the ribs. Trotting down to first base, the player made a few feeble threats.

Johnny O'Donnell, the tough guy.

The number three hitter dug in at the plate. O'Donnell's first pitch caught the inside corner for a strike. Andy called for a curve ball, and O'Donnell gave him a pretty good one. Coming sidearm, his curve ball had a much different look to it.

Strike two.

Usually, O'Donnell would waste a pitch on a 0 to 2 count, but he aimed one for the outside corner, hoping his new delivery would kick it in at the last second. It did. *Strike damn three.*

As the batter headed back to the dugout, O'Donnell checked over at first. His buddy with the sore ribs had taken a pretty big lead. He didn't know Johnny O'Donnell had one hell of a pick-off move. He found out as O'Donnell zipped over a perfect throw and the first baseman slapped down the tag.

"That's two, Johnny babe," Andy yelled. "Let's hear some hobber, infield."

The boys on O'Donnell's side weren't quite convinced. None yelled out a good word for him. Not even a classic *"Hum-baby-hum-babe."* O'Donnell felt like Bob Crosby without the Bobcats.

"Let's see that new pitch, O'Donnell," an ornery voice called out from the batter's box.

Earl Naylor was one of the top players on the Saints. He'd had spent his best years in the American Association. He could hit a ball to Wisconsin, but nipped O'Donnell's first pitch foul down the third baseline. O'Donnell tried to scratch the corner on his next pitch, but missed by inches. A curveball wandered inside. Another curve missed by way of North Dakota. Earl had O'Donnell in a deep hole. He knew O'Donnell had to throw a fastball.

Andy knew it, and O'Donnell knew it.

O'Donnell went through the same motion that he had now pretty much mastered, but when his left foot hit the dirt, he hesitated for a fraction of a second before releasing the ball. The pitch didn't do anything unusual, but he'd thrown Naylor off-stride, and the ball passed untouched, fluttering over the plate. An interesting change-up, O'Donnell thought. Sort of a variation on Satchel Paige's "hesitation pitch."

"What the hell was that?" Earl wasn't pleased.

Alston told him to step in and hit the ball.

"Thought we didn't have but two fingers for pitches," Andy shouted out to O'Donnell, as he laid down three fingers for the next pitch. O'Donnell delivered the change-up again. This time, Earl trickled a weak groundball on the foul side of third base. O'Donnell had him off-stride again and guessing. Earl watched a good, moving fastball on the outside corner sail past him for O'Donnell's second strikeout of the day. Earl's bat didn't move an inch off his shoulder.

Now that O'Donnell had something to confuse the hitters, he gained confidence with each pitch. With the sidearm, submarining delivery, he had the ball nipping on the corners of the plate and dipping down and in to the hitters. O'Donnell made his way through the batting line-up without any serious damage. One banjo hit to right field, and a bunch of piddly groundballs. After the last of the nine hitters looped a weak fly to the leftfielder, Alston told O'Donnell to catch a shower. The Saints's hitters gave him some grudging compliments as he walked into the dugout. Andy trotted up next to him and said: "I'll bet you a beer he re-signs you for the stretch drive."

Alston motioned O'Donnell to sit next to him in the dugout. He filled up the side of his mouth with a sizable plug of Redman chewing tobacco, concentrating on the task of working up the first spit. O'Donnell had never come close to taking a chaw. He'd admit to being prissy on that habit. He stuck to bubblegum.

Alston said, "O'Donnell, I think you've got a comeback in you. Looks like . . ." he paused to wipe off a drool of tobacco juice escaping from the corner of his mouth. "Looks like you can still pitch some." O'Donnell took this as a compliment.

"And?" O'Donnell said.

Alston looked at O'Donnell as though he couldn't add two plus two. "And . . . you start showing up regular for practice, and maybe we'll sign you on in August for the stretch. I'll need more in relievers by then. You got the experience, that's for sure." Was that a compliment? O'Donnell took it that way.

Alston spit a stream of brown juice at his feet, shook his head, and went down to the other end of the dugout to talk with his coaches. O'Donnell sat there on the bench for a minute or so, smiling like an idiot.

O'DONNELL ARRIVED AT THE Y for a post-practice steam and shower about 3:00 p.m. His arm ached from all the throwing, but it was a familiar soreness, not what had put him out of commission in spring training. Nothing to be concerned about—nothing a hot steam room couldn't fix.

He picked up a basket and a towel from Abe Nester, the tote room attendant, who'd been in charge for a couple of lifetimes. He assigned O'Donnell to one of the good lockers near the steam room. The wire basket Abe handed out held a bar of soap, an old pair of shorts, gym shoes, and a very old, smelly T-shirt O'Donnell had forgotten to take home after the last workout. The shirt went in the bin of dirty towels standing nearby. Abe would bitch, but he'd throw it in the wash and then the lost and found. Next time O'Donnell came in, he could claim it. It was an old ruse. Abe would have a conniption, but he never stayed mad for long. O'Donnell tossed his gym shorts in the pile for good measure.

He took his lime-green plastic container with its little bar of Ivory soap to the shower and cleaned up before going into the steamer. When he entered through the heavy metal door, O'Donnell found the steam vents working overtime as usual. Clouds of hot vapor hung heavy throughout the ancient ten-by-ten-foot room, making it impossible to see more than a few feet ahead.

O'Donnell spied the rubber water hose in the corner and sprayed a cool stream over the marble bench slab that ran on three sides of the room. He didn't care to scorch his butt on the bench as so many members did and end up looking like a bare-assed baboon at the Como zoo.

With the steamer all to himself, O'Donnell sat in a corner and stretched out his legs on the bench, allowing the steam heat to work its wonders. He kneaded the sore muscles in his arm and shoulder as the sweat poured out. A fellow steam bath devotee entered through the door and sat in an opposite corner, obscured by the mist. O'Donnell didn't feel much like being sociable, but he couldn't suppress a contented sigh.

"Doesn't take much to please you, does it?" commented a deep voice from the opposite corner of the steam room.

O'Donnell could make out a dark form through the clouds of steam. The shape rose up to its full dominion. Marcus Sanford's chest and arm muscles bulged like a Charles Atlas bodybuilding ad.

"Don't worry, man," Sanford's voice filtered down from the mists, "I don't plan on beating the crap out of you in a steam room. Not my style."

Small favors are always welcome, O'Donnell reminded himself, but shifted his feet off the bench, anyway.

Sanford acted as if being there in the steamer was the most normal thing in the world.

"Nobody to mug today?" O'Donnell asked.

"Careful. You don't want to piss me off, do you?"

No, thought O'Donnell. Sanford outweighed him, out-muscled him, and O'Donnell didn't feel real tough at that moment. Maybe he could squirt Sanford with cold water hose?

Sanford leaned back against the steam room wall and wiped off the sweat pouring down his chest and upper arms. His stomach muscles looked like an alligator's back.

"I read in the news about your golfing buddy getting knocked around," Sanford said, shifting his bulk on the bench. "Looks like you took a few new hits yourself."

"Why are you here? I saw you get on the train."

"Shouldn't believe everything you see. Man, it's hot in here. Let's go grab a shower and a beer."

"Why would I do that?" O'Donnell couldn't believe Sanford's offer. "Last time we shared a precious moment together, I ended up face first in my steering wheel."

Looking at some distant point in the vapors, pointing his finger in O'Donnell's direction, without bothering to look at him, Sanford said,

"You will go with me because I'm a most interesting person with many intriguing stories. Also, my friend, some of my stories have to do with the well-being of you and your buddy.

"Besides," Sanford said, taking a step nearer O'Donnell, "if you don't agree to come along, I'm going to stuff your damn head into the steam vent."

"The beer sounds good." O'Donnell led the way to the shower room.

O'DONNELL AND HIS NEW BEST FRIEND walked across the street to the 427 Club. O'Donnell thought the place lost some of its drama during the day with the sunshine streaming through the windows. He liked it better at night with all the neon signs flashing and the shadows dancing in the corners. In the daylight, the 427 looked like the big bare room it was. The regulars at the bar looked even worse.

O'Donnell selected a table in the back, next to the pool table Chuck installed during the war years. The green felt, stained by beer and whiskey spills, furrows running across it from too many drunks missing the cue ball, took on the look of a farmer's field at spring planting.

Chuck called out to O'Donnell from behind the bar where he was talking with a couple of the regulars. "Hey, Johnny, what can I get for you guys?"

"Beer," Sanford said.

"Couple of Hamm's, Chuck."

"Don't you folks have any good beer?" Sanford asked.

"We got three choices. Hamm's, Schmidt's, and Gluek's," Chuck said. "Unless you want to go across the street and buy a six pack of that imported stuff from Milwaukee, you're out of luck."

Chuck delivered the beers and talked for an embarrassing minute or so about his latest theory on foreign policy. Sanford told him to go away. Chuck looked confused at first, but Sanford's glare convinced him that his bar customers needed immediate attention.

"So what've you got to tell me, Sanford?" O'Donnell asked.

Sanford's mouth twisted in what O'Donnell imagined must have been a grin. "Know my name, huh?"

"You're not exactly a mystery man."

"Let's get down to cases, and this is the straight shit. I do contract work these days. Can't make enough money with the eight-to-five to get where I want to go. Got family, too. So when certain somebodies want something done, I get a call."

Sanford set his jaw, pushing what remained of his beer back and forth on the table surface. "Let's have another of these," he said. "Does your man have any nuts to go along with his diplomatic expertise?"

Chuck brought over two fresh beers and a few packs of beer nuts. O'Donnell knew he wanted to stop and gab, but Sanford gave him another glare that drove Chuck back behind the bar.

Sanford drained a substantial share of his new beer in one easy swig. "So here's the deal. This Butternut character contacts me in Chicago. Says his old man has a job for me. Not much money, but it's enough. Plus, my sister lives over in Minneapolis, so it's a chance to mix business with pleasure. But when I get up here, I find out the mark is your friend, the golfer."

"I wasn't on the list?"

"You were a preliminary." Sanford gave O'Donnell a friendly smile. He fingered a pack of the beer nuts, tore it open, and ate a handful. He finished the rest of his beer, and attacked another pack of the nuts. Chuck brought another beer.

Over the next half-hour, Sanford delivered his short course on the evils of capitalism and exploitation. He spiced the story with bits of his autobiography. O'Donnell didn't get the full background of the man's life and struggles, but had a pretty good idea about the blank spaces. Sanford grew up in Alabama where the "Scottsboro Boys" had met their fate. That episode, along with the degrading Cotton Belt poverty he and his family endured made the Communist Party appealing. The fact that the Communist organizers in the Deep South worked with blacks and stood by the Scottsboro Boys sealed Sanford's loyalty when he was still a teenager. He quit the cotton fields and joined the Party. Not long after, the local police nabbed him on a trumped up charge and sent him off to the chain gang for the next two years. In 1935, he caught a ride up to Chicago with one of the Communist field agents and never looked back.

"Once I got to Chicago, I found things weren't different," he searched for the right words, "just a different sort of the same."

Sanford soon landed in trouble, fell out of sympathy with the Communists and in love with the Public Library. "The more I read, the more holes I found in the Party line. Karl Marx and those boys never lived the slave's life, never had to live the Jim Crow way."

O'Donnell asked him to spell it out.

"It doesn't make any difference, far as I can see, whether you believe in capitalism, communism, or the Republican Party . . . when it comes to getting along with someone who's different—especially white to black folks—it's what's in here." He thumped his fist over his heart for emphasis, and he looked at O'Donnell hard, as if taking a measure. "Most people don't have it in here."

"But you gave the C.P. another chance? You went to fight in Spain against the Fascists didn't you?"

"I didn't go for the Party, that's a fact. I went because I didn't have any future here. I could be my own man in Spain, and so could all the others that went with me. The Party had nothing to do with it. All that "brotherhood of the masses" stuff the Communists prattled—nothing but white man's crap."

Sanford called Chuck over, and ordered a hamburger and fries. O'Donnell walked back to the men's room. From O'Donnell's thirty seconds of contemplation, three conclusions flowed. One, Sanford hadn't told him much yet. Two, O'Donnell needed some answers. Three, beer made for a lot of standing time at the urinal. When he returned to the barroom, Chuck's neon signs had flashed on, and the place was filling up with men and women finished with their shifts at the manufacturing plants. O'Donnell wasn't sure if he wanted any of the usual police regulars to drop in. Despite it all, Sanford seemed to be a straight shooter.

Chuck had placed two more Hamm's on the table in O'Donnell's absence, along with something that looked like shots of bourbon. An empty shot glass already stood next to Sanford's beer.

"Sanford, I can't drink this stuff." O'Donnell pushed the full shot over to Sanford's side of the table. He nestled it next to his beer nuts.

"No problem," Sanford said, gulping down some of his Hamm's.

"I'm beginning to lose the threads here," O'Donnell said. "But I hope you're going tell me something I can remember . . . something useful."

"You should learn to drink more, O'Donnell. Cool you out." Sanford leaned back in his chair, resting his half-empty beer bottle on his stomach. "I'll get to the point. My employer on this little mission thinks your buddy is marching down the wrong ideological road."

"Butternut cares about that?"

"Hell, no," Sanford snorted in disgust. "That two-bit hustler couldn't string two ideas together if he spent a week trying." He let out a deep belch, and O'Donnell could smell the beer and bourbon fumes from where he sat. "I told you. Butternut's the messenger boy for his old man. Daddy Wilkins's the one who's got it in for your golfer friend and his plans."

"Why?"

"I never talked to the man directly, but I got the low-down on him from the boys in Chicago."

Sanford laughed way down deep in his chest. It sounded like a big dog growling. "Daddy Wilkins is one of those pie-in-the-sky 'ideologskis' I was telling you about. He thinks integration and all this Jackie Robinson stuff ain't radical enough." Sanford leaned forward on one elbow, talking now in a confidential tone. "My guess is he wants to screw up your buddy and blame it on the anti-Communists. Pretty smart, huh?"

O'Donnell didn't quite know what to say. His money had been on Jack Clancy until this point.

"Problem is," Sanford said, "Daddy Wilkins called a wrong number for his plan. I don't go after my own people."

"So you didn't have anything to do with what happened the other night?"

"Hell, no. I told Butternut to tell his old man I wouldn't go as far as they wanted. Besides . . . my sister had the relatives over last night for some down-home cooking. I'm not going to be missing that for nothing."

Sanford took a small sip of his bourbon, and followed it with another pack of beer nuts. "I don't like Butternut . . . or his old man."

"Why are you telling me all this?"

"You think about that."

He rose out of his chair, knocked back the rest of his beer, and walked in full control toward the men's room. On his way, he passed a pair of muscular construction workers who stood near the pool table. O'Donnell watched them exchange tight smiles, and return quickly to their mugs of draft beer.

By the time Sanford had settled back into his chair again, O'Donnell's mind remained stuck in neutral. Sanford raised an empty beer bottle a half-inch from the table, and Chuck reacted like a springer spaniel chasing a downed pheasant. "Can I get another brew for you gents?"

"Thank you, my man," Sanford said.

Chuck smiled like he'd won a new car, waiting to see if he could join the conversation. But Sanford ignored him, and Chuck slunk back toward the bar, looking like a springer spaniel who didn't like feathers.

"You and your golfer friend are free and clear with me," Sanford said. "I'm not ready to sign up with the NAACP and be your buddy's caddy, but I like to see things, uh . . . competitive. Guess I'm getting soft in my old age. Hurting guys on pretty much the same team doesn't make sense to me."

Sanford raised the palm of his hand to his forehead, "I hope to hell I'm not growing some sort of conscience." He finished the rest of his beer in a gulp and stood.

"Don't ignore the obvious, O'Donnell."

"What's the obvious?"

Sanford smacked his lips together, coveting what remained in O'Donnell's beer bottle. "It's a process of elimination."

"Right. I can eliminate you from everything except turning my lights off."

"I told you . . . it was easy money. Nothing personal. I figured it wouldn't hurt to take some of Butternut's cash before I told him and his old man to kiss off."

Sanford slapped a fist into his palm, and bunched his powerful shoulders. Donnell had to admit Sanford stood as steady as he'd been when he walked into the bar forty minutes earlier. "I've got a long way home, man. This party's over. You and your buddy watch your ass." He hesitated, reached down and grabbed O'Donnell's beer bottle. He held it to his lips and tilted his head back, allowing the remaining liquid to dribble into his mouth. He held the bottle up to the light, rotating it in his fingers. Reluctantly, he returned it to the table surface.

"I've done more than my good deed for this decade." Sanford gave Chuck a small wave at the bar. Chuck seemed undecided about the leave-taking, and gave a halfhearted wave in return. O'Donnell watched Sanford duck through the door, and down the stairs he went. O'Donnell had the beginnings of a lousy headache.

FLASH HIT PITCH SHOTS on the practice range at the Highland Park golf course. One after another of the practice balls sailed high into the dusk. The 100-yard flag fluttered in the evening breeze, welcoming each shot. Some thirty golf balls clustered within fifteen feet of the flag, and only a few lay outside of that imaginary circumference.

Bobby Borgstrom stood behind Flash, following each shot like some sort of golf pro. O'Donnell moved next to Bobby, trying not to disturb Flash's concentration as he made his way through the practice balls. His shots flew accurately toward their target. Not bad for someone who'd had a gangster body massage recently.

"He's hitting them pretty solid," Bobby whispered. "The amazing thing is how easy he swings . . . and the ball takes off like a rocket."

"You're getting to like all this?"

Bobby watched Flash line up his next practice shot. "I have to admit, golf is pretty interesting. You can have all the technique you want, but it seems like the key is to have your head screwed on right."

"Well, that disqualifies us."

Bobby tossed more golf balls near Flash, so he could hit a few extras before the light faded. Flash stepped away, cocking his head in O'Donnell's direction. "What do you have to say, Ace? Damn. Where have you been? You smell like the Grain Belt Brewery way over here."

"I'll get you up to date when you're done showing off." A quick hamburger had taken the edge off the beers O'Donnell downed at the bar that afternoon.

"Haven't even started." Flash picked up one of his long irons, testing its flex. He lined up five balls, and with an easy but full swing, rapidly drove all but one into the darkness at the end of the practice range.

"Get your autographs now," he said. "There'll be no time for the likes of you after I've won the tournament."

Bobby said. "Let's see how you do in the qualifying."

"Boys, the results are a foregone conclusion," Flash said.

O'Donnell found that sort of cockiness at odds with his ideal of an athlete's behavior. It certainly wouldn't go over well with the fans, not to mention the golf pros. Every time O'Donnell found himself beginning to like the guy, Flash would throw in a monkey wrench.

Flash retrieved his wedge from the golf bag Bobby had slung from his shoulder. He turned back to address one remaining practice ball. "If you have any doubts about my chances, watch this."

The ball shot off the face of his club, flying high and straight toward the practice green. As it soared and then dropped down toward the flag, Flash said, "Keep watching, boys. I've got enough spin on it to dig a trench."

The ball bounced twice, spun backwards, and spurted through the surrounding practice balls toward the flagstick, as if Flash had jerked a yo-yo up a string. Within a foot of the flag, his ball lost steam and stayed put. By that time, Flash had flipped his wedge to Bobby and now bent to loosen his golf shoes. Sweat soaked the collar of his shirt. "Nothing to it," he said.

O'Donnell and Bobby stared out at the practice green. They exchanged looks. "Nothing to it," they agreed.

"Let's head over to my place," Flash said.

WHILE BOBBY AND FLASH went for some beer, O'Donnell volunteered to pick up some munchies. He drove to a small grocery store on Grand Avenue, near Macalester College. Even when school was in session, Macalester never ranked high on anybody's list as a place to party. Most of the coeds spent their time studying, playing bridge, and going to chapel. Their musical tastes ran heavily toward the classics and songs suitable for a church picnic. A good-looking woman with a healthy yen for some fun wouldn't last long in the Presbyterian atmosphere prevailing at the ivy-covered corners of Snelling and Grand. Most of the guys at "Mac" came from small towns and acted like it.

Bobby had a particular fondness for "Fischer's" peanuts—a local, "Salted in the Shell" delicacy. O'Donnell grabbed three bags of peanuts, some pretzels, and package of Ritz crackers. The store had Wisconsin cheddar cheese, so he grabbed some of that as well. Might as well live it up.

A nice-looking girl sorted out his purchases at the counter. She looked up at O'Donnell after ringing each item, like she wanted to tell him something. She had straight, natural blond hair pulled into a ponytail, matched by flawless skin and those ice blue, Scandinavian eyes. A Nordic dream girl. O'Donnell guessed she might be in high school. A senior?

Bingo. She had some boy's high school ring on a chain around her neck.

"Who's the lucky guy?" O'Donnell pointed at the ring.

She kept glancing past his shoulder, out the pane glass window, her forehead crinkling with concern. "Don't look now, but I think someone's real interested in you."

O'Donnell resisted the temptation to turn around and look out the window.

"Quick," she said, "he's pulling away."

O'Donnell wheeled around, soon enough to see the rear end of a dark sedan speed past the window.

"He pulled up in front after you walked in and came back around twice," the girl said.

"Sure it's not your boyfriend checking up on you?"

She blushed. "He doesn't drive. His dad won't let him have the car."

"That's no fun."

She rolled her eyes, and scrunched up her nose. O'Donnell wanted time to see if indeed someone was on his tail, although he doubted anyone would be following him so inexpertly. He nudged the girl into a conversation about the problems of teenage dating without a car. Considerable from what he learned.

The dark sedan rolled past again in the shadows covering the opposite side of the street.

"Mister," the girl whispered. "There he goes again."

Again, O'Donnell could only make out the dark shape of the car, and nothing of who was driving it. "What did he look like?" he asked the girl.

She whispered again, "I can't tell. It's too dark."

"Why are we whispering?"

The girl covered a giggle with her fingers. O'Donnell decided to leave before he gave her his high school ring.

ON THE DRIVE TO FLASH'S apartment, O'Donnell kept watch in his rearview mirror for the dark sedan. Was it the same one from the previous night and the golf course? Nylonhead's? Could be, but there were more dark sedans around town than you could shake a stick at.

At Flash's apartment, Bobby handed O'Donnell an open beer. He grabbed the grocery sack and extracted a bag of peanuts with eager fingers. He tossed the bag of pretzels to Flash, who had draped himself across the sofa. Bobby staked out a claim to an old, but comfy wing chair near the window.

"Find a chair and pull up to the campfire," Flash said.

He'd opened the windows to the street, and the wind rustled the leaves of the large oak that shaded the front lawn. The apartment looked back to normal after the fracas the other evening, minus a broken flowerpot, a collapsed lampshade, and a cracked wooden chair clustered together in a corner. Flash some way had put the phone back in what looked like working order. O'Donnell settled into another chair near the kitchen. He didn't need the beer, but took a small swig to be sociable.

Flash pulled himself up to a sitting position, placing his empty beer bottle on a coffee table in front of him, its wood veneer emblazoned with several beer rings from bottles long past. Flash pointed at O'Donnell's beer, and asked if he had a problem with the brand he served. O'Donnell took another small drink from his bottle. "Yummy. My favorite."

Bobby walked over and grabbed the bottle. He placed O'Donnell's beer next to his, now half full.

"So what did you find out today in regard to our well-being and the forces of evil arrayed against us?" Bobby asked. He now had the cheese from O'Donnell's grocery haul in hand.

O'Donnell talked about his afternoon with Marcus Sanford, as well as what his dad had warned. As he went along, he tried to make sense of what he'd heard during the day, but felt a bit lost—like he needed a scorecard to know all the players in the game and what they'd done. And what slot did the guy in the dark sedan play? Or was he already on the field from well before.

"Okay," Bobby began, leaning forward in his chair, "Marcus Sanford puts Johnny in Lullaby-Land the other night at the 427 Club, but he claims that's his only bad deed. Our favorite local Communist, Daddy Wilkins, and his no-good son, Eldred, hired Sanford to do worse, but he declined the offer."

O'Donnell thought Bobby so far had done a good job herding collective ignorance into the corral.

"If he's telling the truth," Bobby continued his ramble, "we still don't know exactly who punched-out Johnny at River's Edge or who beat up on Flash right here in this venue."

Bobby peeled off a large chunk of cheese, popped it in his mouth, and took a quick drink of his beer to wash it down. "We also know Clancy is a major contender for Mr. Bad Guy in our little melodrama. He definitely doesn't want Flash playing in the Open." Bobby sprawled back in his chair, waiting for the others to pick up the ball.

"But Clancy says he doesn't need to bash people around to get what he wants," O'Donnell said.

"Not giving into the Clancys of this world is what this thing is all about," Flash said. "But more to the point is Daddy Wilkins. That old man thinks of himself as some sort of badass revolutionary. He's not in my corner for integrating the PGA, that's clear. And I buy the theory he's looking for some big propaganda score by putting the blame on Clancy and his sort for trying to keep me from playing. Problem was that Sanford didn't want to play on Daddy's team."

"So Butternut gets a chance?" O'Donnell asked.

Flash and Bobby nodded their agreement. The way Butternut felt about Flash and O'Donnell, he would have had more than enough motivation.

"But who helped him?" Bobby looked to Flash for an answer. "He didn't have time to take on the both of you."

Flash drained more of his beer, and raised himself out of his chair. "My notion is to find more food and drink. Also, I have been dying for some tasty ribs."

"Selby and Dale?" Bobby asked.

"It might be the best place for some answers," O'Donnell agreed.

The three men trundled down the apartment stairs to the first floor. The old lady peered out her half-opened door. She stepped into the hall, wrapped up in a fuzzy pink sweater. "Hello, Mr. Dawkins. Are you feeling better after the other night?"

"Let me introduce you to my friends." Flash smiled for the old lady, pouring on the charm.

She looked thrilled at the prospect of formal introductions and peered up at Bobby.

Bobby murmured a hello.

"I met you briefly the other night. Remember?" O'Donnell took the old woman's hand. "Thanks again for letting me use the phone."

She smiled at O'Donnell, but turned to Flash. "Where's that beautiful young girlfriend of yours? I haven't seen her lately."

The old lady's question took Flash by surprise. "Oh . . . I've stopped seeing her." He leaned down, closer to her level. "She simply couldn't hold a candle to you, Mrs. Hedstrom, so I had to tell her it was quits."

Mrs. Hedstrom giggled like a schoolgirl, thrilled by Flash's teasing. "You and your friends run along. I know you're up to no good."

Flash said. "I'm so sorry we must bid you adieu, madam, but our carriage awaits."

Mrs. Hedstrom covered her mouth with the tips of her fingers before fluttering back into her apartment.

On the way down the front steps, O'Donnell asked Flash, "Who's the girlfriend?"

"You mean the old lady?"

"No. The one Mrs. Hedstrom has tracked coming up to your apartment."

Flash watched Bobby pull up from across the street. "Many a beautiful woman comes to my quarters, I can't keep track. Maybe it was Gloria."

"You must have some charm to get her to come around after the other night at the bar."

Bobby completed a U-turn and stopped in front of the two men. "You driving, too, Johnny. I can't stay out all night, I guess."

"Yeah. I'll meet you guys there."

"Let's go see what we can see," Flash said, and ducked into the back seat of Bobby's car.

AS O'DONNELL PULLED UP behind Bobby's car parked on the Dale Street side of a rickety, two-story frame building with a distant coat of pale-green paint, he checked out the destination. Daddy Wilkins's place crowded the street with nothing but a small ribbon of sidewalk in front of it. The entrance was a cheap oak door with a diamond-shaped, see-through window. No welcoming neon signs for this rib joint. Not many white folks made their way to this corner, unless they were looking for trouble.

It took a few seconds for O'Donnell's eyes to adjust to the barroom's poorly lit interior. Three booths, covered in brown imitation leather and falling apart at the seams, stood along the left wall next to the street. Adjacent ran a small counter with four swivel seats, one of them occupied by an elderly Negro man drinking a beer and sampling what looked to be a delicious plate of beef ribs and fries. The kitchen lay behind the counter. A large iron stove and an ancient assortment of pots and pans were visible through a large serving window. O'Donnell could smell the ribs cooking. To the right, a partition went halfway up the wall, dividing the eaters from the drinkers. The drinking section of the room housed a long bar. A customer could see his reflection within several unframed sections of mirror that ran behind it. A new Wurlitzer jukebox, in contrast to the other furnishings in Daddy's bar, stood guard near a door leading to a rest room. A small bandstand and a cramped dance floor were crowded into a corner. A lone couple swayed to the jukebox sounds of Ella Fitzgerald's "I'm Beginning to See the Light." O'Donnell wished he could sing along.

A beautiful black woman, sat alone at a table, dressed to the nines in a ruby-red dress—cut low enough to earn a second glance from any red-blooded soul. She pulled on the shoulder straps of her gown so any and all might enjoy a better view. O'Donnell viewed. She gave him and the others a wave and a grin. They grinned back. She had a Latin look to her, like somebody O'Donnell had seen in the movies.

At the other end of the bar, shadowed and hunched forward, Butternut nursed a whiskey. Next to him, sat an unsmiling, sulky-looking Gloria. Flash joined O'Donnell for a second glance at what seemed to be an odd pairing.

Daddy Wilkins, a bantamweight type with a shaved head and tattoos decorating his forearms, stood behind the bar, polishing glassware and glaring at the three new faces in his bar.

"Lose your way boys?" Daddy Wilkins asked, pointing towards the street. "Grand Avenue and all the white folks are up that ways."

O'Donnell didn't guess the old man would challenge for the weekly WCCO's "Good Neighbor" award.

"Who's this with the white boys?" Daddy said, pointing at Flash. "Must be the black man's Ben Hogan."

Butternut perked up and moved off his barstool. He ambled down the bar with Gloria in tow behind him. O'Donnell guessed she'd had one too many rum and cokes. She stumbled and grabbed at Butternut's shirt to keep from falling flat on her face. Butternut pushed her away, and Gloria fell back against the bar, missing a hold on a bar stool, and descending in slow motion to the barroom floor. She plumped to the dirty linoleum, and her head grazed the side of the counter. She didn't seem to feel the jolt.

"Dumb bitch," Butternut hissed at her.

"You leave that poor gal be," the woman in the ruby-red dress warned him. She had a southern accent, but O'Donnell couldn't place it.

"She's had too much drinking," the woman continued, moving toward Gloria. "Just leave her be."

Flash brushed past Butternut and knelt beside Gloria. He whispered something to her, and held out his hand to help her up. She took Flash's hand reluctantly, trying her best to scowl at him. Flash pulled her up and steadied her as she rocked a bit on high heels. She started to weep.

"Shut up, woman," Butternut said. "You ain't hurt."

Flash shot Butternut a vicious look, and wrapped his arm around Gloria's shoulder, leading her to the table where Miss Ruby-Red Dress sat. Once secured in a chair, Gloria continued to weep, but not so loudly. Every so often she'd whisper, "Bastard."

O'Donnell didn't know if she meant Flash or Butternut.

"What you want in my place?" Daddy Wilkins asked—a dare more than a question. He tilted his head as a signal for Butternut to go sit down. Butternut grumbled something, but went to a neutral corner. His eyes glowed like a tomcat, looking for a dark alley.

Bobby said, "Hey, we only want some ribs and beer."

Daddy Wilkins looked at Bobby like he was someone from another planet, then broke into a wide smile. He perched on his tiptoes and leaned across the bar surface, challenging his unwanted customers. "Sorry, gentlemens. We don't serve Caucasians here. We got us a blacks-only rule."

O'Donnell could hear the others in the bar joining in the laughter. Ruby-Red laughed hard, damn near jiggling herself out of her dress. Even Gloria stopped sniffling and managed the briefest of smiles. Butternut laughed too loud, too long.

Daddy Wilkins dropped the comic routine and the smile. He gave his son a look of pure disgust. Butternut turned back to his drink. No love lost between those two, O'Donnell assumed.

Daddy Wilkins pointed at O'Donnell and Bobby. "You white boys get the hell out of my place."

He glared at Flash. "You too, Uncle Tom."

"Cool it, old man," Flash said.

Daddy Wilkins snarled something, twisting his lip in disgust. "Don't come on my turf and shoot off your mouth."

"We know your game," O'Donnell said. "The police know. The FBI, too." Piling up the "knowers" seemed a good strategy.

Daddy Wilkins looked confused, and his eyes darted in Butternut's direction. Butternut came up next to O'Donnell, crowding him. "You don't know shit, O'Donnell. Shut your face."

Daddy Wilkins turned his attention to Flash. "You're selling out your people, Dawkins," he said, his voice low and acid. "Ain't nothing to be gained by playing white man's games. They using you. Our people ain't going to get what they need cheering on Joe Louis and Jackie Robinson."

Flash looked down at the old man behind the bar. "Who should they be thinking about? Joe Stalin? Karl Marx? Last time I checked, those guys looked mighty white to me."

Daddy Wilkins didn't have a comeback. He had something better. O'Donnell watched as he pulled out an ugly looking revolver from under the bar and made a sweeping motion with its barrel. "Get out of here."

Flash didn't move. "Old man, you must be reading Groucho, instead of Karl."

"I don't need to read nothing to know what you are," Daddy said, waving his gun in Flash's face.

"And what's that, Daddy?"

"You and your 'friends of the Negroes,' " Daddy spat out. "That lawyer . . . Gustafson. He's doing this for his own self and his people. They'll drop you like nothing if you be your own man."

Flash said. "Maybe so."

Daddy jumped on the opportunity. "Maybe so? Goddamn right."

Daddy waved the revolver again at no one in particular. "You watch. They'll be beating the bushes for the Party members and turning them in to Hoover right soon. You and your civil rights is just a convenience for them now. It's the Party stands with the black man and fights for him."

"What makes the Party different from anything else? You think the Party is going to let you run their revolution?"

Daddy Wilkins pointed at Bobby and O'Donnell with his revolver. "Sit down. Join the women."

O'Donnell sat down as ordered. Ruby Red whispered to the others, "Might be a long evening, gents. By the way, I'm Deloris."

"Party ain't perfect, but it's the best we black folks have now," Daddy Wilkins said. "Got more say with the Communist Party than with the Democrats and Republicans, that's for sure."

"Maybe, so," Flash said again.

"Party stood up for me down South before the war. Ain't never going to forget that. Helped me see things for what they are. Like they say, we're a colony inside the white man's empire. I don't want to go off on some boat to Africa or the Caribbean like Abe Lincoln tried on us. I want my own place in this country. I earned it, and I'm going to get what's fair. That's what the Party stands for."

Daddy Wilkins reached under the bar, and fished around for something. He pulled out a political pamphlet. "Read you something. Kind of makes my point," Daddy eyed Flash, indicating a seat at the bar with his revolver.

Before reading anything, Daddy banged a fist on the bar to get his son's attention. "Do something useful. Come down here and keep an eye on our guests while I'm reading this."

By this point, the few patrons of the bar and restaurant had quietly left the premises. O'Donnell hoped one of them would feel a sense of civic duty and call the cops. It didn't seem too likely, though. They'd probably seen worse in Daddy Wilkins's place.

Butternut accepted his assignment with enthusiasm, taking the gun from his old man and standing guard. Butternut seemed more angry and agitated than usual. Daddy Wilkins ignored his son's recklessness and raised the pamphlet up so he could see the print in the dim light of the bar. He read slowly, like a student in a classroom, stumbling over a word or two. "The slogan of equal rights for the Negroes without a relentless struggle in practice against all manifestations of Negrophobia on the part of the American *bourgeoisie* can be nothing but a deceptive liberal gesture of a sly owner or his agent."

O'Donnell figured he couldn't have read that tortured sentence much better.

"You folks better listen good," Butternut ordered.

Daddy Wilkins frowned at his son. "Quiet. Sit down."

Butternut looked outraged, but he followed orders. Daddy eyed his son with no attempt to disguise his disgust. He raised the pamphlet up again to read, glancing at Flash over the top of the page.

"If you think that Gustafson and his bunch be ready to go to bat for you," he said, "you thinking wrong."

He adjusted and smoothed the pages of the pamphlet, and continued his recitation. "Says here equal rights is used by them who wants 'publicity for themselves by appealing to the sense of justice of the American bourgeoisie in the individual treatment of the Negroes.'"

Daddy Wilkins took another deep breath before reading another snippet.

Deloris groaned. Gloria cradled her head on her forearms. O'Donnell wagered the Communist sermonettes were a familiar part of the nighttime entertainment at Daddy Wilkins's. Bobby turned in his chair to read the menu posted on the wall. Butternut continued to fume, his face fretted with anger.

"This is how Gustafson and all the rest of them fooling you all," Daddy Wilkins continued, waving his hand in our direction, demanding our attention. "It says here that those folks 'side-track attention from the one effective struggle against the shameful system of white superiority: that is, from the class struggle against the American bourgeoisie.' " Daddy lowered the pamphlet to the bar, focusing on Flash, daring him to deny anything read so far.

Flash nodded his head.

"You ain't disagreeing with me much," Daddy Wilkins said. "What's your game, sonny?"

"Seems to me that most of what you read sounds like the truth from your point of view. If I was you, I might look at things pretty much the same way." Flash inclined his head slightly at the pamphlet, smiling. "Don't think I'd write it quite like that."

Daddy Wilkins popped off the cap of a Hamm's beer and pushed it across the bar surface to Flash. O'Donnell would have liked one as well, but he didn't think he had established the same rapport as Flash with the proprietor.

"So why don't you wise up and stow all this Jackie Robinson bullshit," Daddy Wilkins said. "That's not where the struggle is."

"Depends on how I want to look at it," Flash said. "You really believe the government's going to let us start some independent Black Belt state?"

Before Daddy Wilkins could answer, Flash continued on his argument, "If you do, you're dreaming. Nothing like that is ever happening. Besides, the army would go down there and shoot everybody deader than a doornail. I know all the theories, and I've read better stuff than you've got there in that silly pamphlet. People writing that can't even speak our language."

Butternut rushed over next to Flash. "Don't you talk to Daddy like that. You show him respect."

With that as an excuse, Butternut did what he'd wanted to do all along, shoving his gun barrel hard into Flash's ribs. O'Donnell and Bobby jumped up, but Butternut turned around fast. "Stay the hell there," he ordered, turning halfway around, keeping his revolver trained on Flash.

"Hold it right there, honey, or I'll open up your head from ear to ear." The threat coming from behind O'Donnell earned Butternut's attention. "You know I can shoot."

Deloris had produced her own weapon from her purse. She held it steady. It looked to O'Donnell like she'd had plenty of experience using it. "Butternut, put that thing on the bar and slide it away from you. Now."

Butternut glowered at Ruby-Red, obviously weighing bloody alternatives, but did what he was told.

"Daddy. You just stay cool, too," Deloris told the old man. She had things under control, and motioned for Gloria to listen. "Gloria, grab that gun. Keep it handy."

Gloria picked up the revolver, and pulled up a barstool not far from an enraged Butternut Wilkins. Gloria seemed to have sobered up a touch. She looked pleased to be holding the drop on Butternut. But why had she been at the bar with him in the first place? O'Donnell couldn't figure it out. He also didn't trust Gloria much as Butternut's warden.

"Let's all get comfy again," Deloris said. "Daddy, you and that handsome young man keep talking. See if you can remember you're both on the same side."

Despite O'Donnell's doubts, Deloris laid her weapon handy on the table. Seemed things to have cooled off.

"Eldred, damn it, I want some answers." An angry Daddy Wilkins yelled at his son, reacting to something Flash had told him.

Butternut hunched his shoulders and glared at his father.

"What the hell have you been up to?" Daddy yelled at his son, pounding on the bar surface. "You come talk to me. Now."

"Ain't done nothing, old man. You get off my ass." Butternut stepped in front of those sitting at the table, ferociously, uncontrollably angry, yelling and cursing at his father. None had counted on Butternut's feral instincts and the speed he displayed in snatching away Deloris's pistol before anyone could react. Cat quick, gun now in hand, Butternut pivoted towards Flash and Daddy Wilkins.

"You always putting me down, Daddy," Butternut screamed. "No more. No more you ain't."

Without a second's hesitation, Butternut shot his old man in the chest. Daddy stared down in disbelief at the blood seeping through his shirtfront. He staggered up against the beer cooler, clutching at his wound.

Butternut thundered against the wounded man. "You damned old devil. I do your dirty work for you. You always treated me rotten. Screwed over my ma. Damn you."

The gun shook in Butternut's hand, but he raised it to finish what he'd started. Deloris screamed at him to stop.

Flash lunged after Butternut, pushing him off balance. O'Donnell and Bobby struggled out from behind the table to help, rib plates and bottles flying every which way. Butternut saw them coming, but a loud report sounded behind him, and the side of Butternut's head collapsed in a bloody mess.

Gloria stared at the barrel of the gun she held.

O'DONNELL HAD SEEN ENOUGH dead men in battle to know Butternut's fate, but he checked for a pulse. Nothing.

People started moving in every direction, like stagehands and actors in between scenes in a play. Deloris scuttled past O'Donnell and the dead body to see about Daddy Wilkins behind the bar. Gloria buried her face in her hands, her body sagging on the barstool. Flash stepped to comfort Gloria, and gingerly took the gun from her, careful not to touch the grip with his fingers. He led Gloria over to a table and sat her down. Bobby took a couple of bar towels and covered Butternut's head.

"I don't want any part of this mess," Bobby said.

"Neither do I, but people know we were in here," O'Donnell said.

Bobby let out a long breath. "Shit. I should have stayed home."

From behind the bar, Deloris called for help. "Daddy's hurt bad. We need an ambulance."

Bobby said he'd call, and O'Donnell went behind the bar to see if he could help Deloris. Daddy Wilkins sprawled on the floorboards, one leg twisted under him. Deloris held some towels from the bar sink pressed on his chest wound. Daddy waved a hand in O'Donnell's direction, motioning him to where he lay. Deloris cradled his head in her lap.

"Get your buddy out of here. Police will make bad trouble for him." Daddy Wilkins coughed deep in his chest, and a small trickle of blood worked its way out the corner of his mouth.

Deloris said to O'Donnell, "Go on now. Do what Daddy says."

"But someone will know he was here."

"We'll take care of that," Daddy managed to say, pain spreading across his face.

"Get going. The police will be coming," Deloris warned.

O'Donnell ran around the other side of the bar where Flash sat holding Gloria's hand and stroking her arm. "Daddy Wilkins says get the hell out of here fast," O'Donnell said. "I'll take care of Gloria."

Flash nodded, but went in the direction of Daddy Wilkins and Deloris.

"Flash. Damn it. He wants you to get the hell out of here." O'Donnell didn't know what quite to do. It didn't feel right at all to have Flash disappear from the scene, but he handed over his car keys.

Flash knelt out of sight behind the bar. In a minute, he emerged again and said, "Everything's cool. Deloris will handle things. Follow her lead."

"Won't be long before the police will be here," Bobby said. He gave Flash a shove to get going.

A siren blared in the distance. Flash ran toward the exit. In a matter of seconds, O'Donnell's car engine roared, tires squealing as he turned away from the increasing whine of sirens coming from downtown.

"Now what?" O'Donnell said to no one in particular. The whole turn of events felt very wrong to him. He felt caught in the middle of decisions he doubted were the absolute right thing to do.

"I'll see what I can do for our favorite Communist," Bobby said. He grabbed some bar towels and stepped over to where Deloris tended to the bleeding man.

Minutes later, a St. Paul policemen barged in the front door, gun at the ready. He made a quick canvas of the situation, and stepped close to inspect the body. The youthful looking cop stared at Butternut. O'Donnell knew it was his first dead body by the expression on his face. He looked O'Donnell's way for some sort of explanation.

"There's a wounded man back there." O'Donnell pointed behind the bar. "He needs an ambulance."

The cop edged over so he could see Daddy Wilkins and Deloris. "The ambulance is right behind me," he told O'Donnell. On cue, the ambulance attendants rushed through the door with their kits and a stretcher.

"You on your own?" O'Donnell asked. The cops in St. Paul usually worked in pairs.

"Partner came down sick about an hour into our shift." The cop frowned, and pushed past O'Donnell.

Officer Groseth, as his badge identified him, looked more like a kid just graduated from college—blond hair in a crew cut, blue eyes, and an open, pleasant, but slightly confused expression. He probably looked the same when he sat down for a cup of coffee and a Danish. But his shaking hands witnessed that he hadn't yet been center stage at a murder scene. Minnesotans didn't kill each other often.

Groseth pulled a small notebook from his shirt pocket and fished around in his trousers for a pen. He laid both items on the table. "Want to tell me what happened here?" he asked.

Gloria was a mess. She couldn't hold her head up. Deloris had left Daddy Wilkins side and clasped Gloria's hands like a mother would with a daughter. "It's okay, honey," she said, "you saved our lives."

"Gloria did what she had to do," O'Donnell followed Deloris's lead, feeling very uncomfortable now. "We'd have all been goners."

Was he overplaying it? Hell, it was close enough to what happened. O'Donnell knew a theme of some sort was in order. There hadn't been time to concoct a script, though. Maybe it was best to let Deloris handle the cop. O'Donnell looked for some help from Bobby, who now left his first-aid attempts in favor of the ambulance crew.

"Best start with her, officer," Bobby said, edging next to O'Donnell. "She had a front-row seat."

Groseth followed Bobby's suggestion. "Your name, Miss? I'm Officer Groseth."

"I'm Deloris Dauphine, Officer."

Deloris leaned across the table, and offered her hand, allowing Groseth a bird's eye view down the top of her dress. He did his best not to look, but his police training hadn't prepared him for the likes of Deloris. She introduced Gloria as her friend. To O'Donnell's mind, Deloris played the demure coquette with substantial skill and a sexy twist. She placed her hand on O'Donnell's arm, still sparkling her charms at the cop. "I'm sorry. I'd introduce this young man, but I don't know his name."

O'Donnell told him, and held out his hand.

"This isn't a cocktail party." Groseth said. A tough guy now.

Gloria sniffled and gave the cop her name when he asked, and let more tears flow. Groseth wrote her name and address on his notepad, and turned back to talk with Deloris. She gave him an expectant tilt of her head.

"Can you fill me in on what happened?" Groseth asked.

Couldn't have asked a better question. O'Donnell breathed a sigh. He, Gloria, and Bobby now could listen carefully to the story Deloris would spin. *Alibi time. Take it away Deloris.* Still, O'Donnell worried how deep the legal hole they were digging for themselves might end up.

As Deloris launched into her version of events, O'Donnell noticed Gloria finally put a hold on the hysterics. She needed to understand the stakes and the fact that Deloris would be setting up the roadmap for everyone's alibis. Deloris gave a reasonably accurate narrative of the shooting, with the sole exception of Flash Dawkins's participation in the drama. Did it really matter if he'd been there? O'Donnell tried to convince himself it didn't. As Deloris continued to spin their story, Gloria and Bobby nodded confirmations to details, but nothing more. Deloris held Groseth dazzled and spellbound. He went for it in typical Minnesota style—hook, line, and sinker.

The ambulance attendants carted Daddy Wilkins toward the door, but he asked to say something to Groseth. He winced in pain as he shifted his body to address the policeman.

"Officer, my son went crazy. Deloris saw it all." He pointed toward Gloria. "She saved our lives."

He drew a shaky breath.

Deloris interrupted with dramatic timing, imploring the attendants to "get that poor man to the hospital." She clasped Groseth's wrist for an added, theatrical twist. Daddy Wilkins exited through a crowd of neighborhood folks who'd come out to see the action. Groseth ordered the gawkers to leave the area, and announced that the Coroner's office was on the way.

"You folks don't need to stay around," he said, his attention still fixed on Deloris. "But don't go too far from your phones. The Department will want to take formal statements from you tomorrow."

This cop had zilch for experience on homicides. A bad night for his partner to go out sick. O'Donnell could imagine the fit Ikola would throw. Groseth would end up on late night patrol at the Como Zoo.

"Mr. Borgstrom, " Deloris said, twisting toward Bobby, allowing Groseth a few seconds more of sightseeing, "can Gloria and I presume on you for a ride home?"

After the gals had gathered up their purses, all made for the door. None ventured a last look back at the body on the barroom floor.

D ELORIS LIVED IN A SMALL, eight-unit apartment building on Grand Avenue near St. Thomas College. Each of the front units had a screened porch, and O'Donnell and the others gathered there to do some homework.

"They'll be sending in the first team tomorrow, and we need to know our lines," Deloris said.

A car idled at the curb, and Deloris leaned over to the window to look down to the street. "Door's unlocked," she called down. Flash had arrived.

"Jesus Lord. I'm still shaking." Gloria shivered and twisted her hands together. The car ride and night air had sobered her up some. Her eyes had lost that dull look of drink and shock. She puffed on a cigarette, her hand shaking slightly.

"I'll never be able to go to work again," she said. "God . . . If they hear about this thing, I'll lose my job. What'll my parents think?" She snuffed out the cigarette in the ashtray Deloris had given her a minute before. "Damn it. What a mess."

"Gloria, you don't like that job, anyway." Flash eased through the porch doorway. "You're too smart to be doing what you're doing, and your parents live way the hell down in Arkansas. They'll never hear about what happened."

Flash placed his hand gently on her shoulder. She slapped it away.

"Don't go throwing a fit now," Flash said. "It won't do you any good, or the rest of us either."

"I could care less what happens to you, Flash." Gloria turned her head and shoulders away as Flash sat beside her on a small day bed, covered with a blue-and-white checked quilt.

"Gloria," Flash said in a soft voice, "Come on, now. I care what happens to you."

Gloria swiveled around and looked at Flash, apparently trying on what he had said. Gloria wasn't a bad kid, O'Donnell had decided, but she didn't have quite the right line on Flash. He didn't like strings it, seemed, no matter what a nice package they held.

"Can we count on the people in the bar not saying anything?" O'Donnell glanced around at the others.

Flash pursed his lips to suppress a smile. Deloris sighed and leaned forward toward O'Donnell. In her best grade-school teacher's voice, she explained the facts of life on the corner of Selby and Dale.

"I can understand the neighborhood viewpoint about the police," O'Donnell said. "What I don't understand is why Daddy Wilkins was willing to let Flash go. He didn't want Flash to play in the Open, so why the change of heart? All he has to say is that Flash was there in the bar, and connect him with the shooting."

O'Donnell didn't feel so off in right field now. He wanted some answers.

"You're right, Johnny. Daddy could do that," Deloris said, speaking like it would be a remote outcome, a hypothetical.

"But he won't," Flash jumped in. "Daddy Wilkins and I had . . . a meeting of the minds tonight." He winked at Deloris.

Deloris smiled at him. The two had discovered each other, and O'Donnell could feel what was going on. Gloria didn't seem to recognize the magnetic force field. Lucky thing, too. They didn't need to antagonize her.

"So we trust Daddy Wilkins on this?" O'Donnell needed reasons.

"Daddy may be a lot of things, but he keeps his word," Deloris said. "It's okay, hear? Besides, I'm his niece, and if he gives me any trouble, my mama will set that old man straight. Be sure on that."

"Johnny," Flash said, his voice edgy. "Be cool. It's going to work out fine."

"Besides there isn't any room to squeeze out of this corner now," Deloris said.

I sure as hell hope you two are reading this situation right." Bobby stood, stretching his arms to the ceiling. "I'm heading home."

After Bobby left the apartment, Deloris supplied some background to what O'Donnell already knew about Butternut and his growing hatred for Daddy Wilkins. As usual, the truth about how Daddy Wilkins had treated Butternut's mother depended on where you stood. Butternut's mother had pulled a few tricks of her own, and Deloris thought that Daddy Wilkins had less blame to shoulder than Butternut would ever allow.

"Daddy Wilkins was hard on Butternut after his mom left. Treated that poor boy like trash. Too harsh with him," Deloris said. "But Butternut turned real bad mostly on his own account."

Gloria remained quiet, and O'Donnell wondered why she was mixed up with the likes of Butternut in the first place. Maybe she thought it would be a way of getting back at Flash, but all she'd gained was one very bad evening's excitement.

Deloris stretched and yawned. "Lord, this has been a night. I'm tired silly. I'm going to make some coffee. She and her ruby-red dress harmonized out of the chair and toward the kitchen. "Anyone want some?"

Flash smiled, and followed her.

Gloria had fallen asleep in her little corner of the daybed. In the kitchen, O'Donnell could hear the sounds of cupboards and drawers opening and closing, punctuated by bursts of laughter. Flash poked his head out the porch door. "Johnny, do me a big favor and take Gloria home," he whispered. "I need to talk with Deloris for a while longer. I can find a way beack to my place."

O'Donnell guessed that further worrying about the night's problems was out of order now.

GLORIA LIVED OVER BY HANCOCK grade school, right off Snelling Avenue, and it made sense for O'Donnell to drop her off. She was still a bit buzzed and half asleep so she didn't seem to care that O'Donnell took her home, rather than Flash. On the drive to her place, Gloria dozed, making strange little sounds in her sleep as O'Donnell turned a corner or drove over a bump. The clock outside the Midway Bank on Snelling Avenue read 12:10 p.m. When the pair arrived in front of Gloria's duplex apartment minutes later, she opened her eyes and gave a little yawn. She angled her face out the open car window, gulping a deep breath of the night air.

Gloria snagged her heel on the car's running board as she got out, and fell in a ball on the grass. O'Donnell gathered her up and carried her to the doorstep. He set her on unsteady feet, and watched as she scrabbled inside her purse for the key. Once inside, Gloria walked down a hallway from a small living room and entered into a bedroom, closing the door. O'Donnell sat on a couch, bathed in light from the night's moon and stars slipping into the room from a front window. He could hear a toilet flush, followed by running water. Gloria stayed in her bathroom for what seemed like a long time before returning to where O'Donnell sat.

"What are you doing here in the dark?" Gloria snapped on a light next to the couch. Dressed in a man's white shirt and a pair of old pants, she'd washed her face and smoothed her hair back. She sat on a blue plush chair opposite O'Donnell, and put her feet up on a small footstool.

"Tonight's like some horrible bad dream." Gloria hesitated, shivered at the memory. "I never imagined doing what I did. Oh, God, I wish I could take back what happened."

She looked at O'Donnell, pleading for something. "He was so rough and scary with me. I hated him. Part of me wanted to kill him . . . was glad I did it. God."

She wrapped both hands around her knees, pulled her legs tight to her chest, and tried to hide herself in the chair. Her face registered all the dread and anguish she felt at this moment. She needed to talk. What she was facing wasn't much different from soldiers O'Donnell knew who'd killed for the first time—himself included. They needed someone to help them through it.

Gloria and O'Donnell talked for a long time. She did most of the talking, explaining why she had been with Butternut in the first place.

"It was so stupid. I thought . . . maybe Flash would hear about me and Butternut . . . maybe he'd get jealous and want me back."

To O'Donnell's way of thinking, Flash had caught Gloria's heart and put it in his pocket along with who knows how many others. O'Donnell bet Flash's women always wanted more than he would ever offer. Their love and desire likely twisted into much different emotions. Maybe Flash wasn't so lucky with women after all.

O'Donnell talked a bit about what had happened at the bar. He told Gloria she'd done what she had to do, given the situation. She really hadn't had a choice. Sort of like O'Donnell's own time in the war. The analogy wasn't airtight, he knew, but most weren't. Gloria needed to hear what he had to offer, and she seemed to feel better about things by the time O'Donnell left.

She gave him a sisterly hug at the door. "You're a nice man, Johnny."

He left her apartment with mixed feelings about that.

40

COSMO LAY NEXT TO THE BED, looking smug and self-satisfied watching O'Donnell struggle to a sitting position. O'Donnell knew the Andersons had wined and dined the dog like he was a foreign dignitary, and Cosmo made no motion at all toward his food bowl, content to lie with his head between his paws and his legs stretched out behind him, his eyes the only moving body part. *Mr. Crocodile*. Even the insistent jangling of the phone didn't phase him.

O'Donnell made the mistake of answering on the third ring. Detective Ikola yammered on the other end. "O'Donnell, be down here by 8:30. We've some murder business to discuss."

"Murder? Come on, Detective. We told Groseth everything we knew last night. Doesn't he know how to type up a report?"

"Yeah, Groseth . . . What can I say? Get on down here. Now. Time to talk with the real pros."

AT THE POLICE STATION, Sergeant McInerny lounged in his accustomed spot. O'Donnell imagined him cast in bronze. The Buddhists would build a temple around him.

"Johnny, old salt," McInerny beamed, "you surely know how to stir up action in this city." He pointed to a bench on the right side of the room where two overweight, pasty looking guys sat together, smoking cigarettes and drinking coffee.

"The gentlemen of the Fourth Estate, representing rags in both of our fair cities, have gotten wind of your nocturnal exploits," McInerny whispered. "They asked me to herald your arrival. But I hate those fools. Go on back."

O'Donnell leaned in close so the reporters wouldn't hear, "Did they bring Gloria in this morning?"

McInerny dipped his head, speaking in a low tone from the side of his mouth, "They detained Gloria this morning on the early shift, and some gal named Deloris, too." He brightened at the memory.

McGee met O'Donnell at the door to the detective's room. They walked past an open office where Deloris and Ikola sat across from each other at a wooden table. Deloris gave O'Donnell a confident smile and a wave. She'd donned a tight yellow top for the occasion.

Gloria was nowhere to be seen. O'Donnell worried that without much urging Gloria might break down and forget the script.

McGee pointed the way into a small interview room, furnished in a way to make any simple soul happy—two metal folding chairs, a card table, and one plastic ashtray. O'Donnell asked the detective which was his favorite chair. He told O'Donnell to sit down.

"We didn't have much to go on last night because of some less than satisfactory investigation," McGee said. "I need to ask you a few questions on the record." He scribbled the time and date at the top of a new page in a notepad he extracted from his sports coat pocket. .

"What's the status on Daddy Wilkins?" O'Donnell asked hoping to postpone the official business.

"Our local Commie is hale and hearty, despite the bullet hole," McGee said.

"So he's out of danger?"

"You bet. He should be back to plotting the overthrow of our fair Republic sooner than we'd like." McGee's voice turned serious and official sounding. "He's already given us a statement."

O'Donnell knew McGee probably was setting him up. He had to trust that Daddy Wilkins wouldn't change his mind about last night. It wasn't easy for O'Donnell to be operating against the police. He didn't like the spot he was in at all. "What do you want from me? I told Groseth everything I knew last night. Am I under arrest or something?"

McGee waved O'Donnell off. "We need a statement for the record, that's all. Tell me what you remember about the shooting?"

O'Donnell gave McGee the account everyone had agreed on. The detective took notes without asking any questions. O'Donnell relaxed a smidgen, feeling like maybe the worst was over.

"Why didn't you mention that your friend, Dawkins, was a witness to all this?" McGee leaned back and watched for a reaction. He'd caught O'Donnell off balance. What did McGee know?

"What are you talking about?" Come hell or high water, O'Donnell decided to stick with the story.

McGee told him the police had received an anonymous call about Flash. O'Donnell had the feeling the anonymous caller might damn well be the guy in the dark sedan.

"I really don't know what you're talking about," O'Donnell said. "This is nutty, McGee. Do you guys always play this game?" O'Donnell didn't allow the detective time to answer. "Some anonymous caller? Sounds like somebody wanting to cause problems. If you remember, we've had more than enough of these *somebodys* lately."

McGee didn't look like he was buying what O'Donnell had to sell. But who said making a sale was easy?

"Look McGee, I told you what happened, and you know who was there in the bar. You've probably talked to Bobby Borgstrom, haven't you? Ask the others, they'll tell you the same thing." O'Donnell crossed his fingers on that one. He hoped the guy tailing him hadn't followed over to Deloris's apartment.

"Yes. I do expect the others would tell me the same thing," McGee said.

"The world's full of cynics these days, I guess."

McGee appraised O'Donnell like he was used car salesman hustling him into a bad deal. Finally, he said, "That's your story?"

At that moment, Ikola thrust open the door and stalked into the room. He stood behind McGee's chair, hands on hips. "Deloris has confirmed that Dawkins was in attendance for Butternut's last moments. Are you ready to come clean with us?"

"Jesus, Ikola, who writes your dialogue?" His bad acting was the tip O'Donnell needed, confirming that Deloris hadn't given them a thing.

Ikola took offense and stumbled at O'Donnell from behind McGee's chair. McGee grabbed him, pulling him back by the arms. Ikola squirmed in McGee's grasp, then spun on his heel and left the room.

"Sorry, Johnny," McGee sat down again, reaching to retrieve his notepad and pen from the floor. "We've been at this most of the night." He read through his notes for a minute. "I'm too tired to play any games here. If we need more help . . ." he looked up. "You'll be available, right."

"I don't have any big plans," O'Donnell said, except he sure as hell wanted to find out more about the anonymous source.

"Before you go," McGee said, "answer me something. What the hell were you doing at Daddy Wilkins's? Strange place for you to be."

"Best ribs in town. Right?"

O'DONNELL DIDN'T LEAVE the police station feeling all that confident about the collective will of his fellow travelers to uphold the alibi. He wanted to see if Deloris had any comforting news, so he drove just around the corner off 11th Street to where he could spot Deloris when she came out. She sashayed down the steps ten minutes later with half the police department hanging out the windows behind her.

Deloris continued walking down 11th street towards O'Donnell. He scooted over to the passenger side and rolled down the window so she'd notice him. She gave the slightest nod of her head to acknowledge his presence as she opened the door to a beat up, green Studebaker. Sliding into the driver's seat, she said loud enough for O'Donnell to hear, "Como Park Pavilion."

O'DONNELL CONSIDERED the Como Park Zoo one of St. Paul's greatly unappreciated treasures. He particularly liked the gorillas—tricksters supreme. Zoo-goers would gather around the gorilla cage to stare, and the grand simians would pretend to go about their everyday business—like picking at each other's fur for fleas and critters. All the while, the gorillas would keep a close eye on the spectators. O'Donnell was sure they singled out people making idiotic faces and otherwise acting stupid. Someone always proved more obnoxious than others in the crowd, and that's when the gorillas seized the moment, scooping up a handy glop of feces and hurling it. Their dexterity made O'Donnell optimistic about the direction of evolution.

After visiting the zoo, folks could walk over to the Conservatory and visit its domes packed with tropical trees, plants, and flowers. Sometimes couples held weddings there. Mostly, people visited the Conservatory in the winter months to remember what flowers and green, growing things looked and smelled like.

In addition to a picnic grounds, carnival rides, baseball diamonds, and the golf course, Como Park had a dance pavilion, overlooking a small lake. The Pavilion was a sizable structure, painted white, with a dance floor open on three sides and a stage at one end for bands to perform. As far back as eighth grade, O'Donnell and his buddies went there on Friday nights to meet and dance with girls who came from all parts of the city.

O'Donnell found an empty bench on a porch overlooking the water. Deloris sat down beside him a few minutes later. She had a bag of popcorn and two Cokes.

"Want some? It's fresh popped."

O'Donnell took a handful from the bag she offered. He and Deloris sat awhile watching kids and parents maneuver on the water in bright colored pedal boats rented at the dock. In the winter, the Park Board shaped a smooth oval on the ice for the speed skaters. Winter seemed a long way past on this splendid summer morning—so, too, for the moment, did the trouble from the preceding night.

Deloris crossed her legs elegantly. "You remind me of somebody famous," O'Donnell said, "but I can't remember her name."

Deloris fluttered her eyelashes, "Betty Grable?"

"I'm that obvious?"

"Actually, people say I look a little like Carmen Miranda."

"That's it." O'Donnell watched a Carmen Miranda in a movie musical before shipping out to the war zone.

"That's quite a compliment. I'd love to be as beautiful as her." Deloris leaned close. "But you know what? I can sing better."

"And you don't have to wear a fruit bowl on your head to do it."

"Don't have to wear a lot of things."

O'Donnell took another handful of popcorn, and a big swig of his coke. Deloris ruffled her fingers through his hair.

"You're blushing," she teased. She drew her feet back toward the bench and posed on the edge of it, placing her hands primly in her lap. She looked off toward the water. "I want a career in show business more than looking like Carmen Miranda. If I can find the money, I'll be able to go to New York and Chicago for auditions. Daddy Wilkins promised my mother he'd take care of me." A trace of worry crossed her smooth face. "Now, I'm not so sure."

"I'd say you'll make it big."

"I hope so. Maybe I should have given those police detectives a song or too." She laughed with great delight. O'Donnell felt it wasn't hard to like Deloris at all.

"Now that I think of it, I did throw them a pretty good song and dance this morning," she said.

"Did they buy it?"

"They're a tough audience, honey." Deloris thought for a minute. "I don't think it makes much difference any way you look at it."

"What do you mean?"

Deloris didn't answer O'Donnell's question right away. "If we were in my hometown, the police would say, 'It's a bunch of them boys shooting each other. Happens all the time.' Police would figure it's one less of us to worry about, and they'd let things be. Maybe they're thinking that here, too. I hope so."

Deloris nibbled around the edge of a popcorn kernel. "If you had more murder and mayhem in this little city of yours, we wouldn't be sitting here worrying our fool heads off, would we?" She put her hand on O'Donnell's arm. "You know St. Paul better than I do. What'll the police do? Will they dog us to make an example? Try and keep the white folks happy maybe?"

O'Donnell's best guess was the cops would quietly crack down on Daddy Wilkins's "business interests" and generally make things extra unpleasant for the folks in the Selby-Dale. O'Donnell and the others would go a few rounds with Ikola, but that would just be sport for him. O'Donnell figured if everyone stuck to the story, Ikola had nothing to go on really. O'Donnell knew the next few days would tell the truth of that tale.

"You hear anything about Daddy Wilkins's condition?"

"Oh, he'll be fine, that old coot," Deloris smiled, plucking out some pleasant memory of Daddy Wilkins from what must have been a small inventory. "Tougher than hickory. I saw him this morning at the hospital."

Deloris rolled the coke bottle over her cheek to cool down. The sun bathed her and O'Donnell now. "Johnny, let's move down to that bench in the shade over yonder by the water."

O'Donnell followed her to a wooden bench, shaded by a huge weeping willow tree. "Tell me why you're so trusting Daddy Wilkins won't change his mind?"

Deloris thought for a time. "You have to understand that all this Communist business is less important to Daddy than it looks. Sure, he's loyal to a point. They stood up for him and other black folks down South when nobody else would. Communism gave Daddy a way to look at his world that made sense for him."

"You think the Communists are right on all that?"

"They have parts of it figured out, that's for sure, honey. They've just forgot that hating us comes natural to most white folks. The 'triumph of the Proletariat' and all that won't make any difference. People will still think and hate the same way." That sounded like Marcus Sanford to O'Donnell.

"I hope it won't always be so bad," she added as a melancholy after-thought.

Deloris looked at O'Donnell, and a big smile broke through. Her laughter trilled over the surface of the lake. Two swans swimming near turned their heads, treading water, eyeing the pair on the bench for possible conspiracies.

"It all tickles me silly. Daddy talks this world revolution, Communist ideology with the best of them. But when it comes down to it, Daddy is a dyed in the wool capitalist. The man sure loves money, and he knows how to make it. He'll take it from anybody—Communist sympathizer, Republican, and Democrat." She grabbed O'Donnell's arm, steadying herself from another burst of laughter. "Tell you what, Johnny, there ain't no socialism in Daddy's bank account."

"Okay, but . . ." Deloris put her hand across O'Donnell's lips to interrupt.

"Old Daddy Wilkins loves his money . . . but he likes to get back at the world, too. Flash figured that, so he told Daddy two things. Number one, how much certain white folks would have heartburn over Flash winning that golf tournament, and number two . . ." Gloria smothered another fit of the giggles, "that Flash might just pay him part his purse for winning."

O'Donnell couldn't help but join Deloris's laughter. Couples and children by the shore stared back at the two of them, wondering what the big joke was.

"Some big bad Communist," O'Donnell said.

"But, comrade, he's *our* Communist," Deloris said, laughing again.

O'Donnell and Deloris talked for another five minutes or so, about nothing in particular, simply enjoying each other's company. Finally, O'Donnell said he needed to get a move on to the ballpark.

"Where's that golf course here?" Deloris asked. "I'm meeting your handsome friend."

Deloris stood and gave O'Donnell a curtsey. He liked her company. Before he let her go, O'Donnell decided to share his doubts about Gloria towing the line with them.

"Honey, Gloria knows that lying is the better side of truth on this occasion," Deloris said.

O'Donnell thought a bit before asking his next question. "Will she change her mind if she finds out about you and Flash?"

If Deloris didn't care for the question, she didn't show it. She smiled and waved a little goodbye, but before walking away, she said, "I think Gloria knows what's best for her."

MAX SCHMIDT, THE SAINTS'S ancient pitching coach, watched with an expert eye as O'Donnell warmed up in the bullpen. Max had retired a couple of years back, but he usually came over from his apartment nearby up Lexington Avenue when the Saints had a practice. He couldn't keep himself away from the game. After a cup of coffee with the Dodgers, Max had spent almost fifteen years in the minors. Like most good coaches O'Donnell knew from his playing days, Max taught baseball better than he'd played it.

The older man couldn't bend his arm to light a cigarette from all the pitches he made over the years, so Max sat on the bench next to the bullpen mound talking to his pitchers. He liked O'Donnell's new delivery, and set to fine tuning the release. At the end of fifteen minutes of instruction, O'Donnell's pitches had some real mustard on them. He felt like a kid with a new toy.

"You keep coming out and throwing everyday, and we'll have you pitching in the big leagues again." Max's encouragement drifted out from deep in the bullpen shade. "You need a real change-up, though."

O'Donnell and the older man fiddled around with different grips to throw the change for ten minutes. Nothing earthshaking developed.

"Maybe I need to think a bit on this one," said Max, shifting and fitting a baseball within his arthritic claw. "Go grab a shower, kid, and come out again when the team gets back from the road trip. We'll see what we can do then."

On the way in, O'Donnell talked to Al Brancato and Buddy Hicks. Both players lounged around in short left field, occasionally scooping up a batting practice ball and lobbing it back in toward the mound. They had a bet on each throw—closest to the ball bag behind the mound won a dime. O'Donnell knew where he'd like to be in his life. No need for a college degree and a wristwatch here. None of the players showing up for practice early said anything about Butternut's demise and O'Donnell's box seat for the event.

On the way home, O'Donnell worried about what the newspapers would report on the adventures of the preceding night. Maybe the crime reporter had missed the deadline for a story. The sports section was the only place O'Donnell wanted to see his name. Too bad they didn't do witnesses to murder like the baseball box scores. In very small print, there'd be a list . . . *w: O'Donnell, Dauphine, Rowan, Borgstrom.* Like baseball fans, only the most devoted followers of crime would read the small print.

The phone rang as O'Donnell entered the cabin. "Have you seen the paper?" Abby asked.

"You mean the article about my homemade zucchini bread? Sorry, but I can't give out the recipe until after the State Fair."

"Very funny, Mr. Eyewitness. I'm coming out to see you. I'll bring the newspaper."

"Abby, hold on . . ."

"Forget it. I'm on my way. I can be your press secretary and answer the phones. Besides, I'm bringing you fried chicken, cold slaw, and potato salad—the sole fruits of my culinary talents. Is that mixing my metaphors or something? Anyway, I have a new two-piece swim suit I'm dying to try out."

"Now that's a different story." O'Donnell hadn't eaten a decent dinner for days, and he always had a soft spot for a new swimsuit. "I'm warming to the idea."

"You should. I'm stealing my family's dinner for tonight. Daddy said some lame things about you, so I figured he didn't deserve my cooking."

"Do I need to press grapes for a quick bottle of wine?"

"A six-pack will do."

O'Donnell spent the next thirty minutes cleaning up around the apartment. As he swept a mound of dog hairs out the kitchen door, he mulled over recent events, and what he knew—or thought he knew. Butternut's death left several questions unanswered. Was it Butternut who'd knocked O'Donnell around on the road outside of River's Edge? O'Donnell didn't think so, but if not . . . who? What led Butternut to contact Sanford? What would Jack Clancy do if Flash played in the Open? Who was following O'Donnell around in the dark sedan last night? What the hell is that growing on the side of the kitchen sink? O'Donnell scrubbed it clean.

Abby arrived around four o'clock, lugging a large picnic hamper. O'Donnell helped her empty out the goodies, and they stashed the fried chicken, cold slaw, and potato salad in the icebox for after a swim. Abby changed in the bedroom, and emerged from it clad in a new white swimsuit which she modeled for O'Donnell, striking some comic, but seductive poses. O'Donnell had to admit, she'd chosen her aquatic outfit well.

"Let's see how it holds up in the lake," he suggested.

They walked over by the Anderson's cabin. Cosmo bounded ahead, anxious to see his friends down the way. The elderly couple had a swimming float anchored about thirty yards from the shore. The grandkids usually showed up for the weekend, so the Andersons had their beach area cleared of weeds and rocks. O'Donnell had never taken the time to do it.

Abby ran into the water and dove in. She stayed underwater for a long while, emerging halfway to the swimming float, screaming. She'd swum under the surface far enough to tangle with the lake seaweed. The two strands wrapped around her head added a mythic touch to her ensemble. O'Donnell dove in to join her at the swimming float. Cosmo decided to take a nap on the warm sand of the shore.

The swimming float rode a couple of feet out of the water, without a ladder attached to help swimmers climb on. O'Donnell boosted himself up, and let Abby struggle to climb aboard. After two failed attempts, he said, "You need to start a full regimen of pull-ups if you're going to hang around with me."

"Help me up, you clown."

O'Donnell did. Abby returned the favor by pushing him into the lake.

They spent the better part of the next hour sunbathing. The warm sun sliced through the afternoon haze, its reflected rays winking off the lake's rolling surface. Small waves, puffed by a breeze, splashed against the float, rocking the sunbathers gently back and forth. O'Donnell dozed off. Some time later, a shadow fell across his face.

"So what really happened last night?" Abby asked.

"I'm really not supposed to say anything about it." O'Donnell had no intention of sharing the details no matter how much he might trust the woman next to him.

"I understand if you can't talk about it. The newspaper didn't give much detail, but it sounded like an awful thing." Abby touched O'Donnell's arm and gave it a squeeze. "I'm just glad you're okay"

"Thanks, Abby." O'Donnell didn't quite know how to feel about her.

Abby jumped up and dove off the float, surfacing a few yards away. "Let's go in and see about that dinner."

"It's a deal."

Back at the cabin, Abby went to change in O'Donnell's bedroom while he sat on the porch and drank one of the beers. Five minutes later, the screen door squeaked and Abby came out to join him.

"I took one of the beers. Okay?" she asked, leaning up against the porch railing.

"Sure. Are you hungry now?"

"Let's sit out here and listen to the lake for a few minutes. It's so nice and peaceful." She handed O'Donnell a copy of the afternoon St. Paul paper, folded to the second page. "Here's the paper if you get bored."

The headline read—"SON SLAIN AT FATHER'S SALOON"— followed by a tagline below, "Argument Leads to Double Shooting."

Late last night, Charles Eldred Wilkins, Sr., a Negro saloon owner in the Selby-Dale area was shot and wounded by his son. Eldred Wilkins, Jr., apparently enraged by a disagreement with his father, pulled a revolver and fired once, wounding the elder Wilkins in the upper right chest area. St. Paul Police confirmed that witnesses, Deloris Dauphine of New Orleans and John O'Donnell of St. Paul, reported that Gloria Rowan ordered Wilkins Jr. to stand aside, but he ignored her warning. Miss Rowan fired once in apparent self-defense. According to the police coroner, Wilkins, Jr., died instantly from a bullet wound to the head.

Wilkins, Sr., is reported in good condition at Ramsey County Hospital.

Police Detective Daniel Ikola issued a press statement early today. Detective Ikola told reporters the investigation of the incident would continue, but added that no charges would be filed against Miss Rowan at this time. According to Ikola, "Miss Rowan acted in self-defense."

Gloria Rowan refused to talk with reporters. The police have not located any other witnesses, although they are trying to locate anyone who might have seen the shootings.

According to police, the Selby-Dale area has been a trouble spot recently. Police files indicate that several serious incidents have occurred at Wilkins Sr.'s bar and restaurant, 'Daddy's Ribs and Liquors.' A spokesman for the St. Paul Mayor's office stated that the St. Paul Police would be 'making every effort to crack down on crime and misbehavior in the Selby-Dale area.'

Funeral services for Eldred Wilkins, Jr., will be held later this week at the Rondo African Church.

N OT THE KIND OF CELEBRITY you bargained for." Abby sipped on
her beer, watching O'Donnell closely.

"Not exactly. I'd like to climb into a hole and forget it all."

"Okay, but let's eat first before you do."

While O'Donnell and Abby sampled the chicken and potato salad,
the phone kept interrupting. First it was O'Donnell's father, followed by
a call from Floyd's at the pharmacy, and capped off with questions from
several people not heard from since high school. Abby nibbled at the food
on her plate, watching O'Donnell and enjoying his evasive answers. She
uncapped another round of beers, and handed O'Donnell a bottle as he
tried to end a conversation with some woman who claimed to be a
reporter. He hung up and buried the phone under a cushion on the
couch. But the muffled tone of its ringing intruded again.

"I'm not going to answer it." O'Donnell said.

Abby dug underneath the cushion for the phone. She answered,
pinching her nose so that she sounded like Gracie Allen with a bad cold.
"You've reached the residence of Mr. John O'Donnell. May I take a
message please?" She handed the phone to O'Donnell. "It's Flash."

"I'm calling with the opportunity of a lifetime and some good news."
Flash sounded upbeat to O'Donnell.

"What's my alternative?"

"None.

"I thought as much."

"You know that day after tomorrow is qualifying for the Open," Flash
said. O'Donnell agreed he knew that much. "So, here's the deal," Flash
said. "You caddy for me. Bobby can walk along with the gallery and watch
for any funny business."

O'Donnell didn't much care for that sort of assignment.

"Do you get it?" Flash asked, a hint of mischief in his voice. "You'll symbolize a new day in race relations."

"I can't wait." O'Donnell set a time to meet Flash the next morning at Keller Golf Course, the site of the St. Paul Open.

"Be on time. Okay?"

"So tell me what's the good news?" O'Donnell asked.

"They let Gloria go late this afternoon. Deloris said she thought Gloria seemed anxious to leave town if she could and forget things."

"Was she okay?"

"I guess so."

O'Donnell felt bad for Gloria having to leave.

"She said not to worry about her," Flash said, "You must have made a good impression last night. What did you do?"

"Nothing. Nothing at all."

"You must have done something right." Flash seemed to want to pursue the subject.

O'Donnell didn't. He asked Flash about the qualifying. Apparently, O'Donnell had to be there at 8:30 for some directions from the caddy master and one of the PGA officials.

"I want to tell you something else, too." Flash hesitated before he continued. "Friend of mine saw Jill Gustafson and her ex-husband sharing a drink at O'Gara's. Looked like they had more going on than joint property settlements."

O'Donnell didn't like what was going on in his imagination. What was with Jill, anyway?

"See you bright and early," Flash said as he hung up.

"What did Flash want?" Abby asked. "You look like you lost your best friend or something."

"What's this with your sister and her ex?" O'Donnell's question came out sounding like an accusation. Abby flinched at his question.

"Sorry," O'Donnell said.

"Jill's been acting strange lately," Abby said. "Part of it is seeing Brad again. He's the one who brought her home the other night. I hate to say it, but I'll bet she's using him for something." Abby frowned. "He's such a sleaze, and she never liked him that much in the first place. I'm sorry, Johnny, but it seems like Jill uses most of the guys she's ever known."

But not every man, if what Jill had told O'Donnell the other night was true. "No one's ever turned the tables on her?"

Abby thought for a second. "I think she met someone when she was out in San Diego. Something went wrong, and they split."

"Did she ever talk about him? Say who he was?"

"No. She made like it was a big secret romance. Daddy worried whoever it was might be married."

Cosmo had come over to Abby, and she scratched his head. He sat and pressed against her knee.

"I thought it was another way for Jill to make Daddy and Mummy feel bad. She had them so worried when she quit school and joined the Women's Reserve."

"She told me about that. It seems out of character."

"She wasn't doing well in school. Bored, I guess, and Daddy threatened to bring her home. So, to spite him, I guess, she and her friend Holly joined up. From what I could tell, it was a good experience for her. But . . ." Abby shook her head.

"What?"

"When she came back from San Diego, she didn't want to do anything or see anybody. Daddy tried to get her back in school. Then he had her talk with some counselor over at the U."

"How did she and Brad get together?"

"Brad didn't have much but good looks and money when Jill latched on to him. I could tell the marriage wouldn't last, but my parents seemed pleased she'd found a man and settled down. But it wasn't long before Jill and Brad were fighting all the time. Brad accused Jill of going out on him. Jill moved home again." Abby frowned and fell silent.

O'Donnell wanted to hear more of the story. "What happened to Brad after she left him?"

"He started hanging around with all sorts of bad company. I overheard at the club that he's in debt to some local gamblers. Then he takes up with Jack Clancy and that crowd. He and a bunch at the club have been making life miserable for Daddy and his friends."

Cosmo worked his head under Abby's hand. She played with his ears.

"Now that Jill's been seeing Brad again, it's embarrassing for Daddy. For all of us, in fact. I'm not sure what she's doing. It doesn't make any sense."

O'Donnell couldn't make any sense of it either.

The more he listened to what Abby had to say about her sister, the less he cared to hear anything more about it. He promised himself not to give Jill another thought. But she wouldn't be easy to forget. O'Donnell didn't trust his resolve all that much.

O'Donnell opened the icebox door and checked the beer supply. "How about another cold one and a little twilight fishing? I hear it's the thing to do in these parts."

"Ugh. I hate fishing." Abby said. Cosmo looked back and forth between the two, his tail wagging in anticipation of some activity that might include him.

"We aren't big on fishing, but we like the lake," O'Donnell said. Cosmo's tail whacked the furniture and Abby's knees with his tail. "We can go out in the boat and pretend we're fishing."

Cosmo crashed the screen door open with his head. He paced on the porch and turned little circles, whining with each step.

"Grab the beers, Ahab," Abby said. "Let's hit the high seas."

She favored O'Donnell with a quick smooch as she passed through the door, and ran to the rowboat with Cosmo barking and jumping beside her. O'Donnell uncapped two beers and followed them out. He tried to leave the image of Jill and Brad Hoffman behind.

Once out on the lake, the moon and stars made a dramatic appearance, and the night shaped up as an astronomer's dream. Abby reclined on the bench slat in the rowboat's stern. She'd propped her head up with a boat cushion, and stared up into the night sky. Cosmo laid his chin on Abby's outstretched leg and stared at her with dreamy eyes.

"It is a wonderful night," Abby sighed.

O'Donnell had to agree, despite everything that had happened. He'd enjoyed being with Abby again.

● ● ● ● ●

LATE THAT NIGHT, the phone jangled. Cosmo had found a place again near the bottom of the bed. O'Donnell couldn't feel his toes, so he withdrew them from under the dog. Cosmo gave an irritated grunt and lifted himself off the bed, padding off toward the sofa. O'Donnell reluctantly walked out of the bedroom to pick up the phone.

"O'Donnell?" The voice on the other end sounded angry as a hornet. "You have just bought yourself a load of trouble. Do not appear on that golf course as your friend Dawkins is proposing. A caddy? What the hell is wrong with you?"

"Commies in your closet or something, Clancy?" O'Donnell could imagine the man's expression—a very angry one no doubt. "Is this a warning or a threat?"

"Listen up," Clancy yelled. "I know damn well what took place at Daddy Wilkins's place the other night. Unfortunately, the police refuse to follow up the perfectly good intelligence I gave them."

"So is that Arnold driving around in the dark following me? How'd he ever pass the written exam?"

Clancy waited before he spoke again. "My patience is exhausted. Do not underestimate me." He carefully enunciated each syllable so O'Donnell wouldn't miss his point.

"Heaven forbid." O'Donnell said.

"I will play my hand."

"Well, deal us in," O'Donnell said. "But always bet on the good guys. And in case you didn't know—that's us"

Clancy let out a long, exasperated stream of breath. "Have it as you will."

O'Donnell had no doubt Saturday's qualifying round wouldn't be a carefree recreational outing.

KELLER GOLF COURSE SAT ASTRIDE a set of hills far to the north of downtown St. Paul. The public track might qualify as a pretty fair eighteen holes, with its small greens and relatively tight, tree-lined, rolling fairways, but O'Donnell doubted the course marked much of a challenge for the seasoned professional. The PGA officials always toughened up the layout for the tournament with play from the back tees and to the most difficult pin positions, but such changes wouldn't hold against the likes of Jimmy Demaret, Floyd's Mangrum, Jim Turnessa, and Ellsworth Vines. The pros signed up for the St. Paul Open would fire away at low scores. O'Donnell wagered Flash Dawkins would be grabbing his share of birdies, if not an eagle or two.

Before driving over to Keller that morning, O'Donnell retrieved his service revolver from the top shelf of his closet, figuring it wouldn't hurt to bring it along. O'Donnell hadn't fired the weapon since the war, but he'd kept it cleaned and well-oiled. He shoved the revolver into his belt, allowing his tee shirt to hang out loosely over it. He would transfer it to Flash's golf bag as soon as possible.

A number of golfers and their caddies clustered around the entrance to the clubhouse. O'Donnell wandered over toward the putting green and spotted Flash at the far edge. He looked confident as usual.

"Late again," Flash said, not looking up from his chipping practice.

"But I have an excuse from home, teacher."

Flash chipped a practice ball within inches of the hole. "Bobby has some ideas for our day, O'Donnell. Listen up."

Bobby Borgstrom suggested he could trail Flash around the course, staying hidden from view, on the lookout for anything strange. He'd be close enough to signal O'Donnell if he found trouble.

"If a big lug like you can stay undercover, it'll re-write the detective manuals," O'Donnell said, using his friend as a screen from the golfers nearby while he stashed the revolver in a side pocket of Flash's golf bag.

Flash watched O'Donnell deposit the gun. "Is that what 'shoot a good score' means?"

Bobby took the occasion to advise Flash on the upcoming round. "Speaking of which, you don't need to be the number one guy. Just make sure you qualify."

Flash thanked Bobby for the advice, but told him, "I'm going to be the number one qualifier. No doubts."

Bobby made a face and drifted off toward the first tee.

O'Donnell decided to grab a cup of coffee and a donut at the bar section of the clubhouse. But it was time for a something more pressing, so he walked past the bar and downstairs to the locker room. The toilets stood against the wall near the showers, behind a row of steel lockers. Behind the first row of lockers, O'Donnell could hear a pair of voices talking in low but agitated tones. One of the voices sounded familiar. It was Gustafson.

"You're lying to me for obvious reasons," Gustafson said, his voice straining for self-control.

"Believe it."

"You watch what you say," Gustafson answered. "I will not listen to such filth—especially from the likes of you."

"You can choose to believe what you want. I know it's a fact."

O'Donnell could sense Gustafson struggling with his emotions. Nothing more was said for the moment. When the guy with Gustafson spoke again, his voice was low and hard. O'Donnell couldn't make out what was said. Then footsteps sounded by the row of lockers where O'Donnell now stood. He jerked open a locker, pretending to look for something inside, shielding his face from view. After a brief pause, the footsteps continued a steady cadence up the stairs. O'Donnell waited a couple of counts and followed. On the other side of the locker row, he could hear Gustafson fighting for a breath and banging his hand against the wooden bench.

At the top of the stairs, making his way through a crowd hanging around a portable table filled with coffee and donuts, O'Donnell caught a glimpse of Brad Hoffman about to sit down at the bar—looking smug and pleased. What was his game?

O'Donnell poured a cup of coffee and found a glazed donut—his favorite confection for morning confrontations. He doctored up the coffee with some sugar and cream, bit off a healthy chunk of donut, and headed over to where Hoffman sat.

Hoffman punched the arm of the man sitting next to him. "Phil, see this washed up piece of shit? O'Donnell here used to be a big hero type. Thinks he still is."

Phil looked at O'Donnell, already having difficulty focusing from drinking his vodka and orange juice. Phil didn't say anything, and turned back toward the bar.

"Cat got your tongue, Phil?" O'Donnell asked. "You're supposed to say something equally smart-assed."

Phil seemed to think about it, the little wheels spinning, but couldn't come up with anything he could add to the conversation.

"Imagine." O'Donnell chucked Phil on the shoulder. "A jerk as big as you, Hoffman."

But Hoffman refused to take the bait, preferring his response to be a smug, confident smile. The revised model of the man sitting before him put O'Donnell on edge.

45

FLASH DIDN'T TEE OFF for another thirty minutes, but O'Donnell saw him heading for the driving range. Like a good caddy, O'Donnell followed and retrieved a bucket of practice balls for Flash to hit. He then retreated to the shade provided by a nearby oak tree. All around, in every direction, golfers, their caddies, and the fans now crisscrossed paths in a busy swirl, advancing toward their destinations.

Through a tangle of legs, O'Donnell caught a brief glimpse of Gustafson, standing in the clubhouse door, his face contorted with anger, looking with purpose toward the driving range. Gustafson identified his quarry, and walked to the spot where Flash practiced his irons. Flash stopped in mid-swing when Gustafson barked something at him. Flash stepped back a pace, holding his hand against Gustafson's chest to restrain him. The older man brushed the hand aside with an angry swipe. Flash spoke to the indignant, defiant man before him, but it didn't seem to solve anything. Gustafson spun on his heel and walked away. After a few steps, he turned around, pointing a finger at Flash, saying something. Flash stared back without a reply.

Gustafson stomped by where O'Donnell sat, his face florid. An elderly gentleman in a yellow golf shirt greeted him, but Gustafson barged by without a word. At the entrance to the clubhouse, he pushed his way through a group of men gathered there. O'Donnell walked over to where Flash stood.

"What was that all about?"

Flash raked one of the practice golf balls toward him, and maneuvered it to a tuft of grass. He sent the ball flying with a ferocious swing. He did the same in quick succession with the two other balls nearby. At last he said, "Gustafson doesn't want to sponsor me anymore."

"What happened?" O'Donnell knew Hoffman had something to do with it.

"It doesn't much matter now," Flash said, angling his golf bag up so he could shove his golf club into it. "I can't turn back now."

"Why would you have to turn back?"

"Gustafson heard some news he didn't like, that's all." Flash handed the golf bag to O'Donnell without looking, and walked toward the crowd bordering the first tee.

O'Donnell hurried to catch up with him. "Something to do with the other night at Daddy Wilkins's?"

Flash stopped, his shoulders slumping. "Yeah," he said, walking away.

That *was* it. Now O'Donnell could see how things worked. The guy in the dark sedan following O'Donnell around? Not Walter, Clancy's stooge. It had to be Brad Hoffman. Clancy had the guy over a barrel didn't he? Gambling debts . . . and maybe more. Hoffman gave the police the tip about Flash being part of the mix at Daddy Wilkins's bar, thinking the cops would make an arrest. Instead of teeing off at the St. Paul Open, Flash would be in jail. When that plan fizzled, the next step was to plant some sort of nasty bug in Gustafson's ear as another way to pull the plug on Flash's St. Paul Open dreams. The opposition had a notion that Gustafson, the prominent lawyer and citizen, wouldn't risk his reputation at this point in the game. O'Donnell wished Gustafson's commitment to doing things right would hold, but maybe that was only a lesser part of the man's motivation.

O'Donnell caught up with Flash. "To hell with Gustafson. You don't need him."

Flash paused outside the circle of spectators at the first tee. He tugged at the fingers of his golf glove. "Time for the big show."

A PGA official introduced Flash to his playing partners for the day's threesome. O'Donnell figured the PGA had it in mind to put some pressure on the upstart entrant. They had Flash playing with two strong golfers, Bob House, a professional from the Rochester Country Club, and Chuck Bahn, state amateur champion and member of the prestigious Minikahda Country Club. Both men gave Flash a perfunctory handshake without any eye contact. O'Donnell figured Flash would thrive on the challenge.

The presence of a controversial black golfer guaranteed a much larger gallery than normal for the St. Paul Open qualifying round. Flash's group was scheduled next, and the spectators buzzed, anticipating a good show. O'Donnell hoisted the golf bag and advanced to the side of the tee markers.

The first hole was a short, moderate dogleg to the right. Golfers teed off from the top of a hill, and the tee box was set forward for the opening day rounds. A safe tee shot carried down to where the fairway turned right. The next shot had to soar uphill to a small green. Both Bahn and House hit good but cautious drives to the left corner of the fairway at the bottom of the hill, allowing a ninety- to 100-yard second shot to the green.

Flash set up to drive his ball, aiming directly at the green from the tee. The fans edged closer, anticipating a show. To cut the dogleg, Flash would have to hit the ball one hell of a long way uphill, clear an outcropping of pine trees, and then carry a sand bunker protecting against such heroic attempts. O'Donnell didn't see how such a bold drive could work. The only bright spot was an early morning, gusty wind blowing in the direction Flash had aligned for his tee shot.

Flash smacked his drive, the ball shooting off like a rocket, gaining height, and sailing with the wind towards the distant target. His shot easily cleared the trees, seemed to stall at the sand bunker, but dropped a few feet beyond it. Reaction to this magnificent drive among the gallery failed to find an immediate voice.

Someone standing near O'Donnell at last broke the silence, shouting out a simple, but befitting, "Wow!" Flash nonchalantly flipped his driver in O'Donnell's direction, and waved for him to follow, like a general leading his troops.

Bahn and House missed their second shots to the green by a wide margin. They followed up with poor pitches to the green. From where his ball lay in the short grass beyond the bunker, Flash studied what looked to be a straight line down a slight incline to the hole. O'Donnell could tell he intended to land his ball just on the green and have it roll like a putt. He eyed his line one last time before placing his club behind the ball and deftly clipping it off the grass. His chip rolled directly at the target, struck the flag, and settled neatly into the hole. An improbable eagle two.

Flash marched away to the next tee without a backward glance, and with most of the spectators in tow. House and Bahn stared after the departing mass. Not exactly golf etiquette, O'Donnell thought, but effective gamesmanship. It would be Flash's show from that point on.

While Flash waited on the second tee for House and Bahn to show up, an elderly black gentleman, with a neatly trimmed, white beard and wire-rimmed glasses, stepped forward and tapped at Flash's shoulder.

"Enjoying the golf so far, sir?" Flash extended his hand for a formal handshake. He encouraged the older man to stand with him, apart from the rest of the gallery.

"I am indeed enjoying your bold play." The older man stood with his shoulders pulled back in a dignified posture. The two of them remained that way until House and Bahn pushed through the crowd to the tee.

"Excuse me, but I have to get back to business," Flash said to the older man.

The man nodded. "Play on, young man," he said. "You do us all proud."

Keller's second hole was a par four of some 375 yards with a slight bend right at the green. No risk-taking for Flash on this hole as he placed a drive smack in the middle of the fairway. House duck-hooked one into the rough, and Bahn hit a weak shot to the right that barely stayed in-bounds. Walking off the tee, both golfers looked worried and anxious. House growled something at his caddy as the pair tracked into the tall grass in search of his ball.

O'Donnell checked the yardage and picked out a wedge. Flash took the club and made some practice swings, checking the position of his hands as he drew the club to waist level, and then completing the swing in slow motion. As he waited for the others to play, he brushed his club head across the grass, staring off toward the side of the fairway. O'Donnell followed his look, and spotted Deloris in the gallery, resplendent in a shiny red blouse and black slacks. She waved energetically, and performed a mock golf swing.

"Mind if I caddy for Deloris?" O'Donnell said. Deloris practiced another swing to the delight of nearby spectators.

"Deloris plays a game the likes of which you'd be quite unfamiliar," Flash said, his gaze fixed on the woman, and a proprietary smile on his lips.

"I understand," O'Donnell said.

Flash poked him in the stomach with the handle of his golf club. "No, I don't think you do."

O'Donnell slapped the club away, and bit back his irritation. "It's your shot. What club does His Highness want?"

Flash went back to business. His iron shot sounded sweet off the club head, and it raced skyward. O'Donnell lost the ball in the background of white clouds, but re-sighted it drifting down . . . locked on target. The ball stuck into the green's surface like an arrow, but spun in its divot hole and spurted out, stopping a few inches closer to the flag. Flash had a three-foot putt left for birdie. Deloris' war whoop of encouragement could be heard over the cheers and applause. Flash waved at her with a wide grin.

Flash made his birdie putt. After two holes he stood three under par. House made his par after a nice chip, and Bahn missed a short putt to card a bogie. Deloris approached Flash as he walked off the green.

"My hero," she said, giving Flash a theatrical hug. He didn't look uncomfortable with the attention. Some of the spectators clustered around clapped their appreciation. Others whispered among themselves, disturbed by the lack of decorum.

Off to the side, behind a group of men and women, O'Donnell had seen at River's Edge, he caught a glimpse of Jill. As Deloris gave him a friendly hug, O'Donnell waved in Jill's direction. She looked distracted . . . perplexed. Had she spoken with her father? She turned briskly, and walked back toward the clubhouse.

"Let's go," Flash called from down the path to the next hole. O'Donnell hustled to catch up. "Forget that," Flash said, inclining his head back toward where Jill had been standing. "The excitement is right here."

Flash had in mind destroying par at Keller Golf Course, O'Donnell thought, and damn if he wasn't on his way to doing that very thing working through the front nine. Sinking his par putt on number nine, Flash stood at thirty-one strokes. A fantastic beginning to the qualifying round. O'Donnell knew the score could have been lower. On a par five, Flash knocked it on the green in two, but missed a long putt for another eagle by a fraction. He seemed to brim with confidence, and soaked up the spotlight.

Deloris volunteered to grab a couple of cokes as a celebration for a job well done. Flash and O'Donnell continued past the clubhouse area to the tenth tee.

46

SPECTATORS SPILLED OUT of the bar to picnic tables populating the garden terrace near the practice green. The word was out. Flash had established a four-stroke advantage on the nearest competitor. As O'Donnell passed some small tables with sun umbrellas set up outdoors he spotted Jill again, sitting with Hoffman, having drinks, deep in conversation. She glanced up as O'Donnell drew near. Hoffman followed her gaze, and his eyes clouded over with contempt. Jill whispered something to him, her hand resting on his shoulder. Hoffman brushed her hand away, but Jill said something that turned his full attention back to her. What the hell? O'Donnell's face burned with anger and embarrassment. He walked quickly to the tenth tee.

Deloris caught up with Flash and O'Donnell, and handed them bottles of Coca Cola, still frosty from the ice tub. She'd also snagged a couple of Butterfinger candy bars.

"Honey, you sure know the way to a man's heart," Flash said.

Deloris whispered something back, and gave Flash a quick pat on his arm. "You keep your mind on this golf game, sugar."

Flash laughed and cupped her chin. "Watch me go."

On the back nine, O'Donnell turned into a spectator as much as a caddy. Flash's drives burned down the middle of the fairways. His irons shots spiked the greens. Seldom did he need to putt from any distance or from any great difficulty. He launched his second nine with three birdies in a row, and negotiated par on the other holes with no problems.

At the seventeenth tee, with the first qualifying spot well in hand, Flash's drive on the par 4 landed long and in the middle of the fairway. His next shot would be an eight iron to a platter-like green, bolstered in the front by a low stone wall. O'Donnell expected Flash to hit another fine shot, but as the ball sailed down toward the front half of the green, an unexpected gust of wind blew it back. The ball rolled to the bottom of an embankment close to the gnarled roots of a large oak.

O'Donnell struggled down to where the ball rested. He saw no way Flash could attempt a shot. The ball lay close by a large root at the side of the tree. An impossible task, it seemed. A penalty stroke wouldn't hurt his score now, so O'Donnell guessed the best decision would be to take an unplayable lie.

Flash paced around the ball, muttering something. He tried out various stances and swings, but none offered any real solution, it seemed. He stared at the ball as if willing it to roll out of trouble. "Give me the nine-iron, Johnny."

O'Donnell pulled the club for him. It didn't seem the right thing to do. "Flash, take a drop. Why take the chance?"

In return for the advice, Flash grabbed the nine-iron out of O'Donnell's hand. He took a reading of the distance up the bank to the green, and turned his back to it.

"What's the percentage?" O'Donnell asked again.

Flash began to practice a shot that, to O'Donnell's way of thinking, would be no less than a miracle if it worked. He stood with his back to the target, the nine-iron in his right hand, and the ball near his right foot. He intended to backhand a shot that would jump over the tree root and carry the steep bank to the green. He'd also have to clear the stone retaining wall. Crazy. A number of responsible, caddy-like suggestions filled O'Donnell's head. He settled for the obvious: "Don't do it, Flash. You have this thing wrapped up."

Flash continued practicing. O'Donnell felt like that sidekick in *Don Quixote*, the book he'd read for the freshman humanities course. Well, he'd only read a few of chapters, but that wasn't the point.

Several spectators rushed down for a closer look. Others, up near the green, craned their necks and murmured about the possibilities for such a difficult shot. All waited for Flash to give it a go. His club head jerked up, and Flash pulled it back down toward the ball at a steep angle. He caught the ball solid, and it leapfrogged high into the air, ascending to the green. As it reached the peak of its remarkable flight, another gust of wind funneled down from the ridge behind the green. The ball wavered and plunged, striking the retaining wall stones again and rebounding back to a few feet from where it once rested at the bottom of the hill. The spectators emitted a collective sigh of regret. Their hopes for an amazing shot scuttled by the unruly breezes.

Flash held his arms out in a gesture of "What can I say?" The elderly black gentleman and Deloris applauded his effort, and the gallery joined in. But O'Donnell noticed several among the crowd cackling and taunting. Flash hadn't won over all the spectators with his swashbuckling style.

"Okay, " Flash said, clapping O'Donnell on the shoulder, "it's back to business now. Hand me the wedge."

He opened the blade wide, took a long easy swing, and this time lofted the ball high into the air over the offending stonewall barrier. Yells and applause from the spectators by the green foretold Flash had dropped his shot close to the flagstick. He marched up the hill.

As O'Donnell's slipped Flash's wedge back into the golf bag and moved to join the parade, Bobby Borgstrom grabbed hold of his elbow.

"Give me a second here," Bobby said in a confidential tone.

For such a huge lug, Bobby had kept himself hidden from view for most of the day, wandering through the trees bordering most of the fairways and staying at the back of the gallery. In the excitement, O'Donnell had lost track of him for a couple of holes.

Bobby backed off a couple of steps into the shade of the oak tree that had blocked Flash's shot. "Just a feeling, but I think we may see some trouble soon," Bobby said. "I'll keep an eye on your left flank on eighteen and scope out the crowd at the green." He retreated further into the trees. "Keep heads up, Johnny," Bobby called softly, and made his way further into the shadows.

O'Donnell hustled after Flash, who'd already marked his ball on the green, and stood chatting with a couple of spectators. He had a good chance for bogey, with a no frills, six-foot putt to navigate. O'Donnell scanned the crowd, looking for anything unusual. They all looked like normal

Minnesotans. No axe murderers or crazed rednecks. A fat woman in a tight pair of baby-blue shorts, with pink, sunburned arms, looked a bit out of sorts, but O'Donnell doubted she had it in mind to blubber Flash to death. He wondered if Bobby had taken his reconnaissance role too much to heart.

Most everyone seemed pleased as Flash drained his putt for a bogey. After House and Bahn cleaned up their putts, the spectators rushed to the eighteenth tee to watch the drives.

"Nice going," O'Donnell said to Flash. "Forget I ever questioned your judgment."

Bahn, who'd earned the honors with a rare par, configured his tee in the grass and prepared to hit. He slapped a nice drive up to the bend of the dogleg. House was next on the tee box.

Flash whispered, "Think about Jackie Robinson. He can't play ball without stealing home and sliding in hard. It's his natural game."

O'Donnell had to agree.

"So why should I be any different?" Flash said, moving forward to tee his ball.

"So why not drive over the dogleg then?"

"Now you've got it, man."

Flash took a couple of exaggerated warm-up swings, exciting more commentary and stir among the spectators. As he set-up, aiming at a cluster of tall pines guarding the right corner of the dogleg, a murmur of anticipation drifted through the crowd. Flash took a wide, slow backswing, shifting his body direction while still pushing the club toward the top of its arc. He pulled the club head down hard and fast through the ball.

"*Whoa!*" a voice behind O'Donnell declared as the ball skyrocketed away.

"It's going to clear," yelled someone from the other side of the tee.

"Easy," Flash declared for all to hear, walking ahead, confident he'd cleared the danger. Everyone else stayed put, watching the ball streak towards the treetops that stood guard at the top of the hill. Soaring over the pines by a wide margin, the ball plunged to earth, bouncing to a resting place on the upper fairway.

"Let's go, caddy," Flash said. "Time to finish this round."

The gallery jostled O'Donnell to get going as they clapped and cheered what they'd witnessed. Some shook their heads back and forth, staring into the distance.

Anti-climatic, of course, but Flash drilled a nine-iron to within two feet of a back pin placement. Even O'Donnell could sink the putt necessary for a birdie and a first place finish in the qualifying round. As Flash took the victory path up the fairway to the eighteenth green, O'Donnell estimated the crowd around the green and spilling out on the borders of the fairway had grown to two or three hundred people. Most seemed excited and favorable to Flash's impending victory, but once more, groups clumped in the margins of the crowd stared as Flash approached, their eyes hard with disapproval.

In the distance, a kitchen crew of two black women cooks and a young busboy, jumped up and down waving their arms in salute. A tall waitress, dressed in her blue uniform and white cap, stood a little to the side, observing their antics.

O'Donnell glanced at the tables where Jill and Hoffman had been earlier in the day. He expected they'd left by now.

Flash kneeled behind his ball to survey the short distance his putt would travel. He went through all the motions with the dinky putt, playing the drama of the moment with the crowd. O'Donnell checked to see if Bobby was among those watching the final putt. He wasn't visible in the group of spectators closest to the green.

At the moment Flash chose to tap in his winning putt, a woman's voice bawled out behind the green, near the clubhouse.

"Let me go."

Most of the crowd turned in the direction of the shouting and caught a glimpse of Bobby grabbing hold of the waitress. Head down, the waitress fought against Bobby's grip on her wrist, beating at his chest with her free hand, screaming at him to let go of her. Bobby maneuvered her away from the onlookers toward the side of the clubhouse building, allowing a brief but recognizable view of the struggling woman.

O'DONNELL PUSHED HIS WAY through the spectators who seemed divided on whether to watch Flash win the tournament or check out the ruckus behind them. A tournament official solved their dilemma by yelling at the spectators to stand in place while the players finished. Good Minnesotans all . . . they turned around.

Bobby and Gloria moved their one-sided wrestling match to the parking lot. By the time O'Donnell caught up with the belligerents, Gloria was still squirming and mouthing some pretty nasty stuff at Bobby. He looked frazzled. O'Donnell's friend had little or no training for this sort of combat situation.

"Just relax, Gloria," O'Donnell said. Gloria gave him a furious glance and called Bobby something that made both men wince—an epithet O'Donnell was certain no self-respecting classicist would use in an academic treatise on Oedipus.

"Get her purse, Johnny, and take a look," Bobby grunted, parrying Gloria's attempts to bash him over the head with it.

Gloria eyes scanned wildly back and forth, shaking her head in disbelief. "Are you two crazy? What are you thinking?" She stopped struggling, pushing away to arm's length from Bobby. "God . . . you creeps. All I wanted to do was see him play golf. I didn't want to leave town without knowing if he'd win."

"You sure that's all, Gloria," Bobby said, still holding her wrist.

"Here, Johnny. Look in my purse. You won't find a machine gun." O'Donnell took her purse and opened it. No weapons. Only a wallet, some loose change, bobby pins, and the usual bunch of crap women lug around.

Gloria pulled out of Bobby's wristlock and glared at him, angry as hell. Bobby tried to ignore Gloria, but she nailed him with a swift kick to the shinbone. Bobby yowled and hopped backward, groping at his injured leg. Gloria and O'Donnell watched him struggle for his balance.

"You ass," she said to Bobby, smiling with satisfaction at his discomfort.

O'Donnell stepped between the two, holding Gloria by her shoulders, forcing her to look into his eyes. "Gloria, we were trying to protect Flash. What are we supposed to think when you show up masquerading in a waitress outfit?"

Gloria peeked around O'Donnell at Bobby. "You ass," she repeated, but this time she said it with a hint of a smile. Bobby rubbed his shin, wearing his best hangdog look.

"I didn't want Flash to know I was watching him." Gloria frowned, and twisted out of O'Donnell's hold. She stared off toward the golf course. "He's got such an ego. He acts so nice, but loves having women chase after him all the time. I didn't want him to know I cared about his winning this stupid golf tournament." She kicked at the gravel surface of the parking lot.

"My Uncle Morris works here in the restaurant." She hesitated, looking off to the side, her breathing ragged. "He said I could borrow the uniform and watch from the back porch. I couldn't see, so I tried to mix in with the crowd. Then Monster Boy grabbed me.

"You scared the hell out of me," she hissed at Bobby. "Then you drag me away like some damn hunter with his prey." She dug her nails into O'Donnell's arm. "Did he know it was me?"

"Flash?"

"*No* . . . Mr. Muscles here," Gloria said, making a face. "Did Flash know?"

"No," O'Donnell lied. "But let's get you out of here before he does find out."

Gloria nodded in agreement.

"Did you drive?" O'Donnell asked.

She'd parked near the back of the lot. As O'Donnell escorted her there, Bobby called out an apology. Gloria waved him off as she unlocked the car. "I need some distance from Flash and everything that's happened. I can't get the other night out of my head yet. I need some time. I made such a mess of things."

"It's not that bad, Gloria."

"I'll be okay" Gloria slipped her arm around O'Donnell's waist. "You can be such a fool, Johnny. Don't you know anything?"

"What are you saying Gloria?"

"Forget it," she said, climbing into the driver's seat of her car. Gloria rolled down the window, looking at O'Donnell with concern . . . as if trying to decide something. She opened the door again and stepped out of the car. "Flash is a wonderful person in so many ways. God knows he has my heart."

"What is this all about, Gloria? Tell me what you're thinking." Fragmentary and abbreviated images flickered out of focus in O'Donnell's mind's eye, like a high speed, non-stop string of movie previews.

"Forget I said anything," she shrugged, and offered another quick hug.

She slid into the car and without another word backed out of her parking spot. O'Donnell watched her car coast down the hill toward the main road. He didn't imagine he'd ever see her again. She'd crossed a bridge in her life, and wouldn't be crossing back.

O'Donnell walked between parked cars towards the clubhouse. Bobby waited on the edge of a crowd gathered outside on the practice green. Flash talked with a couple of reporters. His arm dangled over Deloris's shoulder. The scoreboard behind him indicated the triumph of his qualifying round. He now had a chance to grab the big prize . . . The St. Paul Open Championship.

"Are we watching a little piece of history in the making here?" Bobby asked.

O'Donnell thought so. But it wouldn't be easily written.

F lash and the gang of reporters set up camp by the bar. He was riding high from what O'Donnell could tell, busy talking a blue streak, and happy to accept drinks from a crowd of admirers clustered around the end of the bar.

O'Donnell took a couple of beers from a cooler the bartender had forgotten to guard and passed one to Bobby before they waded through the other drinkers to where Flash held court. He beamed at their approach, directing the reporters and the hangers-on to make way. Jerry Dale, a sportswriter O'Donnell knew from the St. Paul *Pioneer Press*, jostled near. "Hey, O'Donnell, how'd it feel to caddy for your buddy today?"

Sportswriters always managed to ask at least one dumb question in an interview, O'Donnell had long since concluded. Jerry had used up his allotment, and O'Donnell gave him his dumb interview question stare.

"You haven't changed a bit, have you?" Dale groused. O'Donnell guessed he hadn't.

"Now, Johnny, be nice to our journalists," Flash said, now holding aloft a hefty shot of whiskey. Courtesy of some newfound fans, another shot and a beer waited on the bar surface in front of him. The star of the qualifying round tugged at the front of O'Donnell's shirt as he approached, pulling him into the noisy group.

"You all know Johnny O'Donnell, of course." Flash clapped O'Donnell's shoulder like a father showing off his eighth-grader. "Looks like he'll be back in a Saints uniform soon, so I might need to find another caddie."

O'Donnell grabbed an extra bottle of Hamm's the bartender had brought over. He figured Flash didn't need all the free beers, and he was too busy yakking to notice. A beefy guy, with a red flush spreading across his cheeks gave O'Donnell a half-lidded, evil eye for sneaking the beer.

O'Donnell slipped out of the crowd and sat down at a table near the fireplace. At the bar, Bobby snared another one of the beers Flash's admirers had provided, plus a handful of peanuts from a large bowl on the bar. "Flash says to meet him over at the 427 Club." Bobby popped the whole load of peanuts into his mouth. "The lovely Deloris is going to join us."

On the wall behind the bar, a clock with red neon hands hung over a collection of scotch and whiskey bottles stacked on glass shelves for display. The clock read 2:00 p.m.

"A little soon to start a party, isn't it?" O'Donnell asked.

"Not for me. Ellen's still at her mother's in Rochester for a few days. I'm a free man." Bobby sucked down the remains of his beer and looked at the bottle like it had a hole in the bottom.

"You go ahead," O'Donnell said. "I'm going to go home and relax. I'll meet you around six at the club, okay?"

O'Donnell wanted some time alone. Throwing down beers all afternoon at the 427 Club didn't seem to match that end very well. Besides, he'd decided to call Abby about another night together.

O'DONNELL MADE A STOP at "Manny's Lakeside Groceries" on the way home. Manny had an outdoor stand set up on nice days, and he offered a good selection of fresh produce from the small farms nearby. O'Donnell bought a can of tuna, celery, a red onion, and some bib lettuce. He found a nice jar of homemade pickles, some farm fresh eggs, and another loaf of Wonder Bread. Tuna sandwiches, anyone? He hadn't eaten anything but pastries, candy bars, and peanuts all day.

Cosmo watched with great interest as O'Donnell prepared his special tuna sandwich recipe. The dog didn't much care for the smell of the canned tuna, but he'd eat it if any dropped on the floor. He liked eggs, and recognized them even in their natural covering. O'Donnell placed a few into a pot of boiling water. The saliva ran down Cosmo's chin, and he wagged his tail round and round—a sure sign of Epicurean intent. He had to be dragged out of the kitchen to sit on the porch while the eggs hard-boiled.

Later, O'Donnell ate his tuna sandwich and munched carrots on the porch steps. Cosmo lay close by, alert for any crumbs. O'Donnell allowed him the last bite of each half of the sandwich. The dog snuggled close, happy to be a companion.

A phone call to Abby didn't promise the same outcome. She sounded a bit distant . . . pre-occupied. She couldn't meet O'Donnell at the 427 Club. When she asked him about the morning's golf match, he gave her the play-by-play. She listened carefully about the incident with Gloria. O'Donnell asked her again about getting together.

"I don't know yet." Her voice had a serious tone. "I saw Daddy at lunch, and something's made him all melancholy. I want to see if I can cheer him up a little."

"I think your father and Flash had a falling out about something."

"Tell me what you know. He's awfully sad."

"They had a pretty heated conversation before the golf started, and your father stormed off the course. Flash said they'd cancelled their agreement."

O'Donnell wasn't sure he wanted to tell her more. Abby might find out what her father knew, but O'Donnell didn't feel right about revealing what exactly he'd overheard. If he could get Hoffman alone, O'Donnell would sure as hell find out the rest of the story.

"Talk to your father. It'll be okay" O'Donnell said, but wasn't ready to guarantee that outcome.

"Call me tomorrow?" Abby asked.

"You bet." O'Donnell employed the classic, ironclad Minnesota pledge.

He climbed into a pair of swim trunks, and wandered out to the lawn chair—a beat-up wooden slat contraption that should have been firewood long ago. O'Donnell mulled over the morning's events. Clancy had made his move, and it hadn't worked. All he'd succeeded in doing was to cut the bond between Flash and Gustafson. If Flash won the Open, he'd have enough people on his side in the community to make his own fight against the PGA.

Maybe Flash knew that all along? Anyway, it seemed that Clancy had pretty much played his hand. It was Hoffman who bothered O'Donnell . . . a wild card in the deck. He couldn't believe Jill hanging around with that fool again. What was she thinking? Why did he care?

50

THE CROWD AT THE 427 CLUB split between those at the bar and those sitting at tables near the front windows. Chuck maintained his usual station where he uncapped beers and poured shots in rapid order. He looked pleased with the business. He held out a bottle of Hamm's for O'Donnell, craning it above the head of a patron sitting at the bar. The guy didn't seem to mind the foam dripping down on his shoulder.

"Come on over and join the big winner's table here," Flash yelled at O'Donnell from across the room where he sat with Bobby Borgstrom. Both men wore witless smiles on their faces, and beer bottles littered the table in front of them. O'Donnell noticed they hadn't slowed down much from before. Bobby looked the better of the two. He could put it away for hours and still walk a straight line.

"So, what's on Chuck's menu this evening?" O'Donnell was hungry again.

"What's he always have?" Bobby regarded O'Donnell like he'd walked in from somewhere in Iowa. "He makes hamburgers, cole slaw, and french fries. Saturdays he makes chili. If you're lucky he has pickles to go with the hamburgers. Sometime in the next thousand years, he might learn how to cook something else or find a dessert he could make." Bobby drank some beer, daring anyone to argue his point.

"Sorry I asked," O'Donnell said. "So, let's go over to O'Gara's."

"I can vote for that," Flash said, slurring his words a trifle as he pushed away from the table. He wobbled as he stood, working to keep his balance.

"You guys order a drink on me." Flash said. "I need to make a phone call." He set sail for his destination, listing slightly to the leeward side.

"How many has he had?" O'Donnell asked Bobby. "Looks like he's tried to keep up with you this afternoon."

"I think he's a couple ahead, but I'm gaining on him." With that, Bobby signaled Chuck to send over the waitress.

Flash returned and drifted toward the bar. He'd spotted Jerry Dale. Anxious to cut off any interviews, O'Donnell walked over to where the pair stood together in conversation.

"You ready to go to O'Gara's?" O'Donnell asked, with a quick nod hello in the reporter's direction. No reply, so O'Donnell pushed Flash lightly on the shoulder to get his attention. Flash tipped off-balance, and leaned for support on the reporter, spilling his beer on Dale's arm. O'Donnell ratcheted Flash around to face him, and steered the boozed golf ace a few steps away from the bar and the reporter. Flash stepped carefully, as if each shoe had been set in concrete blocks. He giggled at himself and his halting progress. "Whew, the Prince of Putts is stepping out."

"More like the Prince of Putz," O'Donnell said, and propped Flash against the side of a cigarette machine.

"Screw off, O'Donnell. I climbed a damn big mountain out there today."

"You did. It was quite a round of golf."

Flash wobbled toward the rack where Chuck kept his decaying assortment of pool cues. He sighted down one, trying to assess its worthiness for play. "This thing's more cocked up than me." He racked up the balls and sent the cue ball wide.

O'Donnell had to laugh as the ball ricocheted off the pool table, spun crazily across the floor, and rolled past a guy wobbling out of the men's room.

"Flash, you need to slow down and sober up. Why don't you come with Bobby and me . . . have something to eat."

Flash gave O'Donnell an odd look—trying hard to be less drunk than he was. "You're right. I'll meet you over at O'Gara's. Don't worry, I'll make it. I'm not that ploughed . . . just excited by today. Deloris has to do some

stuff over at Daddy's, and then she's going to call me. You guys go on."
He tilted his head back toward Jerry Dale. "Besides, I need to finish
talking with my faithful scribe."

●●●●●

MARVELOUS MARVEL, A FAVORITE among O'Gara's waitresses, always
bragged about never steering a customer wrong in two decades, so she
instructed O'Donnell on what he should order from the evening's menu.
She had the same prescription for Bobby. The two diners would have salads,
pork chops, baked potatoes, and what Marvel called the "mystery" vegetable.
She returned to the table about five minutes later with salads and a message.

"Honey, you've got a phone call," Marvel said, pouring French dressing
on O'Donnell's salad. "You can get it on the bar phone."

It was Deloris calling. She sounded rushed, very upset. "Flash was
supposed to come and pick me up at Daddy's. Is he there?"

O'Donnell glanced at the clock on the wall behind the bar. It read
7:05 pm.

"When he called me . . ." Deloris searched for the right words, "he
sounded like maybe he'd had too much to drink."

No kidding. A number of possibilities ticked through O'Donnell's
mind, not the least among them that Flash was still boozing at the 427
Club. But Deloris was a good kid, and O'Donnell didn't want to
disappoint her. "Hey, Deloris, I'll make a couple of calls. Don't worry, he
might be outside your door right now."

"No, he's not, Johnny. I'm looking out the damn window. You make
your calls, and I'll wait to hear from you."

O'Donnell started by dialing the 427 Club.

Chuck said that Flash had received a phone call about 10 minutes
after Bobby and O'Donnell cleared out of the 427. Flash left after that
call. Chuck said, "And Johnny . . . whatever that phone call was all about,
Flash didn't like it one bit."

Chuck continued with his theory that bartenders could always
understand what their clients were feeling. O'Donnell tried to cut him

off, but got a minute anyway on bartenders' extra-sensory perceptions. When he succeeded in interrupting the liquor industry's link to a larger world of spirits, O'Donnell asked Chuck if he knew anything that would help point to Flash's whereabouts.

"Whereabouts?" Chuck thought about that for a few seconds. "That sounds like some corny detective novel, Johnny."

"It means, where do you think he might have gone?"

"Am I supposed to say that I don't have a 'clue'?"

O'Donnell hung up before Chuck could extend the conversation, called Flash's apartment. No answer. Was the phone fixed? When he dialed again . . . a busy signal. O'Donnell waited a few minutes. Same thing.

"Anything wrong?" Bobby asked when O'Donnell returned to their booth.

"I'm not sure."

"Come on, Johnny, not much to worry about. He's a big boy. Let's eat dinner."

O'Donnell worried if Flash decided to go pick up Deloris, he might get in a wreck or the cops might grab him. Flash didn't need any more trouble. Neither did O'Donnell.

"I'd better go check on him, Bobby. I don't want him out driving around if he's bad off. I'll be back as soon as I see how he is."

"What should I do with your dinner?"

"Tell Marvel to keep it warm for me." But O'Donnell guessed that wasn't what Bobby had in mind. "Call Deloris and tell her I'm going over to check on Flash."

Bobby nodded as O'Donnell wrote out Deloris number on a napkin. He then speared O'Donnell's baked potato with his fork.

O'DONNELL WALKED OUT of O'Gara's smack into the middle of a driving thunderstorm—the kind of fast moving summer weather Minnesota residents knew all too well. The rain pelted down, blown crazy sideways by gusting winds. O'Donnell raced across the parking lot, keeping his eye on a long, jagged flash of lightning that sizzled along the tops of the telephone phone lines. The lightning flash, followed instantly by rolling tympani of thunder, lit up the slick, rain-drenched pavement of O'Gara's parking lot.

O'Donnell ducked into his car to start it, but the engine refused to obey orders from the ignition. Every hard rain his car would balk at starting. He flooded the engine most times, and ended up hoping for an automotive miracle. This time, he managed to talk himself out of his usual "give 'er another try." O'Donnell kept his fingers away from the starter, determined to wait at least three minutes. He huddled in the car seat as the rain pounded against the windshield.

He figured the storm must have blown out the electrical power at the substation. A few slowly moving auto headlights provided the only light on Snelling Avenue. No street lamps. No house lights. No neon signs. O'Donnell pictured the gang in O'Gara's groping around by candlelight. At least they were dry and warm.

He pressed the accelerator pedal to the floor once, and let it all the way up. Next, he depressed the clutch, pressed the starter, gave it a tiny bit of choke, and yelled at the engine to work. A few fitful coughs, two chugs, and . . . success. He kept a steady pressure on the gas until the engine ran smooth. He flipped the car into gear and turned out of the parking lot. His wet clothes and soaking feet left him cold and uncomfortable. He turned on the defroster.

The storm hadn't let up one iota by the time O'Donnell pulled up at Flash's apartment. Once he turned off the ignition and doused the headlights, darkness ruled the neighborhood. Once inside the front entrance, O'Donnell felt along adjoining wall and flicked at the light switch. That proved a wasted effort. It would be blind man's bluff up the staircase and down the hall to Flash's apartment. He moved along the lower hallway, past Mrs. Hedstrom's door. Didn't hear anything from inside. Maybe she'd gone to visit her sister. Up one flight of stairs he went, gripping the wooden banister all the way. At the top of the staircase, he paused and placed a hand on the wall to get his bearings. The situation reminded him all too much of a few days ago when he'd found Flash beaten in the same apartment.

A few halting steps later O'Donnell could hear muffled voices sounding inside. He rapped his knuckles lightly on the wood. "Flash? You in there?"

No answer, but O'Donnell could make out the scrape of furniture and urgent whispering.

The door opened a crack.

O'Donnell could make out the outline of Flash's body backlit by a candle flickering on the end table. His voice sounded unsteady, and he reeked of booze. "What the hell are you doing here?"

"Deloris called when you didn't show up at O'Gara's," O'Donnell told him, looking past Flash's shoulder into the darkened room beyond. "She's worried about you. I told her I'd come by and see what's up."

Flash said, "I got back here from the bar and passed out on the couch, man. I'm fried."

O'Donnell stepped closer, trying to get a better look into the apartment. Flash shifted, trying to cut off any view.

"Thanks for checking up on me," Flash said. "Go on back to O'Gara's. I'll call Deloris and see if she's still up for it."

"Go ahead and call. I'll wait and give you a ride. You probably shouldn't be driving." Playing the pest didn't suit O'Donnell, but he wanted to make things difficult for Deloris's sake.

The electricity surged back on all of a sudden, flooding the living room with light, revealing a woman in Flash's living room. She sat crumpled forward, sobbing. She pushed her hair back from her face, looking up at O'Donnell with tear-filled eyes he knew all too well.

"Johnny . . . " she whimpered, gasping for breath, the tears streaking her cheeks.

Flash stepped back towards her. "Don't you pull that shit."

O'Donnell grabbed Flash by his shoulder and spun him away.

"What's going on here?" O'Donnell spit out the words. Anger coursing through him, he shoved Flash again, and in return, received a half-hearted defense. Flash's eyes were bloodshot and bleary, but he sidestepped O'Donnell's attempt to grab him.

"Stop, man." Flash plopped down on the couch, holding his hands up. He'd left his golf bag against the arm of the couch, and he steadied it from falling on the floor.

"I'm not getting into any fight with you, Johnny. Don't take all this the wrong way."

That unexpected response leeched some of the heat out of O'Donnell's anger, but his mind brimmed with unwanted images. O'Donnell felt like someone had whacked him square in the stomach. He couldn't swallow. He couldn't get his breath. He couldn't get the movie reel of the two out of his head.

Flash pounded the arm of the couch, and the golf bag tumbled to the floor. "It goes back a long way, Johnny . . . it's her idea of revenge."

"Don't believe him, Johnny," Jill wailed, her face blotched and reddened from crying. She moaned sadly, her body rocking in a strange dance.

"Tell him the truth, Jill." Flash said, his voice softer, comforting.

"Why didn't you come back?" Jill asked him, her voice far away. "I would have done anything to have you come back."

"What are you talking about?" Flash asked.

O'Donnell knew.

THE LIGHTS CUT OFF AGAIN. A loud roll of thunder rattled the apartment windows. Something rock-hard smashed at O'Donnell's left shoulder and sent him crashing forward. Flash broke his fall, but O'Donnell ended up on the floor next to the couch, the golf bag digging into his back.

The boys over at the electric company must have been tinkering with the right wires because the lights came on yet again. Flash's radio sputtered to life for some reason, and the voice of Marty O'Neill informed listeners the Saints had fallen behind in the away game at Toledo. But it was the business end of a gun held by wild-eyed Brad Hoffman that had O'Donnell's attention.

A strange, nasty smile locked on Hoffman's face, and he swiveled a gun between Flash and O'Donnell. He stepped back near where Jill sat on the floor, curled tightly into a frail shape.

"You bitch," he said, trying to lash at Jill with his free hand while keeping a watch on the others. She backed further into the corner, pulling the torn curtain around her body, as if it might shield her. Hoffman scored a glancing blow on the side of Jill's face. She screamed, but the storm outside made it a wasted effort. A sharp clap of thunder shook the windows to make the point.

"Scream all you want, you damned bitch. Nobody's going to hear you." Hoffman waved the gun in O'Donnell's and Flash's direction. "Nobody's going to hear me take care of these two boys, either." He stepped closer, his attention locked on Flash.

O'Donnell shifted his position on the floor, shielding Flash's golf bag with his body. He reached behind to the ball pouch and inched the zipper open.

Flash recognized the play, and tried to buy some time. "Why didn't you kill me when you broke in here before?"

"That wasn't me," Hoffman said in an angry rush, jerking the gun momentarily in O'Donnell's direction. "I was busy with this son of a bitch."

Hoffman leaned down, his rage focused on Flash. O'Donnell watched the hammer of the gun moving back . . . cocking. Hoffman waited for a reaction from Flash, taunting him.

As the storm raged without a second's pause, rain pummeling down and rolls of heavy thunder unceasing, Jill created an unexpected opportunity. She'd crept forward on her knees from behind Hoffman. He couldn't sense Jill coming at him. She grabbed his gun arm, yanking it down with all her strength.

Hoffman struggled to keep his balance and push Jill away at the same time. She clung to his wrist, bending him down, off-balance. He couldn't raise his gun to fire.

O'Donnell came off the deck at that instant, slamming his fist into the side of Hoffman's face. Solid contact. Hoffman crumbled at the knees. Jill gave a last, violent pull on her ex-husband's wrist. He fell and crashed headfirst into the wall, his weapon clattering to the floor as his skull met an unyielding oak paneling.

The flash from a bolt of lightning over-powered the synthetic light, and every corner of the room filled with a brilliant whiteness. Jill knelt on the floor. Her face and hair smeared with blood. Her scream caught silent in the crash of rain and thunder outside.

O'Donnell didn't figure Hoffman would be doing much damage or anything for a long time.

FLASH PUT A HAND on O'Donnell's shoulder. "Sweet Jesus. I thought we'd had it."

"Is he dead?" Jill stared at the body now lying next to her.

"Close enough," Flash said. He kneeled over Hoffman's body. "I've seen a hundred just like him. He's fine. Just like you were, O'Donnell. Remember?"

O'Donnell remembered. He knew that the man on the floor wouldn't be moving anytime in the near future.

Jill started shaking. Too scared to cry anymore. O'Donnell helped her to the couch. She dug her fingers into O'Donnell's upper arm, like a child waking from a horrible nightmare.

"We need something good for the cops," Flash said.

O'Donnell couldn't help but think—once more around the Mulberry bush.

Jill stared at Flash, confused as to what he said. O'Donnell had few doubts about how she still felt about Flash. Parts of the story she'd told O'Donnell the night at the lake floated back.

"Jill, listen to me." Flash knelt in front of Jill, like someone explaining something to a little kid. "We are all in trouble here. What we tell the cops about tonight can't include anything about you and me. Do you understand?"

She nodded.

Flash continued talking in a low, earnest voice. He placed his fingers gently under her chin, turning her face to him. "If the cops find out anything about the two of us, it won't be good at all—especially for someone like me."

Jill shoved his hand away, angry now, and her cheeks flushed. "Don't talk like that. Don't say that."

"Listen. Damn it." Flash said. "Too many people are going to suffer in all this mess if we tell the whole truth. Mostly, it's my ass on the line. I'm the outsider around these parts. This jealous, damn fool tried to kill me. That's me . . . not you two. I've got a right to decide how this ends."

"Johnny, please," Jill pleaded.

"None of us asked for it to happen," Flash said to O'Donnell, following up Jill's cue. "If one piece of the whole story is still missing, so what? We're going to say Hoffman was after you, Johnny . . . because of Jill. Hoffman was in a jealous rage about it. Right? Jill can play that up to the cops. No one is going to believe what that fool might say. The jealous husband. Right?"

O'Donnell knew Flash had written himself out of the scene. *What was the truth?* It would ruin Flash; it would ruin Jill. That didn't seem right to O'Donnell. Maybe not "right" in a legal sense, but lately . . . he found it hard to see much that happened in life neatly divided into rights and wrongs. The war had changed all that. The straight and narrow path wasn't easy to find. O'Donnell knew that he and Jill would play a game of make-believe for the cops and everyone else. At least Jill had lots of practice at it.

"I'll do what you say," Jill promised, gripping Flash's hand. "I'll say that Johnny and I met for a date . . . that he needed to stop by here to tell you something." She hesitated, working hard on a story. She seemed excited about the chance to write it. O'Donnell didn't feel like he knew her at all.

A soft moan came from the man lying on the floor. Flash checked on Hoffman again, placing one of the sofa pillows under the injured man's head. Hoffman lay still again. Normal breathing; no outward signs of distress. Lullaby lane.

The three conspirators worked out the small details of their story. O'Donnell conceded it was close enough to the truth again to make it an easy one to tell. He thought it might stand up against any theories Ikola might stumble on. The detective didn't have any direct proof about Jill and Flash. Mr. Gustafson sure as hell wouldn't go public with that particular tidbit. After what O'Donnell saw and heard at the golf course, he didn't think the doting father, respected lawyer, and budding politician would be volunteering a thing. Anything the man lying on the floor might say would only be the word of a highly suspect someone, soon to be corralled for attempted murderer—not to mention being a drunk, a gambler, and a jealous fool.

"Does anyone else know anything?" A sliver of doubt remained for O'Donnell. Was Clancy a possible wildcard?

"Nobody knows who would say anything, right?" Flash looked to Jill for her confirmation.

"No one," Jill said. "Daddy will keep things tight in the family if he must."

Flash and Jill agreed their secret relationship had been well kept. O'Donnell wasn't completely confident, but they'd sure had him fooled. He tried to let that ride, wanting nothing more that moment than to get as far away as possible from the troubles they all faced. Fond hope. The three would be tied to one another for a lifetime by a tangle of lies woven by strange necessities.

Flash checked the phone line. He nodded his head, his mouth set in a grim line. "I'm going to make the police call. Before I do that," Flash looked at Jill, "you've got to quick talk with your old man. We're going to need him to help out."

He passed the phone to Jill. She recoiled from it like he'd offered her a handful of snakes. All the fears she carried at that moment marked her expression. O'Donnell couldn't see how she'd make any sense in a call to her father.

"I can't. I can't do it." Jill pulled her legs under her and moved away from Flash and the phone he held. Flash placed it next to her on the couch.

"I'll dial the number," he told her.

She stiffened, but reached out and took the receiver to her ear, her hand trembling. O'Donnell listened to Jill make a tearful, anxious call to her father. When she completed her assignment, Jill collapsed back into the sofa cushions, eyes blank, lost in her thoughts.

"Is he with us?" Flash clasped Jill's shoulder, trying to gain her attention.

"Yes, damn you." Jill made a crying sound, twisting away from Flash and to her feet. She left the room quickly. Flash motioned for O'Donnell to keep her company.

"My turn on stage." Flash retrieved the phone. "Time to call our good friends at the St. Paul Police. It'll take a while to get here in this storm. They probably have a lot of things on their plate tonight."

Hoffman moaned again softly. He turned slightly to his side. Resting peacefully, it seemed.

O'Donnell felt bone-tired. All he had to look forward to was another round of telling half-truths and lies at the St. Paul Police Station. If he ever played for the Saints again, the team would probably sell a ton of tickets to thrill-seekers. O'Donnell could imagine the pre-game headlines: "Saints Pitcher Aims to Shoot Down Toledo." The future never looked brighter.

He found Jill sitting at the kitchen table, dabbing at her nose with a corner of a towel. She brought out a compact from her purse, and began to apply her make-up. She didn't have a mirror, but seemed to know where everything went without one. Satisfied she'd done what she could under the circumstances, Jill snapped the compact lid closed, and slipped it back into her purse. After a second thought, she fished out a lipstick tube and spread it on. After a deep breath, she looked in O'Donnell's direction.

"I'm so very sorry about what I did to cause all this trouble." Jill averted her eyes when O'Donnell looked at her. Her finger traced imaginary circles on the table surface.

"Being in love with him has caused me to do some awful things . . . stupid things. I didn't want it to end so horribly. But I couldn't stop."

She spoke as if each word would open a wound. "I used you in the most shameless way, Johnny. I was so frantic, and I wanted to hurt Flash."

"Is that what you did with Brad?"

"Yes," she said, and let her breath out in a slow sigh. "I had no idea he would carry things so far."

She reached out and clutched at O'Donnell's arm. "It's the last thing I would have wanted. I can't believe he'd go so far." Her eyes focused in an understanding of something. "God, he must have felt like . . ." She didn't finish her thought, and buried her face in her hands.

Jill leaned toward the kitchen window next to her. The storm had relaxed to a gentle shower, and Jill pushed the window up several notches, breathing deep of the rain-freshened lawns outside. O'Donnell could hear Flash speaking on the phone again. He was calling Deloris.

O'Donnell joined Flash to wait in the living room for the cops to come. Every so often, Flash would look down at Hoffman on his apartment floor and mouth a swear word. O'Donnell couldn't help but agree. He phoned O'Gara's, hoping Bobby had stayed late at the bar. He had done so, and O'Donnell gave him a brief warning about what had happened.

Detectives Ikola and McGee, accompanied by a St. Paul police officer, stormed into the apartment building within fifteen minutes of Flash's phone call. O'Donnell knew they meant business. Jill's father, and one of the younger members of his law firm, joined the party five minutes later. The ambulance team arrived shortly thereafter to complete the guest list. They checked Hoffman and loaded him on a stretcher. He still had nothing to say.

54

THE KID LEFTHANDER had run out of gas. For seven innings he'd thrown his heart out, but ran deep into almost every count and whacked three batters pretty solid with stray fastballs. Still, he'd held the Aberdeen team to a handful of hits, and the home team infielders had turned a couple of double plays to checkmate any big innings. The Eau Claire nine led by one run, but Aberdeen had filled the bases. O'Donnell had spent the last two innings warming up in a ramshackle bullpen down the third base line.

O'Donnell would take throwing warm-up pitches to sitting on the rock hard bullpen bench any day. The bullpen also hosted some of the meanest looking insect critters he'd ever seen. He and his bullpen mates crunched roaches and huge spiders by the dozens. The day before, a five-foot black snake glided out from under the water barrel and oozed down the length of the bullpen bench. Guys scrambled into the stands to get out of its way. The umps had to stop the game while some farmer came down and chased the snake back to its hidey-hole. The bullpen crew spent the rest of the week sitting at the opposite end from the water barrel. The home team fans in Eau Claire had a ball with the incident, calling O'Donnell and the other relief pitchers the "city slickers." Some of the faithful took to dropping off glass jars filled with baby garter snakes.

A conference on the mound between the manager and the young pitcher drew O'Donnell's attention. He knew the boy wonder would be heading for his shower sooner than later. The Skipper would signal it was time for O'Donnell to come in and make things right. *Yep.* Time to raise the curtain on another late inning drama, starring Johnny O'Donnell— the sidewinding, golden armed, right-handed twirler—darling of the St. Paul Police Department.

"Time to roll, Johnny. Go save the day." The bullpen coach pushed open the gate, and clapped O'Donnell on the back, sending him towards his latest relief appearance for the Eau Claire minor league nine.

O'Donnell strolled toward the mound at the Municipal Field, snugging his cap low, ready to throw strikes. Out here, he was just the strange-throwing relief pitcher from the Twin Cities and the new boarder at Miss Lilly Stinson's house on East Locust Street. The local reporter, who covered everything around town from sports to town council meetings to obituaries, hadn't a clue about O'Donnell's most recent adventures with the law. O'Donnell was that ex-minor leaguer making some sort of comeback, not the guy mixed up in dramatic events over there in St. Paul. He was the welcome newcomer who'd thrown ten scoreless innings since he'd joined the team two weeks ago.

A smattering of applause from the locals trickled down as O'Donnell arrived at the mound. The manager tossed him the baseball and ordered him to "throw strikes." Originality wasn't the manager's long suit. He'd spent the better part of his life in small towns managing kids and guys on their way out. He'd never go any higher and he knew it. He'd learned to keep it simple.

O'Donnell tossed warm-up pitches without any pain or stiffness. A couple of weeks after the showdown at Flash's apartment, O'Donnell had called the Saints. With all the stir about Butternut's demise and Brad Hoffman, the team's front office didn't dare sign O'Donnell to play in St. Paul, but agreed to find a contract for the rest of the season for him to pitch for the Eau Claire Bears, a Class C team in the Northern League. That sounded damn good to O'Donnell. After a few days, he'd closed up the cabin, packed a suitcase, and hit the highway. Cosmo went over to the Anderson's for the time he'd be gone. He didn't seem to mind that much. O'Donnell missed the silly mutt, though. Sometimes talking to a dog made as much sense as anything.

Aberdeen's first batter was much too anxious, digging in deep and white-knuckling his bat. O'Donnell threw him a change-up on the first pitch, and he went for it, topping a weak grounder down the first baseline. Eau Claire's first baseman handled it easy, tagging out the batter half way to the bag. The next two hitters lifted weak fly balls to left, so O'Donnell marched into the dugout to the applause of the fans and the stares of his teammates. O'Donnell guessed they still wondered how he managed to get anyone out with his hinky sidearm delivery. So far, it hadn't sunk into their young minds that throwing heat wasn't everything there was to good pitching. The Skipper had a different understanding, and gave O'Donnell a satisfied nod.

Leaning against one corner of the dugout, O'Donnell relaxed, allowing the sunshine that still remained to warm his bones. He felt easy for the first time since leaving St. Paul and all the mess there. Flash and he had ended up spending hours at the police station, waiting for Ikola and McGee to grill them about what happened. On the other hand, Jill's father had her out of there faster than lickety-split. As one of St. Paul's most respected attorneys, Gustafson's clout made a big difference in matters of justice. It helped that Jill played the hysterical female role like a Broadway star. O'Donnell could imagine her carrying on as her father railed against "Gestapo tactics" and how the cops were intimidating his "traumatized daughter." Jill gave a short statement to the city attorney, with her father and a chorus line of his law partners monitoring the proceedings. She left two days later on an extended trip to stay with relatives in New York City. She was still there. O'Donnell doubted she'd be back in St. Paul soon—maybe not for a very long time.

Ikola wanted to hold O'Donnell and Flash in jail, but Gustafson launched some snazzy legal moves on their behalf once he'd rescued his daughter. Extricating the pair from the clutches of the St. Paul Police made the best sense to Gustafson . . . no matter how much he hated doing so. The election season wasn't far off, and Gustafson wanted to be in the mix. The relationship between Flash and Jill remained a deeply buried secret.

Behind the scenes, Gustafson and his NAACP colleagues asked the mayor and the district attorney to pressure for Flash's release. The black newspapers in St. Paul and Minneapolis raised a hell of a stink on Flash's behalf, shaming the St. Paul *Pioneer Press* into a brief editorial about misguided justice. It all helped. In the end, Ikola didn't have anything concrete. O'Donnell thought the detective would have rather quit smoking cigarettes than turn anyone loose, but he had no choice. All he had left was a rather uncommunicative Brad Hoffman.

Hoffman had taken up residence in St. Joseph's hospital, gliding along in his own world, unable to regain full consciousness, his doctors reporting their patient had suffered a "severe traumatic brain injury" leading potentially to a condition called "retrograde amnesia." The news reporting about the incident cast him as the villain—a deranged and disreputable soul. Not far from the truth at all, O'Donnell thought.

By the time O'Donnell and Flash were free of questioning, the pros had already teed off at the St. Paul Open. Flash quietly left town, traveling to Chicago for an upcoming golf tournament there. The fans and the newspapers placed his St. Paul Open qualifying round victory in the old news bin. The galleries cheered on the likes of Sam Sneed and Jimmy Demaret, perhaps happy to forget the black golfer who'd caused such a stir.

O'DONNELL REMEMBERED HOW HE'D driven out to Keller Golf Course early on the day set for the final round of the St. Paul Open. He'd spent the hours after his release holed up with Cosmo at the cabin, waiting long enough, he hoped, not to attract unwanted recognition when he ventured out. Long before the big crowd showed up for the golf tournament's climax, those players out of contention would be teeing off early to finish their four days of competition. Some of the pros may not have done all that well in the St. Paul tournament, but they were still among the best in the business. O'Donnell wanted a chance to judge how well Flash would have faired against the tour players.

When O'Donnell showed up, it was raining a steady stream. Only a few cars claimed spaces in the parking lot. The grounds crew hustled about despite the rain, mowing fairways, tending to the greens, and doing their best in the hope that a late afternoon start might be possible. Looking for a cup of coffee, O'Donnell slipped into the clubhouse bar area.

Jack Clancy sat alone at the far end of the bar, wearing an amused smile. Maybe it was more like a smirk. O'Donnell wanted to keep walking, straight out the other door, but he needed answers.

"Ah . . . the dangerous Mr. O'Donnell. I so hoped to run into you. What luck."

"Right. You just happened to be in the neighborhood."

A guy O'Donnell assumed might be the bartender walked into the room from the kitchen, carrying a steaming mug of coffee. He looked like he'd be more at home in a heavyweight boxing ring than tending bar. O'Donnell asked him for some coffee. The bartender shot him a dirty look. O'Donnell put a hold on a request for cream and sugar.

Clancy pointed to the bar entrance. "Frankie, why don't you lock the door. We need some privacy here for a few minutes. Mr. O'Donnell and I have some things to talk over."

O'Donnell decided to float a trial balloon. "So, tell me," he asked, keeping his voice low. "Did Hoffman pay off what he owed you?" Jill had mentioned Hoffman's gambling debts, and that piece of information had stuck in O'Donnell's mind. He watched Clancy for a reaction, and the man rewarded him with a smug, winning smile.

"Yes, indeed, Johnny-boyo. Hoffman is paid up. But, gosh. That won't do him much good from what I hear." Clancy leaned into the padded back of his barstool, gently swirling the coffee in his mug. "Been doing some thinking, eh?"

O'Donnell didn't answer.

"How did you find out about the unfortunate Mr. Hoffman?" Clancy asked. "Professional inquisitiveness, if you will."

No doubt about it, O'Donnell thought. Clancy had used Hoffman. The conversation in the locker room made all the sense in the world. Hoffman setting out on his own to intimidate the father of the woman he so coveted made no sense. It should have been the last thing on his list of things to do. But Clancy had Hoffman over a barrel. Jill's former husband didn't have any choice but to deliver Clancy's threat. Hoffman's revelation about Flash and Jill had worked quite nicely. Her father had been shocked and angered to the core. Gustafson reacted as Clancy knew he probably would, rushing out to confront Flash on the golf course. O'Donnell could only imagine how much Clancy enjoyed humiliating someone like Gustafson. Driving a permanent wedge between Flash and Gustafson also would put a brake on any plans to end segregation in professional golf and create another civil rights hero in sports.

O'Donnell thought maybe it was his turn to twist the truth. "Hoffman had some secrets to tell us the other night, Jack. I guess he wanted to get a few things off his chest. Your boy had much to tell. A case of 'loose lips' like they warned us about back in the war. Too bad we couldn't use him to sink your ship."

"Yes, the young man often talked too much for his own good. But he won't be gabbing anymore if it can be helped. One never knows what he might say." Clancy pointed a finger at O'Donnell, "You would be well-advised to remember that I'm not fond of any loose ends."

"Gee. Thanks for the warning. Any more words of wisdom?"

"Bring me some coffee, Frankie," Clancy yelled out to the kitchen. "I need to stay awake for this entertaining moment."

Frankie, the obliging muscleman, appeared in a few seconds with a replacement mug of coffee. Clancy took a sip, scowled, and ordered Frankie back into the kitchen and to make a fresh pot. Clancy pushed his mug away, waiting for a better brew.

"So, to continue," Clancy said. "Hoffman often became quite chatty about intimate matters after a few drinks at the club. Of course, I lent a sympathetic ear, and the poor young fellow came to regard me as sort of a father figure. He'd fallen into a rather huge gambling debt to one of the local mobsters. Of course, you knew the late and lamented Butternut."

O'Donnell let Clancy go on. He wanted to brag . . . to show himself as the great mastermind. The man harbored, no doubt, a dangerous, confusing mix of motives that could bring on further damage. Was Clancy a taste of what the nation had become or . . . might go in the future? O'Donnell didn't know the answers.

"I shouldn't have assumed the debt for Hoffman, of course," Clancy continued. "If I had known what destiny had in store for Butternut, I could have saved myself a considerable cash outlay. Still, it all worked out nicely."

"So you had your hooks in Butternut, too?" O'Donnell asked. If only he had a witness for Clancy's disclosures.

Frankie reappeared at that moment with the fresh coffee. No friendly witness possibility there. The brawny flunky jumped at Clancy's every whim and lurked close by like a palace guard. He damn well knew what to hear and how to keep his mouth shut.

Clancy's gaze met O'Donnell's over the rim of his coffee mug. "I discovered soon enough how much Butternut liked to make money for himself, and how much he hated almost everything and everybody—

especially his own father. Butternut was no Communist, but he had a thug's mentality old Joe Stalin would have loved."

O'Donnell tapped his index finger on the bar to get Clancy's attention. "So you couldn't turn down the opportunity to run Butternut like one of your agents back in the good old days, could you?" O'Donnell wondered how many of those agents had ended up dead on account of Clancy's egotism.

Clancy wore the same expression O'Donnell's teachers had when students asked the right question—the one allowing them the chance to show off, to demonstrate how much more they knew. Clancy needed an audience, a cheering section. All his scheming and manipulating might be fun, O'Donnell reckoned, but not as much fun as when he could crow about his victories.

"I can't tell you how much I miss those days," Clancy said. He slapped the bar. "Right, Frankie?"

"Those were good years, Mr. Clancy."

Clancy dragged his coffee mug back and forth on the wood surface of the bar, lost for a moment in whatever memories he treasured. He asked O'Donnell, "Don't you miss it?"

"No." O'Donnell didn't have the answer Clancy wanted. "Why would I?"

Clancy continued staring into the distance. O'Donnell thought of him lingering still on some select moment in his past—like planning an undercover assassination or pulling the wings off insects as a kid.

"Of course, I didn't quite have to go to all the trouble I did for this operation," Clancy said. "I suspect the PGA would have stiff-armed Flash Dawkins and the other troublemakers, anyway."

He let out a loud stream of breath, holding his arms out in a gesture of deep self-appreciation. "But, alas, I needed a taste of the old times."

Clancy's mood shifted in a flash, and the jovial face changed to one that more suited his baseness. "Besides, it was a wonderful opportunity to give a rather profound mortification to a whole range of deserving parties. A 'black' eye, as it were. One must keep in mind the larger issues, as I've told you already. And yes. I must say. Butternut's proclivities could, theoretically, be used to good advantage. He wanted money, and he wanted out from under his father's heel. Revenge on his father—an ancient motive, eh? I supplied Butternut the opportunities he wanted."

Clancy rested his chin on his thumb and forefinger, favoring O'Donnell with an impish look. He looked like a depraved Wizard of Oz.

"You met the late Mr. Sanford of Chicago, didn't you?" Clancy asked.

"Late?"

"You haven't heard? I'm afraid the poor boy met with a bit of foul play in the Windy City. It's such a pity. Those Negro neighborhoods are so dangerous."

O'Donnell came off the barstool ready to put a twist in Clancy's fat neck. Sanford had proved a decent guy.

Clancy's stooge couldn't get out from behind the bar to help, but his boss already had a small revolver in hand, aimed at O'Donnell's chest. Clancy had been expecting fireworks—ahead of the game as usual. His jovial public face had vanished now, replaced with a cold glare. "Sit down, O'Donnell, maybe you'll learn something."

O'Donnell sat down.

"That's better." Clancy motioned for the bartender to stay near. He regarded the weapon in his hand with affection. "Tools of the trade," he said, grinning. "'Small, but deadly' . . . to borrow a phrase."

Over the next few minutes, Clancy took great pleasure in describing every detail of his local venture into anti-Communist, anti-Liberal, anti-civil rights undercover schemes. Butternut's hatred for his father and the lure of a payoff made him a willing, if unlikely partner, according to Clancy. It was Butternut, at Clancy's instigation, who'd called Marcus Sanford in Chicago. Butternut initially fooled Sanford into thinking that Daddy Wilkins wanted him for a cut-and-dried, strong-arm operation. Clancy knew all about Sanford's background. "J. Edgar's a good friend," he said, and winked at Frankie.

O'Donnell's anger remained at full tank. He worked hard to keep it in check. But in the back of his mind, he knew there wasn't much he could do. He wasn't going to forget, though.

"It was a neat setup," Clancy said. "The police would receive an anonymous phone tip, and Mr. Sanford would end up in the arms of the F.B.I. Flash Dawkins would be incapable of playing golf in the tournament. Sanford would be tied to Daddy Wilkins and the Communists, who'd in turn be blamed for subverting the dreams of your Negro friend and his backers." Clancy beamed at his stooge behind the bar. "*Whew.* So many puppets on a string."

"It was a neat package, sir," Frankie told his boss.

Clancy revealed that when Sanford refused to cooperate and play his role, the second team—Butternut and Hoffman—had to take over. The memory didn't sit well with Clancy. "Those two damn fools." Clancy studied the scratches on the bar surface before him, his mouth drawn in an angry line.

He hadn't accounted for human nature. Butternut and Hoffman had brought too many emotions to their assignments. Clancy couldn't control them, and that made him less gratified than he wished at the end of his game. Butternut and Hoffman had screwed things up. Spoiled a larger plan and its greater ends. The puppetmaster wanted much more.

Clancy allowed himself a brief flare of anger, slamming his palm down on the bar. His coffee mug slid to the edge of the counter and fell, crashing into the bar sink below. Clancy's muscleman made no move toward the mess. He watched O'Donnell like a hawk.

Clancy gave O'Donnell a brief sideways glance, allowing himself a minute to regain his composure. "Poor Hoffman," he said, playing up his phony remorse. "A young man in the throes of passion will do almost anything for love's object. He lost his bearings. A tragic end."

Clancy had pulled the strings, using Hoffman to do his dirty work one way or another. Things just got out of hand. Hoffman let his jealousy and desire for Jill overwhelm him. O'Donnell couldn't work up any sense of regret for the man's fate.

"At least the dear boy delivered the intelligence about Gustafson's daughter and her illicit affair." Clancy grinned in Frankie's direction. "I imagine Daddy Gustafson wasn't ready to see that sort of integration. What I wouldn't have given to see the man's face when Hoffman told him."

Clancy leaned back and regarded O'Donnell like an insect caught in a web. "How about you?" He couldn't keep a straight face. "Any new thoughts about integrating the races?"

Clancy broke into great, loud gasps of laughter. O'Donnell had provided the man with more than his share of amusement. Clancy caught his breath, but not long enough to say anything before his laughter echoed again in the room. At last, all he could do was wave O'Donnell away, pointing toward the door.

O'Donnell knew he looked pathetic, standing there in front of Clancy, like some panhandler on Washington Avenue. Any threats he might make now would be equally pathetic. For the time being, he couldn't do a thing.

"You miserable, stupid fool," Clancy said at last. "Go back to throwing baseballs. As they say . . . you're way out of your league here."

THE HOMETOWN EAU CLAIRE BEARS went down without a peep in the bottom half of the eighth inning. Like any relief pitcher, O'Donnell would have liked a couple of insurance runs. But damn it, he could hold a one-run lead. He was more than just a rally killer, right?

The first Aberdeen batter grounded out, and the next hitter swaggered into the batter's box. He hadn't heard about O'Donnell's dangerous past and laced a line drive right back up the middle. O'Donnell jerked his head aside just in time. The ball screamed by him and through the hole. It skidded past the Bear's centerfielder and bounced toward the "DeKalb Corn" sign painted on the wooden fence. By the time the second baseman's relay reached third base, the batter had arrived without even having to slide. The umpire called time, and O'Donnell hiked back to the mound and kicked some dirt around. He played with the resin bag, bouncing it off his forearm a couple of times, resolving to get his mind on the ball game.

Since he'd joined the team, O'Donnell kept pretty much to himself, thinking about what had happened. One thing that kept repeating through his mind was Flash. O'Donnell knew it could be more than jealousy swarming through his heart when he'd discovered Jill at Flash's apartment. O'Donnell didn't like where he'd landed. He didn't want to think like that.

Flash showed up at the cabin just before O'Donnell left for Eau Claire. He and O'Donnell sat on the porch and talked. Flash had played in a Chicago golf tournament—a first place finish—and he'd compete the rest of the year at various cities where they had a spot for Negro golfers. Joe Louis wanted him back in action as soon as possible. Flash assured O'Donnell he wasn't done with his challenge to the color line the

PGA had set in golf. "They dodged the bullet this time around, but there's always next year. I'll be more than ready for them. We'll see if Clancy and his buddies can stop me."

O'Donnell didn't doubt it. Flash already had promises of backing from all around the country. Shooting such a great score in the qualifying round for the St. Paul Open hadn't hurt. A host of Negro newspapers around the country planned articles on Flash and his fight against the PGA. Offers to play golf and speak to civil rights groups turned up every week. Maybe things would change for the better. Maybe he could beat the likes of Jack Clancy after all.

The two men didn't speak for a few minutes, each immersed in their own thoughts about what had happened. The night seemed exceptionally still. Even the ever-present loons had nothing to add. O'Donnell wanted to bridge the divide between himself and the man sitting next to him. He wondered if Flash felt the same—or even gave it a thought.

"Just move on, Johnny," Flash said. Nothing more added. No explanation for breaking the silence. He stared hard at the dark water of the lake.

"I don't expect I'll be moving on down the same road if I can help it."

"All you can do is try to make things different, Johnny."

A small boat with an outboard motor passed by not far from shore. Two men trailed fishing lines in the gentle wake that followed the boat. O'Donnell heard the clinking sound of someone reaching into a cooler for a couple of brews. One of fishing lines pulled taunt. A sizable fish surfaced and leapt above the water, whipping its body in a fierce attempt to free itself of the hook. O'Donnell and Flash heard a curse echo across the lake, the fisherman's line now slack.

Flash said, "That's what we have to do."

"What's that?"

"Keep on keeping on."

"Like that guy fishing?" O'Donnell gibed, trying to keep things light.

"You and that fish have a lot in common, O'Donnell."

"How so?"

"You're all wet."

● ● ● ● ●

THE NEXT ABERDEEN BATTER WALKED on four pitches, and the home crowd grew restless. O'Donnell could hear a few voices from the stands suggesting he pack his bags and head back to St. Paul. Such fickleness should never go unanswered, of course, so O'Donnell resolved to get himself out of the inning.

The cleanup hitter popped up to first on a sharp breaking curveball over the inside corner. He threw his bat in disgust and said something nasty to a group of fans yelling at him by the Aberdeen dugout. The crowd started up yelling and clapping for O'Donnell to finish off the threat. *Now they're on my side*, he thought.

The next hitter stepped into the batter's box, and spent a ridiculous amount of time digging in with his spikes. He backed out, took a couple of practice swings, and gave O'Donnell a tough-guy look. The umpire reminded the hitter he was playing in Eau Claire, not New York City. Adding to his embarrassment, he swung like an old lady at one of O'Donnell's change-ups, delivered out of the strike zone. The umpire pumped his right fist and bawled out "Strike"—emphasizing every syllable. The batter gave him an anguished look, and the ump said, "Just like the Big Leagues, huh?"

In the background to all the crowd noise, O'Donnell could make out the steady bark of a dog down the right field line. The batter fouled his next pitch, a fastball, over the small grandstand and out to the main street. While O'Donnell rubbed up a new ball, he took a few seconds to look out where the dog kept barking. There, past the picket fence, a small clump of fans had set up camp chairs to enjoy the game for free. Bouncing up and down against the rickety fence, a dog that looked very much like Cosmo barked wildly and lurched to get free. It was Abby who held the leash for dear life with one hand, waving at O'Donnell with the other.

The crowd spotted the two of them and cheered as Abby at last restrained Cosmo with a heroic effort. She had her heels dug in, yanking the leash to keep Cosmo from jumping over the fence.

The ump yelled at O'Donnell, "Throw the damn ball, Pitch. This ain't the County Fair."

O'Donnell threw a nice fastball nipping the outside corner. As he snagged the return throw from his catcher, O'Donnell took in the crowd behind him, most of whom still watched the big dog and the pretty young woman. He couldn't blame them.

The Aberdeen batter was in the box, but also watching the ruckus. The catcher signaled O'Donnell to quick pitch. He threw one over the heart of the plate. A meatball. But the guy stood there with the bat locked on his shoulder, too surprised to take a cut.

The umpire yelled, "Strike!" and walked away from the plate. The fans buzzed about the quick pitch strikeout and another win. As O'Donnell walked in to shake his catcher's hand. The fans swelled up from their seats and roared with what O'Donnell thought was a heart-warming tribute to his pitching performance.

Cosmo hit O'Donnell from behind at full speed, front paws planted square into unsuspecting shoulders. O'Donnell piled into his catcher, and they ended up sprawled on the field near home plate. The dog grabbed O'Donnell's glove and sprinted around the infield. Abby ran up with the broken remains of the leash in her hands and a huge smile on her face. She had dirt and grass stains all down the front of her blouse and on the knees of her white trousers. She looked like she'd gone in head-first stealing second base.

O'Donnell helped Abby to her feet, and wrapped his arms around her.

She looked great.

####